ABOUT THE AUTHOR

Born with an obsession for the written word, Rowena Spark navigated her youth armed with pen, paper and an overactive imagination, characters whispering to her from the shadows.

Rowena weaves romantic tales of flawed heroes who fall hard and love deeply, and strong, passionate heroines courageous enough to take a risk.

She lives on her farm with her husband, doing her best writing against the backdrop of Victoria's breathtaking South Gippsland hills, surrounded by cows, sheep, and one crazy dog.

For more information about Rowena Spark and her books visit www.rowenaspark.com and facebook.com/RowenaSparkAuthor

I0593489

COPYRIGHT

PRUDENCE

BY ROWENA SPARK

NATIONAL LIBRARY OF AUSTRALIA

A catalogue record of this book is available from: www.trove.nla.gov.au

ISBN (print): 978-0-6489089-9-9
ISBN (eBook): 978-0-6489089-7-5
Editor: Sharyn Constantine
Cover Design: White Clover Creative
Cover Image: Shutterstock: Petar Paunchev
Interior Design: White Clover Creative
Print typesetting and eBook production: Adobe Indesign

BOOK TWO OF THE SCARS OF CREDENCE SERIES

ROWENA SPARK

LIME TIGER ENTERPRISES

CHAPTER 1

WILLOW

I have a bed. So sinister yet so alluring, I'm hesitant to crease it with more than a careful caress. Drawing my knees to my chest, I take in the queen bed with its crisp white sheets and royal blue cover. It feels like I've walked onto a set for a photo shoot. It's magazine immaculate.

I wish I could fall into it feeling as safe and serene as the models in those magazines look.

But I know it's a vicious trap with razor teeth.

A beautiful lie.

I leave it skulking in my space like a hungry wolf, resisting the urge to strip it down and dismantle it on the spot. I'm not ready for the questions that would come from that. It stands taunting me as I pile my old bedding in the far corner of the room.

The sigh squeezes from my chest as I drag my blanket over my shoulders and I find some kind of comfort on the thick carpet.

I blink into the dusk. I have two weeks before I start work. Fourteen days before I can break out of this invisible cell I've existed in for so long. Fourteen days until I can be done with toxic homes for good. My nerves jerk excitedly. I can't recall the last time I was enthusiastic about something that I didn't have to compromise to get.

So far.

It's not that I doubt Rain's intentions, it's that she still appears naive enough to believe that good things just happen. But I know better; everything has a price, and the costs always bite deeper than she could ever understand.

But a job? This could change everything. If I am just able to hide the broken pieces of me, I'll appear normal, like everybody else. Just a normal seventeen-and-a-half-year-old girl with a job and a permanent address.

I feel a smile threaten. In every home since I was twelve, it's been my job to cook and clean, so waiting tables is one thing that I'm certain I can do. I can take orders with perfect recall and deliver an armful to set the different dishes before the patrons who ordered them.

My smile blows out and sits on my cheeks.

A shriveled seed of hope inside me sends up a tentative shoot.

* * *

I hear the deep growl of the motorbike roll in and the hulking footsteps cover the distance to the house with the sharp crunching of stone. Climbing quietly from my nest I creep to the window. The curtain slides aside and makes room for my curiosity. The forest giants surrounding Rain's home break up the moonlight, so I catch only fleeting glimpses as the man moves in languid, arrogant strides towards the house. He shifts his bulk as if liquid; graceful and purposeful like a smooth dance.

Holy hell he's a big man. I hear my own swallow and my mouth slackens. The leather on his jacket creaks as if it's failing to constrain all the muscles fighting against it. He's so tall and broad that my heart races.

He could protect me.

He could kill me.

His steps break and for a second he's as still as stone, head to the ground, and my gaze is glued to him as he turns his face slowly towards my bedroom window.

My stomach smashes against my ribcage and I jail my breaths.

Hidden behind the curtains he can't see me, but he knows I'm here.

The moonbeams don't reveal his eyes, or any clear feature, but I feel his stare. Sense it in the darkest places of me that twist inside and remind me what I am.

Then he gently shakes his head and continues towards the house. He almost fills the doorway as he slips through it, and I race to check the lock on my door. Secure. My pulse slowly eases.

* * *

Much later I wake in panic, pressing my back into the corner and my hands clawing the empty air in front of me. My thin wail bursts from a mouth thick with sleep as I wrestle my eyes open. I need to know where I am, what weapons I have at hand and what sinister threat looms. My inhales rasp over roughened throat and I swallow down my thumping pulse.

I'm in a room. Rain's spare room at her house with the immaculately decorated bed and drawn curtains. There's nobody but me in here. The sound that yanked me from slumber fills my ears still and I gravitate to its source. The motorbike. The huge man fired it up and woke me. I pull in a shaky breath in relief, but the rumble fades out of the driveway and into the distance long before my breaths even out.

Grateful for my respite I slip from my nest and stretch out the aches that grew in my bones as I slept. I dress in clean baggy jeans and a loose jumper and make my way to the kitchen, locating the bacon and eggs easily.

A tune forms in my mind and I surprise myself with the hum that chases it. It's been too long since I've felt a little distance between myself and danger, despite the motorbike guy, and I owe it all to Rain.

I turn at the sound of footsteps to see Rain being led by her wide smile.

"Morning, Will. How did you sleep?" Her voice is a song of joy, and I can't help my smile.

"Really well, thanks. I hope you don't mind me taking over

your kitchen, but I was starving."

She slips her arms around me and squeezes gently.

"I'm so glad you're here, Will."

Her voice takes me back. We're sitting on the bed drawing pictures in a bubble of innocent delight. Rain giggles at some snide comment I make, and our only concern is not having the right shade of blue pencil for the flowers. A broken lifetime ago.

"I bet you are. Cheapest cook in the south." My sly remark tumbles forth unannounced.

The giggle sneaks from her mouth.

"I've missed you so much." Rain grins wide.

"Morning, Willow." Archer sinks into the furthest chair with sleep ruffled hair.

"Morning, Archer. Bacon and eggs?" I quirk a brow.

"Thanks. I'm off to The Broken Keg today to check over the book work, but I could use some fuel before I do."

I get it. They're being patient and giving me time to adjust. I pass Archer his breakfast and linger.

"Hey, thanks for this. It's a fantastic opportunity, and…I won't let you down."

He waves his fork dismissively.

"No, Willow, thank you. The waitresses aren't transferring with the sale of the pub, and it's damn hard trying to find one in a small town like this."

A warmth begins in my stomach and travels through me. If what he says is true, I'm not someone they feel they have to save. I can almost believe I am really, honestly, needed. The hint of a hopeful smile escapes me.

"Rain just wanted me around to balance out the testosterone in this place."

Archer's breakfast muffles his chuckle. I widen my eyes at him, dramatically folding into a chair.

"I'm not kidding! But we'll need to get a few more ladies to properly balance it out, methinks. That other guy is a giant!"

Archer's laughter explodes.

"I know Axe looks intimidating, but he's harmless, really. He lives in the bedroom two doors down from yours. I asked him to give you some space while you settled in, but I'm beginning to think he'll be the one that needs to adjust to you!"

* * *

The afternoon sun slides behind the rugged Gippsland mountains. It really is a beautiful place. We talk for hours, Rain and me. She tells me Sarah died. We share a look. We don't need our voices to rehash our darkest places. It lingers between us and thickens the oxygen. Rain and I shared our home with two other foster sisters, and the four of us were fostered by Kurt. We believed him to be kind and caring, but we'd naively bought into his deceit. We four girls were there to fill part of an order for eleven-year-old girls in the sex trade, and Kurt had been tasked with 'breaking us in' on our eleventh birthdays for the shady buyers. He raped and brutalised Sarah and I. Rain killed Kurt and in doing so spared herself and Katherine from the same fate. Just last year, Rain was instrumental in breaking open the child trafficking ring across every part of the globe, but the victory was bittersweet. The ugly scars left by what they were subjected to never fully heal.

Sarah became a shadow of herself and never recovered. The grim line of Rain's mouth drew the same conclusion I did. Kurt forced us to be Sarah's audience, so we know what she went through. We all saw it. And I felt it, so we knew with the certainty of our shared pain. Our sister took her own life.

We spoke of Katherine, our younger sister, and the foundation she's built to fund legal costs for fosters.

Then we stretch out in comfortable silence. We process, reflect. We remember. We don't talk about the *before* that happened in the times between contacting each other, when we were forced to disconnect while the investigation was carried out. It all worked out okay. The puzzle in Rain's head was solved and some very evil people met their maker over it. Somewhere in the chaos she found Archer. She was blessed with luck. Always had been. And me? I just found different shades of the same demons.

Her glance tells me she can see my ghosts, and she knows I can see the swirling pain in hers.

"Tell me about Archer. How did you meet him?" I try to lift the sombre mood.

Rain snorts, her pretty head shaking slowly.

"It's pretty messed up, actually. He's my foster brother."

I gape openly. "You hooked up with your *brother*? Oh, Rain." I tut-tut in mock disappointment.

"Yeah. We fought it for a while…well, he did, anyway. But…" Her gaze unfocused, and a wistful smile tugged at her mouth. "One day I'll tell you how he chased me down, how he followed me wherever I went and died for me."

I narrow my eyes. Died? She nods at my unspoken question.

"He was shot in the head. The hair that grew over his scar lost pigment."

I swallow the questions that leap to my mouth. She's not ready to elaborate. Her tight shoulders and thinned lips are her tell, so instead, I entice another smile from her.

"Hmmm, clearly a bullet to the head is the only explanation as to why he wants to marry you. What's the story with Andre in there, then?"

She snorts daintily at my reference to Andre the Giant.

"That's not my story to tell. But I can tell you that he's a great guy, and Archer's mate, and he was instrumental in saving me."

I smirk at her. "Was that before or after Archer died?"

"After." She giggles and I roll my eyes.

"Of course it was."

CHAPTER 2

AXEL

*C*ome back to bed, baby." She rolls towards me and offers a sultry smile that fails to arouse anything deeper than waning interest.

"I need to get going." Deadpan.

I brace for the conversation I'm trying to avoid. The woman gathers the sheet around her chest as she sits up, the marks of my lust still colouring her skin.

"That's too bad. What about tomorrow?"

And there it is. I inwardly roll my eyes, regulating my exhale so it doesn't sound like a huff.

"I thought you understood. I'm not interested in anything more."

I watch as her eyes darken. They all imagine that a night with them will change my mind, no matter how clearly I spell it out for them. She frowns.

Please leave it there. Don't make this harder on yourself.

"Of course I understand, baby. What about just another night of fun, then?" She purrs, but the light of hope burns behind her proposal.

I leave the button open on my jeans and slide into my shirt, scanning the bedside table for my wallet and keys. Only when they're tight in my grasp do I turn back to her.

"Listen…" I search my mind for her name uselessly. "I explained to you I don't want anything more, and you agreed, remember? A good time. A bit of fun for both of us for the night. Now it's over, and I'm going home."

"But don't you think there could be something more here between us?"

Then I do roll my eyes at her. I watch her flinch and annoyance flares inside me. I had a good time with her, and she just went and ruined it by making it awkward.

"Look…" Shit. I still can't remember her name. "No. No there couldn't be anything more to it. This is what it is. Not a thing more. I'm sorry…"

The tears well up and I make for the door, shirt still unbuttoned and hanging in my haste.

"You can't even remember my name, can you?"

I flex my fist in frustration. I hate it when things end like this.

"I'm sorry." I slip through the door and walk away from the rage that will inevitably follow.

* * *

I turn on the ignition and my bike struggles for a bit in the cold before firing. My shoulders drop in relief. I couldn't stomach having to be around what's-her-name any longer than I had to, watching those tears, consoling her delusions.

It's the weapon woven through the veins in every woman. Sirens who lure and promise until they have you in their lair, your heart bloodied and pulpy in the cold fist of a smirking female. I could keep away if I turned my mind to it, I have that level of discipline and determination, but their bodies are soft and warm and make me feel so damned good.

I saw what Mum did to Dad when she left that night. The week after I turned thirteen. Didn't even say goodbye to me. Just left Dad and me and walked into a new life. Apparently I have a half-brother who doesn't know I exist. I don't even know his name, so I think of him as Replacement Axel.

I swore I'd never be the cause of that kind of destruction.

I'd do the right thing. That's why in the name of honour four years later, I stepped into the insidious arms of Janice, and she showed me an entirely different level of pain. Vowing never to offer myself to the devil again, I avoid any of the tiny hooks they try and sneak under my skin. It works, but I haven't been able to shield myself from the guilt they make me feel.

I toy with the idea of taking on a double shift tomorrow. If I can't find satisfaction in a woman, I'd rather spend my days seeking out another way to charge my interest. I've been missing the military. I miss the adrenaline, the spike of alertness that comes from facing a foe. Wondering if today is the day you're destined to meet your maker or return to battle another day. There's something pure and raw about the way it makes our blood positively hum with awareness, knowing that at that fraction in time every sense has never been sharper, every muscle has never been tighter. The feeling of being ready. And the euphoric buzz as my body relaxes into safety when the directive is completed. I *should* be relaxed now, not feeling guilty and responsible for that woman's sadness. I growl in my throat.

The wind buffets against my jacket as I lean into the bends. The powerful vibrations fix to shake me off like a raging bronco, but I tighten my thighs around its metal belly and move faster than any human should. The fresh air curls into the helmet vents and blows away the feminine scent of my regret.

The cool night weaves its magic and cleans out the residual tension, leaving me almost happy. I turn my steel stallion into the driveway and coast as quietly as possible to a stop. With a practised flick of a finger, I release the helmet strap and lift it free.

Drawn by the barest movement in the bedroom curtains, I catch sight of the moon's reflection in a single eye.

Rain's friend. The one she lived with when...

I shut off the thought. Of all the tasks I was assigned, eradicating the scum of society alongside Archer was the one that I couldn't shake free of. It wasn't so much the enemy, after all, the enemy is a faceless entity we are programmed to fight. We'd done that a thousand times without thought. It was the intel gathered from the computers we scanned, the details, the videos that curdled my blood. When the noise of the battle cleared, the loudest sound branded in my head was that of the frightened silence as the liberated girls shuffled into the daylight, some carrying babies on their hips. Every step echoed with the terrified screams they never uttered.

Archer knows the sheer size of me can be intimidating to people. Especially to a young woman who already views men as the enemy. He asked me to keep my distance until she feels safe enough to face me. I can give the girl space. I can give her so much space she'll never see me if it helps her. I'd almost be relieved if that was what she needed, because I don't think my soul could withstand another set of haunted eyes like the ones I helped set free, knowing that none would ever truly know what liberty feels like again.

* * *

She watches me every night, probably wondering if I'll be the next to make demands on her she doesn't want. I shiver.

Pulled back into a heavy mood, I slowly make my way to bed.

* * *

Running through the trees, I listen as Archer catches up and keeps pace. We're both retired from the military, but there remains this intrinsic need to maintain our sharp wits. Just in case. Rain joins us most days but when she turns for home way back at the second climb, Archer catches me up and we train together.

"Late home again last night?" His friendly jibe has me grinning.

"Yeah, another damn mistake. I've got to learn to pick them better."

"You and your conscience. They know the deal, just leave them to it." He shrugs.

I huff. "Easy for you to say. I can't spell it out any clearer, but somewhere in the groans and scratches, they think they can change my mind. It makes me feel like shit. I go into it thinking it's black and white, but end up in a damned grey area feeling like

I've done them wrong."

Archer grins at me, and I fight the urge to shove him into the bushes.

"Look on the bright side, Battle Axe. Pretty soon you'll have to try 'em out a second time since you're running out of bodies you haven't slept with."

I pull up and Archer shoots ahead.

"How is that a bright side?" I growl at him.

He shrugs and his smile stretches. "More entertainment for me."

"I think I much preferred you when you were brooding and quiet."

We slip into a comfortable silence of labouring lungs and burning muscles for a time.

"How's the new girl settling in? She adjusting alright?"

He gasps out a laugh. "Yeah, actually. She's not what I expected at all. She'll fit in well, and she'll make a great waitress when she starts. You guys will get along well once she warms up."

I quirk my eyebrow at him, but he won't elaborate.

"Hey, Axe, want to come and check out the brewery with me today? I should touch base with them in regard to our orders, but if you're not doing anything, I thought maybe you can sample some of the beers for me?"

He doesn't drink. Rain's biological mother was a drug addicted alcoholic, so I imagine he keeps away from those things for Rain. I nod slowly. Yeah, I can do with a bit of time away from needy women.

* * *

The smell of bacon and eggs has me finishing up my workout early. I skip the shower and towel off the sweat in my haste, then snag up my shirt with a smirk. I can't have Rain's friend intimidated by my muscles.

Archer is at the table, and I see Rain at the sink. The new girl mustn't be awake yet.

"Oh, yeah. Smells amazing. Can I grab some?"

Rain grins and nods, then a voice stops me in my tracks.

"There's a fee. A fiver for each egg, and ten for bacon."

I stare past Archer's chuckle, and leaning over the stove is Rain's friend. She's tall and awkward looking, her deep blue eyes shimmering with mischief, lank, dirty blonde hair curtaining most of her face. She's not startled by me, probably because she's seen me coming home every night since she arrived.

I close my gaping mouth.

"Okay. I'll have four eggs and…is there an added charge for an extra helping of bacon?"

"No. Flat rate for bacon, but there's an extra fee if you don't want me to spit in it."

I wing my eyebrows at her, but feel the trace of a smile tug at my mouth as she indicates where I should sit and delivers a loaded plate.

I eye it with exaggerated suspicion. "So, do I owe you that extra fee?"

She leans over the table at me and whispers conspiratorially. "Try it and see."

Rain clutches her sides and Archer chuckles. He's right. She's not what I expected either. The girl watches me intently as I take a mouthful, and I play along, chewing carefully.

"It looks like I don't get the extra charge. There's a distinct flavour of malicious saliva in this."

She grins and leaves me to it, dropping full plates before Archer and Rain.

Rain looks up, laughter still lifting her lips. "I guess I should introduce you two. This is Willow, my sister and The Broken Keg's new waitress, and Will, this is Axel, Archer's mate and police officer in Hawker Ridge, the next town over."

She nods and smiles politely and turns her attention to chat excitedly with Rain. Cheeky to demure in a mere second, the shift is like whiplash. Curiosity narrows my eyes as I take the opportunity to study her. Dressed in bland and shapeless clothes, she's perfectly unremarkable. I hope Rain will organise a haircut before she starts work to freshen her up a bit. Otherwise, she's got the right personality for waitressing, snappy and sassy.

I imagined she'd be reclusive, tentative, but she's the exact opposite, and while I'm relieved I don't have to modify my behaviour around her as I'd expected, something about her niggles at me.

Her demeanour is so far apart from the lineup of victims burned into my memory that I'm more than a little confused.

How should a victim behave?

The moment my cutlery rests on my plate, Willow scoops it up without acknowledging me.

"Thanks for breakfast." I murmur. She appears to falter, darting an odd glance at me before joining Rain at the sink.

* * *

The beers go down a treat. It's not often I have a drink. Between work and having my bike as my only mode of transport, I'm rarely able to let myself go. It's difficult to organise a designated driver with a motorbike.

The woman pouring my drinks tops it up and hoods her gaze. Her eyes sparkle with lust and…hope? Disappointed, I empty my smile and turn back to Archer.

"Are we done here, Frostbite?"

* * *

"What was that about?" He asks as soon as the doors close.

"I…I just needed to get out."

"That woman couldn't have been more obvious, Axe. I thought I'd be going home alone." He glances at me sideways and my heavy sigh empties my lungs.

"Yeah. I'm just not ready to have that awkward conversation again right now." The alcohol entices my mouth to keep making noises, much to my shame.

"You know, Frostbite, it would be nice to just have one fling, just one, where the girl actually listens to what I tell her and doesn't make shit weird."

I brace for a sarcastic comment, but Archer wears a strange expression and remains silent.

CHAPTER 3

WILLOW

I leap to my feet at the soft knock on my door. I glance down at my nest with relief that opening my bedroom door won't reveal it.

I crack it, and the body outside blocks the hallway light.

"Yes?" I wedge my foot just inside to brace the door.

The deep rumble of his voice makes me shiver. Everything about him is huge, even his timbre.

His usually graceful stance seems sloppy from being at the brewery, and it sets my nerves on edge.

I don't like drunk men.

His grey eyes lock on mine, and he blinks slowly as if he's concentrating on focusing. He slips a couple of ten dollar notes through the narrow gap, and my heart sinks.

"What's that for?" I grind coldly.

"Four eggs, extra bacon, minus the extra charge because I definitely tasted spit." He slurs.

My tension evaporates with a giggle. I widen the opening a little and push the cash back into his palm, the motion unbalancing him slightly.

"Goodnight, Andre. Go sleep it off." I tell him, then push the door closed. My giggle explodes when I hear him object, irritated, into the hallway.

"My name's Axel!"

Moments later I curl up in my nest with a smile on my face. I know its early days yet, but they all seem lovely and…

I'm instantly fully alert. I just opened my bedroom door to a drunk man, a huge drunk man, and I'm not fighting for breath in a panic attack.

* * *

I continue to mull over his visit when I seek him out the next day. I'm lured by the sound of metal shifting and clunking at the far end of the hallway. I don't make a sound, but the moment I peek through the open door, his eyes snag to me. He must have good hearing.

He's sitting on the bench, wearing only shorts and runners, fists clenching a bar attached to weights that he's pulled to his shoulders. His skin shines with a layer of sweat, and his chest…

He clears his throat, and I realise I'm staring boldly at the impressive display of muscles twitching and tightening. Fear sparks in my stomach. I need something from him, but the utter power of him makes me doubt that I could handle the price. And history reminds me that I am capable of handling a lot. I hesitate.

"Are you lost?" He prompts.

His voice cleans my thoughts. I fold my arms.

"Yeah, Room Service isn't answering so I thought I'd seek them out."

His expression is stone, but I see his eyes shimmer with amusement. It feeds my courage, and I swallow and step into the room, keeping my focus off the steel of his body.

"Last night…" I begin.

Is that glow from exercise, or was he actually blushing?

"Ah, yeah, sorry about that. I'd…overindulged, and I…ah, thought I'd run with your breakfast joke…" It was odd seeing this hulk of a man sheepishly apologise to a small slip of a thing like me.

"It wasn't a joke."

His face contorts into astonishment and I know I've got him. The smile that lingered behind my sharp tongue bubbles out and cascades delightedly over my teeth.

He frowns in defeat and I laugh harder, but when he lets the weights drop with a clang, my amusement strips away and I take a couple of steps back.

His head shakes on his thick neck and he smiles gently.

"You're a nightmare."

It's my turn to clear my throat.

"What I was going to say, is that joke or not, there is something I would like, if you could?"

My mouth dries out as my words fall. This is it. We are alone, and I'm asking…

"What do you need, Willow?"

His tone is gentle, but those words. They are a loaded gun. A phrase sneered at me so many times I've lost count, the next words will be the price I'd need to pay. Goosebumps ripple up my arms and I hold them to my waist, trying to calm the trembling. My focus drops to the ground beside my old runners as I reach for oxygen, but it was a mistake to look away. As I stare down, the presence of every lewd breath and sinister touch stands sharp in my memory before my bent head. They slide from the shadows all prickly, reeking of decaying pain.

"Look at me, Willow."

His eyes are grey granite, and they reach to soothe me without touching.

"What do you need? If I can't get it for you, I'll tell you."

The breath whooshes from my mouth. *If I can't get it for you, I'll tell you.* Those were the words that snap the safety back in place and holster the gun.

Before I lose my nerve again, I hold his gaze and my request stutters out.

"I'm after a sketch pad and some pencils. Please." My next breath shakes with relief.

His eyebrows dart upwards. "Is that…?" He stops himself, and I feel my humiliation crawl up my neck. I know he sees it; how awkward and painful this is for me.

"Of course I can. There's a newsagent two doors from work."

I search his face, waiting for the next part. The bit that stings, but it doesn't come. I detect empathy resting on me as the corner of his lip twitches.

"That wasn't so hard, was it?"

My loud laugh barks into the air, and I leave the gym.

As the distance between us grows, so does my courage. I spin in the doorway and beam.

"Thanks, Andre." And slip away.

"My name's Axel."

I grin.

* * *

Rain was so blessed to have been placed with Heather. I warm to the woman immediately. She's open and loving, and so accepting of the strange circumstance between Rain and Archer.

As they sit around the table, discussing the wedding, I serve coffee and biscuits. Heather watches me with a kind smile as I buzz around the kitchen.

"How did you know how I have my coffee?" She invites me into the conversation.

"Rain mentioned it a few days ago." I shrug. "I've been endowed with perfect recall, so it's easy."

Her mouth hangs open on softly wrinkled hinges, and I smile.

"You'll be an exceptional asset to The Broken Keg next week, then."

I feel a blush rise, and fetch my own coffee to hide it, but I feel so warmed by her opinion that I'm dancing on the inside. Acceptance is like gold to me, and I'm wealthy from her praise.

"So, Willow, what do you think of this wedding? Your sister's getting married!" Her eyes dance in excitement.

"Well, I have my reservations, Heather. I think there's going to be a big decision to make." The room stills. Archer, Axel and Heather contemplate me with caution. Rain leans forward. She knows me too well.

"And what's that, Willow?" The old woman asks carefully. I flop in the chair opposite her and rest my jaw on my palm.

"Whose side are you going to be sitting on? The bride's or the groom's?"

Heather erupts into laughter, as does the rest of the room.

I find Axel's gaze fixed on me. It's the first time I've seen him smile with his teeth. It transforms his face into a gentleness that I feel in my chest.

* * *

When Heather pulls me into her arms, I revel in her embrace. It's a hug that triggers my most precious memories, and I don't let her go for a long time. As I reluctantly pull away I whisper in her ear.

"Thank you for being there for my sister. You've given her what she always wanted; a safe and loving home."

She lands a kiss on my cheek and says nothing, but her eyes glisten with emotion as we pull apart.

* * *

I start work in exactly one week. Rain and Archer are frantically finalising staff, menus, drinks and managing the safety auditors that seem to be swarming over the place, but Rain bounces in with a secret smile on her face.

"Your uniform arrived. Want to try it on?"

My head nods sharply and my stomach twists in excitement, and I lead her into my room without a thought. She pulls up short when she sees the untouched bed, and she scans the room until her attention lands on my nest. I watch it all collide in her expression, guilt, pain and horror. She's studying psychology, and she knows me. She's seen far enough inside me to understand that I'm not capable of finding rest in the linen jaws of a bed. Beds bring only terror and agony. I'm grateful I don't need to explain, but it exposes just another weird behaviour that sets me apart.

She makes a choking sound and I watch the tears fall on her pretty cheeks, and I wrap my arms around her.

"It's okay, Rain. Truly. I'm fine." I murmur into her hair.

Deep sobs that rip open my heart heave from her. "I'm so, so sorry."

She grieves for my past, but that's just what it is. The past is where the ruins of my soul dwells, and I'm hell bent on building a temple from the rubble.

I press consoling lips to her forehead. "I'm here, now, Rain. I'm safe. Now let me try on that dress."

I'm used to baggy clothes that hide my body. The loose fabric is an insulated barrier against unwanted attention, the drab designs dragging the focus away. But this dress is anything but what I'm used to. A classic style, black and clinging that pulls in at my waist, and highlights the shape of my hips. The neat and modest button up neck fits snug over my breasts. I stand before the mirror in disbelief.

"Holy hell, Will. You look amazing! How do you feel?"

I turn side on. I study my long slender legs that look even longer in the uniform.

"Wow." I breathe. How do I feel? I feel exposed. I feel on display, and I tug the skirt down in a useless attempt to cover my exposed flesh.

"I feel naked." Doubt seeps in. I'm imaging the leering faces, the hands that reach and intrude. The expectations.

"Flynn will be there to watch out for you the whole time. So will Archer. You'll be safe."

I study my reflection incredulously. The image before me appears confident, so far removed from how I really feel. I suppose I can liken this to wearing a mask. The uniform creates this alter ego, a different persona I can adopt in the pursuit of stable employment.

Rain's voice tightens in rapture.

"Definitely flats for you, Will. They'll be more comfortable on your shifts, too."

"Can we please get my hair done, too? I've got so many split ends, and I kind of want my natural colour back. You know, new place, new face?"

A natural, neutral brown should help me blend in with the crowd. I know the bleached blonde look with the awful brown regrowth makes me appear trashy. I just want to look like a normal, ordinary person who can be easily missed under the radar.

Rain's face brightens. On a whim she twists my hair into a loose but neat bun, leaving a wavy tendril loose to soften the effect.

"New face! Yes!" She leaves me alone to contemplate the stranger staring back at me and returns with a small metal case filled with cosmetics. She sets to work with unrestrained enthusiasm, and I watch my reflection bloom with a dusting of rouge and dark lines highlighting my eyes. Definitely a mask to hide behind. I look so completely different from who I really am that I feel almost secure imagining that nobody would recognise me in the street.

"Lipstick?" Rain suggests. I grin, and my little sister completes the picture with a flourish.

My mask is on, I think as I absorb my reflection.

"Oh, wow, Rain!" I whisper, watching the shade of my lips move around my words. "You've worked a miracle."

"Just highlighting the talent, Will. And I checked my calendar. The only time I have available to take you for a haircut is next

Sunday, and the hairdresser said she'll stay open so it's done before you start work." She tugs at the loose strand of hair. I throw my arms around her, too grateful for words.

CHAPTER 4

AXEL

I change out of my uniform and slip into my street clothes and power up my phone. My eyes roll as the texts announce themselves loudly, and I scan them. Most are just numbers, not important enough to save into my phone.

Most of them begin with *Hey, it's me. Do you want to catch up...?*

Like I'm supposed to know which 'me' they were. I feel the familiar stab of guilt when I delete them all, I mean, I told them it was only for a night. Why I had to give them my damn number in the beginning mystifies me.

Oh, yeah, because I'm an idiot and a glutton for punishment.

And that deeper, niggling voice that whispers to me.

You want a reason to push them away.

None of the messages comes from a saved number, so I toss it in my bag and shoulder it, walking out into the street.

I have to get the sketchbook for Will. My forehead crinkles when I recall that look on her face when she asked, like a graveyard of ghosts were hovering in her blue eyes. It gave me chills. She's been invading my thoughts all day, the way she sunk into dark memories when she asked for such a tiny favour.

How she bravely stepped up to me, when her whole body trembled like a trapped fawn.

How many scars is she hiding behind that smart mouth?

I sigh and clear my head. That's Rain's problem, not mine. But my thoughts just gravitate back to her. The way she looked at me when she approached me. In my world, there's two kinds of women. The ones who fear me and the ones who want to warm my sheets. Willow is neither. She perused my face and body with a kind of hesitant curiosity tinged with those ghosts of hers. There was fear there, of that I'm certain, but not specifically of me. Her fear was tangled within the words we exchanged. But there was no familiar desire for me, either.

I wander the aisles running my fingers over the selection of sketchbooks. I feel someone slide up beside me.

"Can I help you?" The man looks like an artist. Long, wild hair, round wire-rimmed glasses and long pale fingers that would suit the coloured stains of oil paint.

"Yeah, a friend asked me for a sketchpad, but I have no idea what she's after. I didn't realise there were so many to choose from."

"What will she be using it for? Watercolour? Ink?"

He grins as my expression clouds over. I assumed paper was paper.

Then I blink, finally understanding. "Pencil. She's after some of those, too"

The man nods, selecting a couple from the shelf beside him.

"I think these are what you want?"

I nod my gratitude, and mutely follow him up and down the aisles. He hands me two sketchbooks and a handful of pencils. I frown. A vision of her haunted face leaps to mind and I select the smaller sketch book, then hand him back most of the pencils.

"Maybe only three of these, thanks."

I just get the impression that I should be very careful with what I give her. I know enough about her past to imagine that she doesn't want to feel like she owes anybody.

* * *

I find her in tracksuit pants and a jumper that's two sizes too large. She's cross legged on the window seat with the sun on her back and a book open on her lap. When she spots the sketchpad, a wary smile darts over her face and she sets her book aside. Like a timid deer she approaches.

I offer it to her, and instead of snatching it away, she reaches out a cautious hand, frowning suspiciously at me. I shove it into her hand and keep my expression empty, and when she closes her fingers around it, I shove the pencils at her in the same empty manner and turn away.

"I'm going for a run. I'll be back in a couple of hours."

Her face opens in surprise, and I feel her eyes on me as I leave the room.

I don't normally announce my movements, but I needed to let her know that the conversation, the transaction, was finished. It made me feel good to watch the relief stain her face.

The message tone on my phone drove the train of thought from my mind. Number unknown.

Are you still coming?

Shit. I'd forgotten I had that woman from the brewery lined up for tonight, and I don't usually forget things like that. I'd been too distracted getting the sketchpad for Willow to remember. There is still time to go back to town, though. My fingers hover over the buttons, the cursor flashing impatiently as I consider my options.

Something came up. Sorry. I respond.

Then I spend the next two hours jogging through the forest wondering why I chose running over sex.

* * *

The house is dark when I get back, and I'm instantly on guard. There should be lights on in the kitchen. In the living room. Archer and Rain are out, but Willow is still home. I open my mouth to silence my breaths, and my feet make no sound on the carpet. There's not a single noise to be heard, except...I strain my hearing and move alert and coiled towards a distant sound of a muffled exclamation, and soft, unintelligible murmurs. It leads me to the kitchen, and I peer carefully around the door frame.

Willow sits perched at the kitchen table, so immersed in the sketchpad in front of her that she's squinting through the dimming twilight. My muscles relax. She's fine. She was too distracted to realise it was getting dark. I snap on the light and she tumbles off the chair with a clatter and dives into the nearest corner, her rough-sawn scream ripping open the silence.

Shit.

"Sorry, Willow, it's only me. I was worried when I saw all the lights off."

Her eyes are impossibly wide and the air tears at her throat in frantic rasps. I watch her swallow and her body gradually soften.

"Holy hell, Andre, you need a bell around your damn neck!" She palms the cupboards and pushes herself up.

My attention is caught by the pages of the sketchbook torn out and scattered over the surface of the table. On each one, a perfect image decorates the page in delicate greyscale.

I lift one. Heather's face laughs at me from the page, each wrinkle on her face softened with love, the gleam in her eye filled with her heart. Even her earrings, sunk slightly into the aging lobes, are perfectly drawn.

"Jesus, Will. These are amazing!" I breathe. I reach out a hand and sift through the pile. In this one, Archer stands beside Rain, his lips on her forehead, and adoration saturating from the strokes of grey lead.

It's how she sees them. Those perfect images capture everything in a detail so intricate that it could almost be a photograph. But there's something more in there. I see a dark unpredictability in the lines on Archer's face, a sharpness that Willow captured that explains how she feels about him. I can see she likes him, but she's still wary. The drawing of Heather, however, is as pure and light as the soul she is.

There's one of Rain, clearly a younger snapshot, laughing with an innocence that's now been lost. The next page is of Rain yesterday when she spent the afternoon with Willow.

I reach for one poking out from beneath a small pile. All I can see is the bench of the machine I was using and my shoe. As I close my fingers on it, a knot forms in my stomach, and I pull in a breath. This is me, when she came to me to ask about the sketchpad.

It's incredible. The detail. She got everything perfect. Even the slightly smudged sheen of my perspiration, and the streak of effort that tracked down my face. My face. It shows a strong jaw, determined without being stubborn. My mouth is full and hints at a smile. But my eyes. The simple picture tells such an intricate story. The eyes are deep and soulful. They are kind and patient. They are eyes that invite you all the way in. They hold deep mystery, intrigue, and humour. I catch the hint of doubt in the careful strokes around my waist, but its the pressure she used there that stands out. The tentative, exploratory sweeps of the pencil come from something inside her that unfurls as if for the first time into the image of me.

This is how she feels about me.

With such raw honesty in the lines of her pencil it takes my breath away.

"These are incredible, Will!" I find her eyes and it hurts when I see the suspicion cloud her face.

Her breathing has levelled out and her courage returns slowly. She begins to gather them in a messy pile.

"Thanks. I want to show Rain how grateful I am for everything she's done for me. I'm going to give her the gift of her whole family."

"Oh, Will, she'll be delighted. You're very talented!" I consider. "Do you want me to call Simone so you can draw her, too?"

She relaxes into a smirk then, and taps her head.

"Nope, thanks anyway. Photographic memory remember? I've got Simone up here, too."

She lifts another page sporting a different angle of Heather, and the face of a young girl stares back at me. There's a glow of naivety in every feature on her laughing face.

"Who's this?" I gesture. Willow's face dulls.

"Sarah." Her whisper drags eerie chills down my spine. I change the subject.

"All these faces, and the only men are Archer and I. Wasn't there a special guy for you tucked away in this pile of memories?"

Her snort is sharp and poisoned, and her blue eyes narrow to slits.

"Men bring pain and degrading cruelty."

Willow glares at a memory and shuts down in front of me.

My mouth dries. Her explanation crushes my chest. Man equates to pain in her world. The details she doesn't give are buried in shadows, and they stalk her wherever she goes. There's nothing I can say to her to soothe her. My useless words can't rewind her life and delete the painful parts. Everything she's endured will be clear and unrelenting, and always fresh in the archives of perfect recall.

"Can I keep this?" I hold the image of me. She shrugs nonchalantly and fades into the shadows of the hall with the rest of her drawings.

An urge to follow her appears from nowhere and startles me. I'm deluded if I think anything I say or do can give her relief, but it doesn't stop me from wanting to try to prove to her that not all men are to be feared.

I study the picture a little longer, tracing the lines with care not to smudge the pencil. I can't seem to put my finger on what it is she's seeing, but it's there, mixed with curiosity, and it demands my attention.

Confusion taunts me. This drawing is important, and I don't understand why.

CHAPTER 5

WILLOW

I find my subconscious is hell-bent on seeking Axel out. I try to convince myself that it's because I'm lonely with Rain out all the time, but deep down, I know different. He fascinates me. I should be terrified of him. His height, breadth, and the sheer mass of him should send me screaming in the opposite direction. But it doesn't. Instead there's a quiet gentleness about him, a safe, nurturing light emanating from him that make my shadows lighter. Less important. Instead of retreating, I take delight in teasing him, taunting this giant just to see what response I'll get.

Today, though, I resolve to keep my distance. Every afternoon when the rumble of his bike brings him home, I found myself gravitating towards him, but I must be becoming a nuisance of late, never leaving him alone. He hasn't said as much, but he stands in the kitchen, his glance searching until I walk in, where he lands me a look that seems to say 'Oh, there you are. I figured you'd be here about now.'

I'm almost finished my drawings for Rain, luckily, because I only have one page left blank. I'll save that for something special until I can afford to buy another book. The last two strokes here, the briefest smudge there and it's done. It has to be my favourite. Axel sits astride his motorbike, helmet under his arm and hair all messed up. It's the day he came back early with my art supplies. He has a distant contemplative expression as he seeks answers in the distance.

"How do you do it?" The deep timbre pierces through my thoughts and I scramble away, my pulse pushing my veins open painfully.

"Christ, Andre! Will you stop doing that, or I'll shove a bell so far down that neck of yours that it'll ring every time you breathe!"

He gives me a sheepish grin.

"Sorry Will. I'll try to remember to walk heavy around the house."

My lungs catch up, and my glance explores his body openly. "You'd think with someone of your size, I'd feel you coming through the ground! What were you? Military? Ninja? Assassin?"

I expect laughter. A smile. Not the awkward silence that falls between us. I zero in on his features, suddenly void of all emotion. A muscle in his jaw ticks.

"Holy hell, Axel! I'm right, aren't I? Which one?" He stands impassive, boring into me with those eyes of flint.

I pinch my chin and squint at him, studying him with exaggerated scrutiny.

"Well, you can't be a ninja. The idea of you trying to squeeze that bulk behind a little sapling to hide is nothing short of ludicrous." The image makes me smile. His gaze flicks with a forced vacancy back and forth between my eyes.

"Assassin? No. I don't think you could exist for the sole purpose of killing someone. Besides, you run too much. It would do your head in to have to keep still for too long waiting for that one shot. You were in the military, weren't you?"

I watch his throat bob on indecision, before he allows the slightest nod. I grin my victory until a darker thought dawns on me.

"You worked on Rain's operation, didn't you?"

He blinks, and guilt surfaces.

Shame surges through me and bile climbs my throat. My lungs tighten until it's difficult to draw breath and panic weighs my limbs down.

"You…you know about me."

My pulse thunders and my inhales struggle to keep pace.

He knows my secrets. The box I have padlocked and tucked away in the darkest corners of my soul is open and spilling out at his feet. I'm filthy, disgusting and a creature worthy of pity. He knows what I let them do to me.

He knows because my ordeal was shared with every soldier that fought the war to overcome those depraved enemies. The detectives told me they'd need to disclose the details to assist with the operation, but I never imagined a task force of thousands would be entertained by it. Or that Axel, a perfect stranger until now, knows my ugliest scars.

I try to hide my face, but my hands don't obey me. I'm a heaving out of control mess of horror staring wide-eyed into empty black space in front of me. I feel myself slump to one side, unable to stop.

Suddenly my lungs have a little more space, and I realise it's because I'm standing. Not standing. I'm being held upright, pressed with strong arms against a wall that doesn't give. It's hard and stable, and I lean against it without hesitation.

A voice hovers around my head.

"I'm sorry, Will. They told us in a debrief before we began what these people were capable of. The things we heard, the things we saw. Our pain is different, Willow, but the same kind of demons exist in our nightmares."

I fight to catch my breath. The wall emits its own sound, and I chase it, desperate for something I can focus on besides my treacherous lungs.

Thump-thump. Thump-thump.

The darkness gradually lifts as my senses return, and I let my eyes close in relief. My lungs open wider, bones return in my limbs. I'm aware of a scent so comforting I instinctively pull in a lungful. The smell of raw pine and heady musk. Intoxicating. I soak it up for a few moments, then lift my hand, pressing it against the firm surface next to my head. It's not brick. It gives a little beneath my fingers. And it's covered in fabric.

I snap my eyes open and jerk backwards. Axel has his arms around me. A man is holding me! His arms drop from my shoulders but I stare in horror into his face. His jaw is tight, his nostrils flared. But his eyes…

The silver in them is completely gone, utterly consumed by the black of his blown-out pupils.

That's an expression I know. My heart pumps adrenaline through my veins with a force that I feel in my brain. My chest crushes with the need to escape.

I feel his huge hand encircle my arm, and a thin scream erupts. I know what comes next.

He's trying to talk to me, an imploring tone, but the words won't penetrate, and I can't look away from the depths in those eyes…

His other fist curls and bites into my other arm.

No no no!

I've only been here a week and it's started. Like it always does.

I'm a furious tsunami of kicks and scratches, and the urgency to escape has my muscles straining. A voice booms through the shroud of my panic.

"If I let you go you'll hurt yourself. Just stop for a second, will you."

No way in hell.

I throw myself backwards until my spine near breaks but his grip tightens. I see in his face that he's not even breaking a sweat. His features are hard stone of determination.

Then I realise. He's an immovable mountain of muscle and there's no way I can fight him.

I slump into futility, that protective fog that takes me far away from the pain that follows. The stretched, keening sobs begin as he lifts me off the ground.

"Willow, listen to me. I'm not going to hurt you, but if I'd let you go before, you'd have hurt yourself. Look at me."

I am. I can't not. He fills my vision. I feel wood beneath my legs as he deposits me firmly on the seat.

"I'm going to let you go, and I need you to just sit for a while. Can you do that?"

I can't respond.

Then his grip leaves me. Just vanishes. The blur of his back shrinks into the house, and I can't move.

I know the salacious look he had in his eye, but this is the first time it hasn't ended with my screams of pain. It just ended. I rest my shaking arms on my knees and cradle my forehead in grateful confusion.

I'm absolutely mortified. But unharmed. As my tremors cease, and the adrenaline is replaced by fatigue, I pull my legs into my arms.

And that's where Axel finds me, on the edge of sleep. I'm instantly alert when he intrudes on my vision, but he shoves a wine glass full of water in my hand.

Recovering a sense of normalcy, I take it from him and lift it in a toast.

"To a lungful of fresh air" I smirk.

Axel hisses and jams a hand through his hair. "Why do you do that?" He winces.

I sip and tilt an eyebrow.

"Do what?"

"You use humour to deflect." He frowns.

"Well, I guess there's no avoiding the proverbial elephant in the room, is there?" My tone flattens.

The flint that's returned after his pupils receded narrows on me. I exhale long and slow.

"It's not so different to how you manage." I explain reluctantly. "How can you kill someone in one heartbeat, and then as a cop, treat the public with patience and empathy the next?"

I register his surprise, watch his lips thin. Axel's eyes flick to mine and I think for a moment he won't answer.

"I guess I…detach from it. Pretend there's two of me. The soldier and the man."

"…and why do you do that?" I quirk an eyebrow his way.

His eyes drop to the ground and I can hear the sour tone of guilt.

"To be able to keep going without it eating me up from inside."

My voice softens. I understand his war like it's my own.

"And there you have it, Andre. What's done in the past lurks like a wolf on the edge of consciousness, and if we don't find a way to subdue it when the mood strikes it, the wolf will devour us. So we do the only thing we know how to do. We step past the pain and leave it behind us where we can."

He stares at me almost intrusively, taking a stroll through the ugly parts of me until I turn away from his scrutiny.

He folds his massive frame into the bench beside me, careful to avoid the contact I fear.

"Can I ask you to do something for me?" His rumble inquires.

"Depends." I hear the suspicion in my own voice and shrink away a little.

Glinting silver holds me still. "It's more like a transaction, really. I'll get you another sketch pad, but as payment I want you to draw a picture for me."

I feel my spine straighten in surprise. Just a picture? I can do that. Then I'll have another book of beautiful empty pages hungry for more pencil strokes. Only…

"Of who?"

"You."

"Why?" My tone snaps in defence.

I assumed he'd want one of Archer, or them and Rain together as a family. Axel shrugs, and a light blush travels up his neck.

"I guess I've seen your pictures of the others, and I wondered why your face isn't among them."

I search his face for ulterior motives.

"Okay, but let's get the details sorted. One image, clothes on. And you don't get a private show with it. Just a picture. For one empty sketchbook." I can feel my tone tighten as I stipulate my terms.

When I finish, I find the courage to meet his eyes. They rest on me, wide and coloured with horror.

He angles his huge bulk away from me as if I were dirty.

Because I am.

CHAPTER 6

AXEL

S *weet Jesus! Does she really believe I want those things from her?*

I swallow down the urge to shake her, forcing her to understand I have no intention of ever seeing her without clothes, but I need to proceed with caution. She believes it's something that would be asked of her probably because it's happened before. I decide to approach this with a different tactic.

"Will, that's exactly what I'm after. What you just said. And if someone has asked for, or taken more than that, then it's illegal and you should press charges."

Her derisive snort broke apart her fear.

"And what are you going to do, Andre? Arrest them all?"

I silently choke on the bile that rose. *Them all. There was more than one?* I look at her hard, then. She is shapeless, bland and almost dirty looking with her washed-out bleached hair and nondescript clothes. But as I keep examining her, something new surfaces. There's a sparkle illuminating from her, enhancing the wild and playful oceans of her eyes, her delicate cheekbones, and the mouth she normally pulls into thin lines sits relaxed and almost plump. The sassy jaw that sits firm and brave above the long, graceful lines of her throat. That light emanating from her settles over her like a beacon, and I feel it in my stomach like cold lead. That's what they saw. That's what they took without asking.

Her eyes level with me with that look of dark expectation. She thinks everyone is capable of those things.

"Willow…not everyone is like that." She creases her brow in skepticism. "I'm not like that."

She shakes her head.

"I saw it, Axel. That look was there. It's always there. You are the same."

She slumps with resigned acceptance, and I'm irritated.

"What look, Willow?"

How dare she accuse me of being like every other man? She looks at me with those huge tortured eyes, and with barely more than a whisper she explains.

"It's the dark look. The one that makes your eyes black. That one that turns men into animals that take and hurt and won't leave me alone."

She takes a sip with trembling hands and watches me through narrow suspicion. My lungs empty. She saw it, that wave of… something that took me by surprise when I held her and smelled that frangipani and lime scent.

"Look, Willow, I'll be honest with you, but you need to hear me out. I'm a man, and men like women, but most of us aren't animals. I reacted to holding you. I don't know why, but I did. But nothing happened, did it? The reaction can't be controlled, but the next step can be. By every man. At any given point a man can stop, and nobody has the right to take anything that isn't given willingly."

"How do you know if they're willing?" There is a bitter edge in her tone. Whatever I tell her would be met with mistrust. I need her to see it. An idea forms and I slip my phone from my pocket and hand it to her, open on the messages I haven't yet deleted.

Are you still coming?

Willow hovers over it with open curiosity. She stabs a sideways glance at me before scrolling to the next message.

Can I see you again tonight? I had a great time.

Willow's eyes narrow as if she's seeking a hidden message within the brief text.

My breath hitches as she hovers her slender finger over the third one. That one is quite explicit. The nameless woman gives a detailed description of what she wants me to do for her. I watch curiously as Willow reads it. Then rereads it. Her lips part slightly.

I shuffle with the embarrassment that floods through me. Willow is beside me, reading my smutty messages. Knowing what she's reading and watching her subtle reaction to it is beginning to heat my blood.

I shake my head clear. I have no interest in Willow.

Her eyes have darkened to sapphires as she hands my phone back.

"They *want* you to touch them? To do those things to them?" She shudders, but confusion lingers.

I nod carefully.

"I wouldn't engage in anything without their consent, Willow. It's not supposed to be painful. When it's something you want, it can be one of the most wonderful experiences..." I trail off at the memory of lying panting and sated beside a woman, the feeling of euphoria so wonderfully...transcendent.

"If they're so willing, why do you need so many women? Maybe you're mistaken. Maybe you take from them more than they want to give and that's why you've gone through so many."

What?

"I hear Rain and Archer talk about all the women you go through, Axel. They laugh about it, but it tells me things you don't say."

I feel my jaw stiffen. This is a speech I've made many a time.

"Willow, it's not what you think. The problem I have is that the women do want more from me. They want the relationship, but I do not. Some people just aren't built for relationships, and I'm one of them. I'm not interested in anything deeper than feeling good, and I find that one...interlude...is all I can offer before it starts getting complicated."

She listens intently, and I expect her to object to my line of thought, but instead she frowns her acceptance.

"Doesn't it hurt them? I mean, you're a big man, and I imagine-"

I cut her off abruptly. "They love it. There is no pain. There should never be pain."

I can't have her imagining what lies inside my pants.

"It always hurt for you?"

She nods and her face clouds.

"It was never about what I wanted, Axel. They'd all make excuses. It was my fault. I wanted it. They couldn't control it. I heard it all. But not once did they ask me, or listen when I asked them to stop."

We sit in a thick and heavy silence, Willow overcome by the ghosts of her past, and me with so many horrific scenes playing out that my head pounds.

I stand with mixed emotions. I'm almost overcome as a sudden intrinsic urge to protect her barrels through me. To hold her in my arms until all her demons fall away and she is safe. She looks at me with reservation standing side by side with her courage, and my lungs squeeze, but I catch myself.

Is this just a lure I haven't come across before?

"I am a friend, and it's safe to ask me anything. I promise you, Will, that as long as I am here, nobody will take without consent from you again."

She looks dubiously with those soulful blue orbs and shrugs.

And I burn with helplessness.

* * *

I stare at that message. The one Willow read twice that had her breath shifting faster than it should. She's known nothing besides pain and fear, but I watched as her gaze burned with curiosity at the content.

The woman who sent it; I vaguely remember her face. The words that drew no desire from me before now intrigue me. I sit on the edge of my bed and read it again, my hand wrapping firmly around my raging erection. I use long, languid strokes and imagine a woman in its place, her head thrown back as she impales herself. She wears the face of every woman whose ecstasy I can recall. I work my fist faster as my peak nears. I'm on the edge, but I can't quite get there. Then an image of wide blue eyes, swollen lips parted with heated curiosity intrudes. Willow. Her subtle beauty changed to one of fearless wonder on my lap.

My eyes fly open and I release my hold, but it's too late. The image of Willow carries me over into a powerful orgasm, and I grunt as an avalanche of shock and rapture earthquakes through my body.

* * *

I head down to the art supplies shop again, and the cashier gives me a grin, remembering me. It annoys me that I've been so distracted with thoughts of Willow all damn day. I almost wrote her name on a speeding fine I issued. I caught myself in time, but my partner, Dane, shot me a frown.

"What's up with you today, Axel? Woman troubles?"

"No." I growled back darkly, a little too quickly.

The cashier follows me into the same aisle as before.

"I'm after a slightly larger one this time." I tell him, and he selects one for me.

"Your friend liked the last one? It was the right one?" He inquires.

"I think so. She didn't say it wasn't. She does drawings like this one. Can you tell me if it's the right sketchpad?" I pull out the drawing of me working out. I keep it in my backpack, safe in the back of the work folder to protect it from creases. The man lifts it reverently from my hand and gazes at it in amazement.

"This is incredible. Such powerful emotion in these lines. Your friend is very talented. Here. One of this type would be better suited to her style."

I can't tell the difference, but take the spiral bound pad gratefully.

"Some more pencils, too, please."

He packages the lot for me, and when I find it's too large for my backpack, I shove it down the front of my jacket and turn my bike towards Willow. I mean home.

* * *

I find her curled up on the window seat again, her knees drawn to her chest with her nose in a book. She hasn't noticed me, so I make a display of stomping into the room and clearing my throat noisily. Willow smirks and excitedly eyes the package in my hands.

"Thanks for not sneaking up on me. I've been practising my ninja moves, and you just saved yourself from my fury."

"You couldn't hurt anyone with your moves." I challenge, but I can't meet her eyes. The deep sapphire ones that came to me in my bedroom.

"The bigger they are, the harder they fall, Andre." She cautions, and I shake my head with a smile. I thrust the package into her hands and step away as she opens it. I hear her soft breath linger as she caresses the pages.

"It's…*perfect*, Axel. I don't know how to thank-" At her own words, she stiffens and closes up.

"Did you do the picture I asked for as payment?" I joke lightly. "If not, I'll force you to sit at the table and not move until it's finished."

The grim thoughts leave her with a relieved smile.

"Wait here." She unfurls herself and disappears down the hallway. It's like the warmth in the room left with her. I swallow heavily. My nostrils find the lingering scent of her, and they pull it in, reminding me of the way she felt when she rested against my chest.

Shit.

I need to get her out of my head because she has no business existing in the same place as my desires. I see her book resting open against the cushions and I try to distract myself with its contents.

Ruby arched her back as his kisses burned a trail lower still, his mouth brushing her...

Fuck.

Shit.

I slam the book closed in frustration. Now I sport a raging erection, and Willow's footsteps grow louder. Glancing around the room, I sink into an armchair and scramble to pull a cushion over the bulge in my lap.

CHAPTER 7

WILLOW

*A*xel stares at the picture and his mood grows sombre. He doesn't like it. Of course he wouldn't. It's an image of me. Nothing special. His reaction nicks at my heart. I like it when he looks at my pictures and smiles as if the drawings I make are worthy of him, but this look… He seems disappointed. Then his mouth moves.

"A picture paints a thousand words." He rumbles in a tone almost undetectable. That remark wasn't meant for me. There's a heavy pain in his silver eyes.

"What were you thinking of when you drew this, Will?" He asks softly. I shrug.

"About how excited I am to start work next week."

He blanches.

I moisten my lips. "You hate it, don't you?"

He lands his full attention on me, and I feel exposed. His lips move and a shadow crawls over his expression.

"Honesty, Axel." I warn him. I'd rather feel the immediate puncture of his words than the excruciating twist of the knife later.

I watch his throat bob. Then he nods.

"Will, it's both my favourite and my least favourite. As always, your skill with the pencil is incredible. Each drawing is nothing short of a snapshot of the soul. But that's why it's my least favourite, too. Willow, it tells me how you see yourself."

I feel my forehead pucker.

What?

The calming tones continue low and deep.

"It shows me a picture of a young woman who is incomplete. See the expression you've given her? It's meek. Empty of expectations and bracing for an unseen enemy. It's a beautiful picture, Willow, but the image within is heartbreaking."

I lean in, peering over the top of the page. It's not that. It's just me. I feel his breath warm my face and pull back at the shivers it sends tumbling through me.

"Willow." His voice hardens and bites. "Why are you reading that book?"

I'm grateful that his attention is elsewhere, because my face burns with shame.

I attempt a nonchalant shrug, but he cuts in.

"Honesty, Willow."

I sigh and pick up the book. I stare at the inconspicuous blank cover so I don't have to look at him.

"I…uh, found it hidden in Rain's library. I wasn't going to read it, but, well, after I saw your texts yesterday I couldn't help it. I mean, the texts, the story. These women want it. They don't just accept it, they really, truly want to do those things. Sometimes, they even initiate it!"

My ears strain to catch his low query.

"And how did it make you feel to read that? Did you feel fear?"

I shiver. "No. It made me feel curious, like I could almost understand that look Rain gives Archer sometimes…"

I almost tell him the rest of it, how I've found some of those sites on the internet and just stared at those pictures of the naked men for ages. Then I found the videos. They were fascinating. Full of men in control of themselves and women with that look on their faces like they just tasted the most amazing desert of their lives. Her body leaning towards his. I couldn't stop watching. So many different videos, and in each one the women presented themselves to the man with an open invitation on their pouting lips. My eyes were irresistibly drawn to the man's movements, the rolling of his hips, the part of him that sank and withdrew from his willing partner.

Willing. Like Axel had said.

And the way my own body heated and ached a little more with the conclusion of each video bewildered me.

I realise in the silence that Axel is staring curiously at me, like he's intruding on my thoughts. My face burns and I look away, snatching up my new sketchbook and novel and leave him sitting in the armchair.

* * *

Rain returns with Archer around midday on Sunday. She takes in my pale complexion and slides her arm through mine, leading me to the garden.

"You'll be perfectly fine, Will. It's okay to be nervous, but there's really no need. We'll be there for you, and Flynn's coming this afternoon, too. He's been my security for well over a year, and he's good. You'll meet him after the hairdresser's appointment tonight. Oh, Will. I'm so excited! This is our dream, and everyone who's important to us is right here beside us." Her eyes shimmer and sparkle.

I've heard about Flynn. I'm sure there's a story there, too that will be revealed to me in time. He's going to be staying for a couple of months in the spare bedroom between mine and Axel's, and that alone puts me on edge. A strange man so close to my bedroom makes my stomach curdle.

Rain's so wired with anticipation that I can't help but grin past my doubt.

"I'm looking forward to listening to my sister's beautiful voice again. Do you remember when you used to sing us to sleep?"

She chuckles at the memory. "I'd make up songs about all of

us going on silly adventures. I really miss that." Then the corners of her mouth drop.

"I just wish those memories never ended like they did. We were all meant to explore the world together, grow old with each other."

I squeeze her hand, tilting my lips.

"Nah, that never would have worked. You're going to be a cranky bitch when you're old, and nobody's going to want to be around that."

"I was trying to convince Archer to let me get a kitten." She smirks meaningfully. I nod in playful contemplation.

"Yep, there's the first instalment of your crazy cat lady phase."

We giggle until our tension falls away.

"You ready to go?" She tugs at a limp strand of hair. It feels like the end of a chapter, and the buzz of nerves in my belly dries my throat. I need this chapter to end. With new hair and a cosmetic mask, I can take a lungful of air and begin the next part of my life. The one where I have a stable place to live, where I'm employed and preparing to exit the foster system for good. I can be Willow who doesn't jump at shadows.

* * *

I stare at the woman looking back at me. Her eyebrows have been tamed and shaped into a graceful arch, making her blue eyes seem larger. Her hair is a warm light brown that falls away from the delicate structure of her cheekbones, the loose strand curling under the lines of her jaw. She's pretty. And it makes my stomach clench in fear.

"What do you think, Will? You look stunning!" Her elation stiffens as she watches my response.

"Maybe I should have left it alone." My voice wobbles.

"Honey, you're safe. We are all here to protect you. Archer, Flynn and I will all be watching you."

"Will Axel be there, too?" The question tumbles from my mouth without thought, and Rain zeroes in.

"Axe will be working, but he might come by some nights, why?"

I shrug, as surprised at my reaction as Rain is. I run my tongue over my lips before I find the words.

"He's…big. I'm sure nobody will try anything if he's there."

Her teeth gleam. "He's a great guy, Will. You can trust him." Her statement is smug and certain, and I bite my lip. He's huge, and strong, and unpredictable. But he held me without hurting me, and showed me he could protect me from the dark look, even when he wears it, and I feel almost safe in his company. But still, I'm so tied up in knots that I have no idea how to distinguish between good and evil.

"Can I, Rain? How do I know? Do I simply take your word for it that he won't hurt me?"

She clasps my hand, pressing her lips against my forehead.

"No, sis. Don't ever rely on anybody else to decide if people are likely to hurt you or not. It's a distinction you need to learn yourself. The people who want to be part of your life in any capacity need to prove themselves worthy of you, but it's a two-way street. You need to give them a little, too. I'm not saying open yourself up to everyone you meet, just be cautious about it. Exercise prudence at every opportunity and never give power to someone unworthy of you. You will eventually be able to distinguish between those who give back, and those who take."

The drawings and the art books! Axel ensured that everything was an honourable transaction, that I would not feel indebted to him. He gave back.

As I mull it over, I gather my hair and tuck it into a hat I brought. It's beautiful, but without the rest of my mask on, I feel too exposed to wear it out in public. Rain watches with quiet thought as we head towards the bus shelter.

"You don't have to hide here, Will. The people in town are good sorts."

I want to believe her, but before here, I've never been exposed to people who were anything but evil. Even those who didn't hurt me physically could be mentally brutal. It's not possible for me to have met with all the evil in the world, and Rain all the good. She wants me to see this place as a paradise. But eventually, the cruel underbelly will show itself. I merely dip my head.

"Tomorrow, your shift will start at ten. It will be quiet with only a couple of tables full for lunch. It will give you a chance to adjust and see how the system works. You'll be onto it in no time. I'll be there to help you, but at around five it should start filling up. Your shift should end around ten thirty. I can relieve you for breaks, but it will be a long day. I'll run you through the cash register, but Archer will mostly be doing that from behind the bar, so it will only be settling accounts when he's busy."

I don't mind the length of the shift. I'm used to working harder for longer periods. And this time I'll get paid.

As we close the few metres between the bus stop and Rain's gate, she squeals in delight.

"Flynn's here. You have to meet him. He's a sweetie!"

She snags my hand and drags me inside.

"Flynn!" She calls, and he emerges from his bedroom. He's not as tall as Axel, but taller than me. He's well built with neat blonde hair and a kind face. His clothes are more stylish than the simple jeans and shirts of Axel and Archer, freshly groomed and smelling of spicy aftershave. Everything about him shows he didn't move in the same circles as the other boys.

He shows all his teeth and scoops Rain into his arms.

"You look well, and I want to congratulate you in person, too! About bloody time that loser quit his commitment issues and snapped you up before I did!"

Rain's giggle explodes as Archer's voice carries down the hall.

"Quit your whining. You snooze, you lose."

Flynn turns with a cheek tight from the size of his grin, catching Archer in his arms. It's an embrace of hard muscle and loud silence that speaks volumes, and when Archer pulls back his eyes shine, even though his expression remains impassive. He swallows loudly, gravitating to Rain's side.

"It's great to have you back. How is your mum?"

Rain explains that Flynn and his mother are selling up their place and planning on moving to Mountain Plateau. There's a comforting warmth in his tone that eases some of my trepidation.

"Great. She's busy cleaning the place up, but she's accepted an offer on the house, so I'll be hitting up the estate agents before work."

"How wonderful! Oh, and you've got to meet my sister, Willow."

CHAPTER 8

AXEL

*E*ven as I'm bending the kid's head down into the back of the patrol car, Willow's eyes linger in my thoughts.

That picture she gave me. It's terrible. I guessed she'd have a view of herself diluted with the abuse, but the image was hollow. There was nothing deeper than pencil lines. The light that radiates from her wasn't captured. The mischief wasn't even hinted at in the straight lines of the nondescript mouth. I need to speak with Rain about it.

But that's not the only thing troubling me. It's how she's infused in my thoughts. When she's not there I find myself looking for her. When she's close I have a need to be talking to her. When she's gone I chase that frangipani-and-lime scent that lingers around her.

I'm used to women. I find something in each of them I like, then convince the feeling to build into desire, then share it with them. But the way my body reacts to Willow? That came without the interest to warm her sheets first. It crept in unbidden and unwanted. I have no interest in going there with her.

My lungs flutter.

But I do.

I grind my teeth and push the thought away. There is no way that will be happening. Besides Willow being too damaged for it to be on her radar, I couldn't do that to myself knowing we'd be living in the same house with those uncomfortable conversations I don't want to have. She'll want more from me, like all the others. And I will never give that. I can't offer that to anyone a second time.

I'm absorbed into an old bitterness that threatens to grow, so I swallow it away and mechanically read the kid his rights.

Dane frowns at me.

"Come on, Axe. Give it up. Something's eating you."

Dane is already married with his first child on its way. His missus sends him to work with extra baked treats he sometimes shares with me.

I huff and rub the back of my neck, resigned.

"There's this girl-" I break off when he spins towards me with his mouth agape.

"No way! Is it possible that there's a woman out there to reign in the stallion?"

My growl answers him.

"No. It's not like that. I mean, she's got issues, huge ones, and the last thing she wants, or needs is a man around."

"But? There's definitely a 'but' in there." Dane prompts.

My lungs empty.

"But…there's something about her that's under my skin. She's not like the women I bed where I react to the idea of a night in the sack. I don't even think those things, and my body just reacts on its own. It's doing my head in."

"You don't even think about it? Not even when you're on your own?" He smirks, and my face reddens thinking of the other night when her face flashed through my head and took me over the edge.

"You like her." He says.

My blood chills.

"No. She's utterly unremarkable and not my type at all." I seek out slim women with gentle curves, not skinny, nondescript ones.

"It doesn't matter if she's your 'type' or not. You like her. You want her."

I snarl his ridiculous theory away and pull up at the station more abruptly than I intend to.

The kid in the back bangs his head against the window and utters a soft groan. Dane stabs me a dark look and I fall silent, hoping the kid won't mention it.

* * *

"Hey there, Battle Axe!" Flynn greets me with a handshake and winces as I slap him on the back. I automatically scan the room for a glimpse of Willow, but she's not around.

"Ready for tomorrow?" I ask.

"Sure am. Looking forward to being back in that place. It all started there for all of us. Archer, Rain and me. Hey, you haven't heard Rain play yet, have you?"

Rain and her guitar, Wind, used to play at The Broken Keg before she got her big break with Flynn's mate at a club in the city.

"You'll have to come and watch." He invites. "She's amazing."

My thoughts shift to Willow. I'll be going there after work for a while, just to make sure she's safe.

"You met Willow?" I probe.

"Yes. She's quite something, isn't she?" He chuckles, and I slam my teeth together in inexplicable irritation at his observation.

"You'll keep an eye on her, won't you?"

His smile falters a little at my tone.

"It'll be my pleasure."

I detect an edge to his voice and I'm rattled by the heavy warning in my own.

"Just leave her alone. She's been through enough. Just leave her be and make sure everybody else does, too."

Flynn's eyebrows shoot upward.

"Sure thing."

* * *

Flynn returns to his room to finish unpacking and I locate Rain poring over paperwork at the kitchen table. I slide the picture of me Willow drew under Rain's nose. She drops her pen and clutches it, an awed 'ohhh' escaping from her lungs. She doesn't shift her gaze.

"She's so talented. This is beautiful."

I fall into the seat beside her.

"Yeah, she's captured it perfectly. You can see the effort I put into working out. How is it even possible to convey energy spent in a picture?"

As Rain shakes her head, I slip the next drawing over top and watch Rain's forehead crease.

"This...?" She can't finish.

"I know. This is how she sees herself. It's heartbreaking, isn't it? You know her. What can I do to make her see herself like this?" I tap the image of me.

She lingers on the portrait of Willow, then lifts the other one again, scrutinising the detail. Her eyes light on my face thoughtfully.

"Interesting." She mutters and lifts my picture again.

"What?" I press.

Something flickers in her expression before she closes off to me. She pinches her lips together in thought and appears to search my face.

"Just...just be yourself. I think that's exactly what she needs."

* * *

I frown as I make my way to my room. I listen to the muffled bumps and scrapes of Flynn settling in and find a hard knot in my stomach that tells me I don't want him here.

My phone vibrates with a message coming through.

I'm free every night this week if you want to catch up.

The thought leaves a bitter taste in my mouth. I'm not even remotely stirred up. There's a hunger inside me, but it's not for her, whoever she is, or what anything she has to offer.

Sorry, I'm just not interested. I tap out and hit send.

The phone vibrates again.

So you got what you wanted and you just put me out of your mind?

Shit. I lock my jaw and resist the urge to respond. I couldn't put her out of my mind if she were never there to begin with. Now I have that old familiar guilt churning around inside again.

I delete the messages without responding. Then I block the number.

I grab a fistful of hair and growl. How did this get so difficult? I never led them on. I explained what would happen, and when it did I became an arsehole. A player.

I used to have fun, but lately the demands outweigh the release. In the last week my interest in pursuing them seems to have all but dried up. I dig around in my pocket and retrieve a small handful of torn paper, numbers scrawled over each one.

Huh! This one added her name. Tiffany. I feel my lips curl in a grimace at her name.

Willow. I catch my breath.

"Get out of my head!" I snarl into space.

Willow.

My phone vibrates again with another unlisted number. Frustration bleeds into rage, and my phone shatters as it strikes the bed frame. I crush it beneath my boot for good measure and head for the gym.

* * *

I do another set of push-ups and rejoice in the burn of

muscles. My throat is too narrow to fill my lungs fast enough, but I keep pushing through. I discarded my shirt when it reached saturation, and now the sweat pours off me, the drips rolling off my hair forming a puddle beneath my face. I watch it grow beneath me, the moisture rolls down my arms and runs onto the mat at my wrists.

Just keep going until your mind empties, Axel.

My ears sharpen on the sound of someone approaching, and I glance up. Dirty old runners, baggy jeans…

My hand slips in the puddle of sweat and snaps out from underneath me. My chest and chin hit the mat together and I feel my lip bust on a tooth.

The soft chuckle caresses my ears as I fight for breath on my stomach.

"You falling for me?" She gazes down sardonically as I flip on my back to open my lungs.

For once I'm at a loss for words. She has her hair tucked away inside a grey woollen hat that highlights her delicate features and graceful neck. She hands me a bottle of water and I lean against the wall and take a swig, suddenly aware that she watches the bit that I spilled travel down my chest. My stomach tightens and my pulse races faster.

"What do you want?" I bite out, and instantly regret my tone. She's the last person I should want to see right now, yet I'm pleased she's here. She frowns and squats before me. Shit. She's the closest she's ever come to me of her own accord, and my nerves are going haywire. I close my eyes and force my breaths to settle.

The gentle warmth of her fingertips brushes my lip and I groan at the exquisite sensation.

What the fuck is she doing?

CHAPTER 9

WILLOW

*Y*our lip. It's bleeding."

His eyes shoot open and drill into me. I freeze in fear, but he doesn't move. Axel doesn't reach for me, even though all the silver has left his eyes, leaving them blacker than I've ever seen.

It's fascinating, really. Without the terror that expression usually invokes in me, it makes him almost…beautiful. I feel my body respond. I heat up, and my heart races. Parts of me pulse and ache, but in a throb that excites, that promises. Like in the novel. It makes my mind up, and I mull over how to raise the topic as I use the sleeve of my jumper to soak up the blood.

I've finished the book. It ended with the woman willingly offering her mouth as the hero kissed her, and it left me with a residual feeling of curiosity. Axel told me I can speak to him, ask him anything, and I'm encouraged by his display of control. He reacts to me, but he's not seeking to control me. That's the safest I can get. I just need to find the courage to ask him.

He stares at my mouth as the bleeding slows and I move the lip gently with my fingertip to inspect the damage.

"It's not too bad." I decide quietly. He doesn't say a thing. Just watches me with those darkened eyes and caught breath. I feel his hot exhales stroke my finger. I lock on the sudden courage that finds me, and run my fingertip gently over a bead of sweat pooling beside his mouth and trace a path for it over the side of his lightly stubbled jaw. The coarse texture seems at odds with the silk of his lip. A fascinating discovery. I'm mesmerised. I've never touched a man like this and it's so different to how my own skin feels. I lift my other hand slowly, so as not to startle him, and mirror the movements on my own body. Soft and hard. My flesh beneath one hand and his beneath the other, a fascinating comparison. My smooth jaw makes me wonder how his would feel against mine. I lead my finger slowly over the pulse jumping erratically in his neck. My own fires to a similar rhythm. On a surface of sweat, I take my finger on a slick ride over the hollow in the base of his throat and pause.

I search his eyes, and that dark look smolders. There's something there I could almost touch, a flame I'm drawn to.

But still he doesn't move. My breath shudders and his eyes erupt. I hear his swallow as I draw my finger down. It slides between the hard mountains of his chest. His flesh is on fire, and so is mine as my other hand sinks below the neckline of my jumper. On a whim I divert my path. His pectoral muscles are like granite covered with satin. I thought his skin would be rough. The hard peak of his nipple meets my finger. I marvel at how it feels like a smaller version of my own beneath the fingers of my other hand. I flick my eyes to his, and the full force of them is locked on my face, his lips still parted.

I startle when a low moan escapes my own slack lips, and I stagger backwards.

From an arm's length away I feast on him. The power coiled in that body is so incredibly potent that I can smell it. The display of muscle and flesh short circuits my brain and electrical misfires vibrate through my veins.

"What do you want, Willow?" He rasps in a tone lower than I've heard before.

But that look on his face…

"Is this what a man feels like, Axel? Because this is amazing." I murmur in awe.

"What do you want, Willow?" He repeats. The darkness tangles with his voice and sends tremors through me and before

I lose my courage I tell him.

"I…I think I want you to kiss me, Axel."

His eyes narrow and he remains so still for so long I think he won't. Then he moves.

His body comes to life with the languid finesse of a tiger, closing the distance between us cautiously like I'm his prey, and I hear another moan leave me. He remains on all fours, his breath carrying the warmth of his gentle words

"Are you sure, Willow?"

Fresh sawn pine and heavenly musk dives into my lungs, carrying the salty tang of his sweat with it. That scent that is Axel finds something dormant and elusive, shakes it awake and feels its thirst.

"Oh, yes." Every cell in my body shudders with impatience. The space between us fills with inhales, and I close my eyes to surround myself with the sensation.

I feel the warm soft caress of Axel's mouth ghost over mine. The barest touch, little more than a secret glance but my breath hitches and I lean towards it. Then he's there again, another fleeting touch. And again, but this time he lingers, his breath setting pace with mine. His heated exhales fill my lungs, and I send them back to him. It's so intimate, sharing air. It mixes with the fire under my skin and the aching throb in my core and renders it impossible to steady my lungs.

His mouth starts moving, massaging my lips with exquisite torture. He gently tugs with satin pressure on my bottom lip. Like a drawn-out punishment he teases and taunts and I find my own desire demands I seek him out. We're synchronised hunger. His tongue darts out cautiously over my lip and I gasp. It's as soft and warm as his mouth, and I shiver as the tip runs lightly between the slight parting of my lips. I groan into his mouth. He answers with a low growl I feel between my legs and his kisses grow harder, more demanding. I explore the tip on his tongue with my own, and with a groan he dives deeper. I can feel him. I can taste that incredible nectar that can only be Axel. I'm immersed in him, the taste of his mouth, the encompassing scent, the duet of our laboured breaths.

Of its own accord, my hand reaches out and slides over the hard muscles of his shoulder, sliding through the sweat, finding his nape and entwining my fingers with his thick hair, pulling him closer to me. His flesh is scorching beneath my touch. I feel his weight shift and a huge hand cups my face.

He's touching me.

My eyes slam open and Axel fills my view. His eyelashes rest lightly on his cheeks like he's sleeping, or savouring a top shelf wine.

There's a man. Right there!

With a gasp I break the kiss and scramble away.

Heaving fire burns through my lungs as if I'd run through the woods for hours. My hand touches my lips to discover the source of the tingles that still excite them.

Axel hasn't moved. He's still on his knees with a hand hovering where my face was his breaths rasping and that deep dark look. I stare at him in awe.

"Is…is that what it's supposed to feel like?" My words tremble with the effort of holding myself back from diving in for more.

He shakes his head, swallowing thickly. I watch him draw a heavy breath and sit back on his haunches and I'm immediately flat.

"Oh. What did I do wrong?"

His huff explodes like he's biting back laughter. I cringe and draw my knees up to my chest. I want to get out of here, but my legs won't work yet.

His timbre is raw and spills out over gravel.

"Willow, shit. No. You misunderstood. I mean, it feels good normally but this felt-"

"I get it." I snap, humiliation replacing the strength in my legs. I stand unsteadily and carry my shame through the door.

"Willow! No, it's not-"

I close the door.

* * *

What a double-edged sword that was. I thought the kiss was incredible, my nervous system still burns for more, but the mortifying consequences that followed?

I didn't imagine Axel could be so cruel, but I should have known. If experience has taught me anything it's that the cruelty of men comes in many different forms.

I'd hoped he was different, but I've seen the messages he gets. He has his pick of women at his fingertips, none of whom I can compete with. I don't belong in his circles. I'm sure they're all worldly, sophisticated types who aren't damaged and clueless like me.

I shake my head and bury it in my hands. Not that I want him like they do. I just wanted to discover what it was all about. Safely.

The echo of a thundering roar carries through the hall. Axel. I can hear his steps, oddly heavy, pound past my door. They pause for a moment and I hold my breath with a frown. Then they move off and a moment later, his bedroom door slams shut.

I suck on air. My stomach tightens with a compulsion to go to him, but I push it aside. Why would I want more ridicule?

I take off my beanie and watch my new hair tumble free. I love it. My drab bleached look has been miraculously replaced by a golden-brown halo that shines and gleams. This is a woman with a job. A home. A family. This reflection is a strong woman who felt the touch of a man and didn't cower. Well, not immediately.

I'm finding my courage.

Tomorrow is my first day of work.

Butterflies collide and dance in my chest.

CHAPTER 10

AXEL

*W*ith white knuckles I pace the room.

What a fucking shit day! Between that woman messaging me, making me feel guilty, and the kiss...

My inhale hisses between clenched teeth.

What the fuck was that about?

I shouldn't have done that. I should have gently turned her down. After all, I'm not interested in Willow, and it's not fair on her. But...

I couldn't not kiss her.

A part of me thought I'd do a noble deed. Show her it can be nice. So I did. It was only supposed to be a quick taste, a chaste touch. And then she dipped that damned broken innocence of hers into my chest and made me feel her in places I never knew existed. She blew my mind apart with burning temptation and lingering promises.

And I want more.

Just a night of fun to share, to show her how good it can be. It's the least I can do for a friend.

In the shower, I attempt to wash away the scorching trail her finger left. The icy water does nothing to cool my thoughts, and this time, her face encourages and tempts me into my release.

* * *

"Axe, you need to just cool off." Simone squeezes my arm and closes the door behind us. We're in the empty workout room and I groan inwardly. The last time I was in a gym, Willow was there. Images crash through my head and won't clear away.

"Are you listening to me? You can't just punch a fellow officer, even if he is being an arsehole. You know discipline, you understand control. What's going on, Axel?"

What can I tell her? That I lost control and gave that fresh-faced prick a taste of knuckles and retribution because I was already frustrated and his stinking attitude was the final straw? It was just the result of waters running far deeper down. Just a female. The unimpressive girl who burrowed into my veins and messed up my insides. The lacklustre creature that asked for a kiss and blew my world apart. The plain woman that tore open my core at that expression of hurt. I thought I understood guilt. I'd made friends with it along the path of one-night stands, but the shame I feel for allowing her to think she'd done something wrong burned through my stomach like acid.

When Officer Ryan led that cuffed woman to the holding cell, helped her in with a rough shove and muttered about her being trash, I just reacted.

My head thumps from my clenched teeth.

"Put on those gloves and take it out on the bag. You know you're going to be reprimanded for this, and if you come out looking like you've lost control of yourself, it'll be worse."

I snatch off my shirt and don't even bother to tie the gloves. I thunder my frustration into the bag over and over again until sweat soaks the waistband of my pants. After a while I lean against the bag, my lungs burning. It's still there. That image of Willow's expression melting from innocence to humiliation when I couldn't get the words out properly.

I hurt her.

I snarl and put everything I have into one last punch.

Simone opens the door as the bag snaps off its chain and lands on the floor beside her.

I apologise through gritted teeth. Officer Ryan offers a smug smirk through his swollen jaw and puts a limp hand in mine. My superior's nod.

"This is your first warning. You only get two, and we would prefer not to issue a second, so I trust you will learn from this. We can offer you Anger Management support, psychological services to assist where needed and of course, the support of your police family."

Simone interjects; "And of course, Axel, if you require a leave of absence to manage your issues, we are willing to allow you any time you may need."

I feel their kindness like salt in a wound.

* * *

I turn my bike towards The Broken Keg. The afternoon rush would be in full swing and I just want to see how she was doing. That's what I tell myself, anyway.

My eyes adjust to the darkness, and I take in all the changes Archer and Rain made to the modest tavern. The old bar has been replaced by a giant slab of curved timber with a raw edge, highlighted by the soft glow of several strategically places downlights. The tables and chairs have been upgraded, also in timber. Every table is filled. The bar is lined with patrons, and I spot Archer darting between customers with smiling conversation, dispensing drinks with efficient hands.

The stage is a slightly raised platform with a piano at one end, and Rain perched on a stool at the other. She brings her guitar to life with a flick of her wrist, and her beautiful clear voice sails through the air. I listen to the haunting lyrics of Mystery Girl by Roy Orbison as I scan the tables for Willow. She must be in the kitchen while another waitress is weaving around the tables. The waitress moves with a confidence that suggests she's done this work for years. She's made for it, I think appreciatively as I take in the dark caramel tresses piled in a loose bun, the dress that accentuates the most incredible figure I've ever seen. I take more interest, taking in the long, elegant legs, her hips gently swelling with a rear end that's plucked straight from my hottest dream. Her waist is narrow and fragile looking, and I linger on the fabric that clings to it before I slide my gaze upwards. The firm swell of her breasts strain against the buttons. Not too big. Just perfect. My pulse clatters.

Maybe that's all I need. To lose myself in a hot, perfect body to dump all this stress that chews on my nerves. Something to take my mind off her.

I've kept my personal activities away from Mountain Plateau. I know better than to hunt too close to home, but maybe just once, when the prey is as tantalising as this, I can allow an exception.

I realise I've been daydreaming when I clear my vision and the waitress has disappeared. I stab a hand through my hair and make my way to the bar. I don't even need to see her face. It doesn't matter, anyway since I never remember what they look like the next morning.

Archer appears before me with a shot glass and lifts his chin.

After a day like today I need this. I throw my head back and feel the liquid burn its way down my throat.

Archer appears and lingers, a towel hanging at the ready over his shoulder.

"Bad day?"

"You've got no idea."

He slaps me with a sympathetic grin. "I can line up the shots if you want to stick around for a ride home?"

I think about it, but I have work tomorrow. I decline with a frown.

He whips a beer from nowhere and pushes it over.

"How's Willow going?" Even saying her name dries my throat.

The light catches the white patch of hair on his temple as he grins.

"Ask her yourself."

I turn around, and that stunning waitress is walking towards us. A knot forms in my stomach and with a sense of dread my eyes leap to her face.

'Fuck me!" I breathe and Archer stiffens in my periphery. Willow walks towards me like a cat, the stunning figure she's kept hidden beneath shapeless rags paling only to her face. Besides yesterday when she'd had her hair bundled in a hat, she'd always concealed her face behind a curtain of hair. Now she's exposed it, highlighted her huge sapphire eyes and delicate cheekbones, revealed the exotic lines of her jaw. The whole world can see her beauty.

But she can't. She smiles with a shyness that's completely ignorant of how stunning she is.

"Hey Andre. See anything on the menu that interests you?"

Her eyes twinkle as she gestures to a small pack of women standing together at the end of the bar. They're looking at me with familiar, hungry expressions, but my attention is all for Willow.

"Yes." I murmur, but she tilts her head in a laugh that misses my intent. She smiles without jealousy or possessiveness and turns away.

I can't let her go. I reach out and glance a touch on her wrist. She doesn't flinch, just lands me with open curiosity.

"I'm sorry." I mutter. Her grin widens.

"No, I'm sorry. I shouldn't have asked something of you that you didn't want. It's forgotten. Go have fun." She twirls away and is engulfed by the crowd.

When I turn back, Archer stands still as a statue, his eyes drilling into mine.

Shit. I can't deal with this today.

I don't meet his gaze. I just drain the glass and make for the door.

My ride roars to life.

The stars mock me from the safety of the night sky as they watch me try without success to empty my head.

She thinks I didn't want to kiss her. She's forgotten it.

But it's all I can think about. Every damned second of the day.

CHAPTER 11

WILLOW

I curl up in my nest of blankets with a happy sigh. The mask worked. I felt courageous, capable and worthy. I felt normal. I got everyone's orders right and was able to service them in good time.

Rain has the vocals of an angel. My little sister always had a good voice, but it's richer with maturity of use and years. I'm so proud of her.

There was nothing to fear, as it turns out. Besides Axel's barest contact at the bar to catch my attention, nobody touched me.

I can still feel his skin on mine, and I absently rub it.

He apologised for kissing me then left. Probably with one of those women. The thought that he'd never want to touch me doesn't stop me from imagining how it would feel to have him touch me like he would them.

How would his hands feel on my skin?

* * *

"Can I ask you something?" I ask Rain shyly.

She smiles reassuringly, and I fill my lungs.

"I'd, ah, like to take a self-defense class. Um, in town, sometime." I frown and tap into my widening pool of courage. "You know, so I can throat punch anyone who doesn't like my service." I drop her a wink as she giggles.

"Absolutely. You don't have to ask me, Will. You are your own person and can do what you want with your own money."

A warmth spreads in my stomach and widens my smile.

"Oh, Rain, that sounds like music to my ears. My own money, my own decisions!"

"If you like, though, have a chat to Axe or Archer. They might be able to give you some useful tips to feel safe."

'Oh, and Will? Archer and I have been talking, and we thought that it might be good for you to have Monday's and Tuesday's off to do your own thing, if you'd be happy to work the other days?"

A lump burns in my chest. First Axel regrets our kiss, now I'm not good enough to waitress every day.

"I'm sorry, Rain. I'm trying, but I can do better."

Rain spins and grabs my shoulders, landing a stricken expression on me.

"Jesus, no, Will. That's not what we mean at all! You're better than we expected. Your service is flawless, and you're so efficient you could be mistaken for having been doing this for years. We just think you deserve a rest like everyone else in every other job."

I nod and manage a weak smile. I wonder how long it will be before I 'deserve' more days off. Maybe as soon as they find someone to replace me.

I can't shake the knot of dread that ticks like a stopwatch counting down the minutes until it all falls apart again. Like it always does.

* * *

The crowd is thick on the floor as I weave through the bodies, trying to make my way to the kitchen without touching any.

"Table eight. Rib eye, medium rare with mushroom gravy, vegetables and a side of chips."

Archer taps it into the register while he's there, and lifts his eyebrow for the next order, but I shake my head.

"He's on his own." And I flit out the doors again.

The completed order is plated by the time I return and I snag it, delivering a jug of squash to another table on the way.

"Here you are, sir, enjoy." I slide the plate in front of the man.

"Wait." His deep voice halts me and I meet his eyes, deep brown and fixed hard on me.

"When does your shift finish?" He inquires.

"When the last table empties." I turn away but his hand snakes around my wrist. My pulse leaps and I jerk free, staggering backwards in my rush to escape. My blood roars in my head.

"I'm sorry. I didn't mean to frighten you. I just wanted to see if you'd join me for a drink later."

He's one of those guys with perfect teeth who never has a problem attracting attention. Fine, dark eyebrows that give a suggestion of innocence, strong, proportionate features laid out beneath naturally olive skin. With a figure built from power, and his wide smile, he seems like the boy-next-door type, the one promising safety and reliability.

But something seems off.

He wears that dark look. It chills me and locks my breath in my chest. My skin still prickles and squirms from his touch and everything inside me claws at me to get away from him.

I shake my head and let my feet carry me away.

Flynn steps in front of me.

"You okay? I saw him touch you."

I allow my lungs to empty at Flynn's friendly expression, nodding slowly.

"Yeah, it's okay. He was just trying to get my attention. He wanted to meet me later for drinks."

Flynn searches my face, then steps away.

"Don't worry, Willow, we're all keeping an eye out for you."

He's back again a few nights later when The Broken Keg is at capacity, but doesn't try to touch me again. He orders a pasta and snatches conversation where he can.

"I'm Danny. I'm staying in town so you'll see me around for a while. You a local?"

I try to ignore the tightening feeling in my chest. The one that urges me to avoid him. He's being polite, and I'm supposed to be friendly with the patrons.

"I'm new to the area. I'm a friend of the pub owners, so I'm sorry, but I can't even give you any suggestions of the main attractions."

"Ahh, I should have known." He jerks his head backwards, but doesn't turn, just pulls his neck further down into his upturned collar. "They're all watching out for you, you know. Especially that big fella behind us. He your boyfriend?"

I frown. How Danny noticed their protective glances when he never seems to be facing them makes my stomach tighten. I lift my eyes, but I already felt the air shift and knew who he was referring to. Axel stands just inside the doorway, searching the room until he finds me. He notices me talking to Danny and his eyes narrow. I smile at him in greeting while answering Danny.

"No. He's not my boyfriend."

"Interesting." His tone is tight. "Because he seems to be showing you a great deal of interest. Here. Keep the change."

I widen my eyes on Axel. He's just looking out for a friend. I start to object, but when I look back, Danny's seat is empty. I shrug off my frown, scooping up the cash. I leave the meal there for when he returns.

"Hey Andre. Burgers are good tonight. You'll have to skip the spit though, I've already dished that up to a table of rowdy customers."

His face splits and reveals his teeth.

"My name is Axel." He smirks. Then his face hardens. "Look, Will. We need to talk."

"Okay" I say slowly.

A soft blush rises on his cheeks, and as much as I want to listen to his voice, I have to prove to Rain and Archer that I don't need to be replaced.

"Look, Andre, can we do this later? I gotta get back to-" I freeze as his hand encircles my wrist. I pull a breath. The panic begins to coil and I dart my eyes down. His huge hand closed on my skin looks like it could break my bones with a single squeeze. The wave of panic threatens and I snap my attention back to his and that dark look settles on me. But it's not frightening, like Danny's was. It's...electric. My pulse reminds me of the feel of his lips on mine and burns to feel it again. My mouth sags as breaths race through the space, and my tongue darts out to moisten dry lips.

His thumb gently strokes the inside of my wrist and my breath explodes, but I don't pull away. It's Axel who breaks the contact, leaving me shivering with the loss of his touch.

"Later." His mutter agrees, and I watch his huge frame stride out the door.

As I clear the tables, I notice Danny at table eight watching me from the shadows, the meal untouched on the table. That table only seems to fill when there's no other seating available. It's tucked behind a pillar with awful lighting and a limited view of the pub. If you're fortunate enough to be seated against the wall you get a pretty good view of Rain's profile, but you lose the atmosphere, but Danny doesn't seem to mind. I make my way over.

Indicating his plate with a smirk, I say, "found that rat, huh? I was wondering where that little fellow got to."

His cheeks lift on soundless laughter.

"I ate the rat, left the rest. Cooked to perfection, with just the right amount of seasoning."

My laughter dies when I notice his meal. It hasn't been picked at, so much as dissected and strewn about his plate.

"Was it not to your liking?" I keep a neutral expression, but criticism leaves me feeling queasy, even if I'm not the one responsible for it.

His eyes flash to mine with unsettling clarity.

"No, I honestly just came for the ambience, and felt guilty for taking a table without ordering anything. And I was hoping to convince you to have a drink with me."

"Thanks for the invitation, but I'm not looking for anything."

Undeterred he offers me a slippery smile.

"Not even a friend? Just a little conversation?"

I sigh. It would be rude not to indulge a customer a harmless invitation. The tables are empty, anyway, and soon enough Rain would call on me to come home.

"What do you drink?"

He smiles his victory.

I bring Danny a beer and sit opposite him.

"So, what do you do when you're not providing the town's best service?"

"I sneak up on old men in wheelchairs and push them down the hill."

Danny chokes on his beer.

"Seriously, I have a collection of the false teeth that fall out when they scream."

He sniggers.

"Well, I'll ensure I don't include Mountain Plateau in my retirement plan. Although I do enjoy travelling fast downhill. I found that my Mustang loves diving down the slopes of this town."

"Is that your car?" I have limited understanding about cars. I realise a personal passion for a make and model of car is a very normal thing to possess, but in a world of threats and looming pain, I had no time to entertain 'normal' things.

Danny's face flashes with hurt and I chuckle.

"Oh, I'm sorry. This is where I'm meant to be impressed about whatever it is that makes a Mustang special." I shrug and try to hide my embarrassment behind a smile.

"I'm sure your Mustang is amazing. I guess I'm just not your average girl who 'gets' cars."

Danny leans forward, and instinctively, I push back into my chair.

"No, Willow, you are certainly not 'average.'"

With his smooth flowing tone, I gulp down the rest of my lemonade to settle the threatening bile and stand.

"Thanks for the talk, Danny. I heard my boss call. See you later."

I know I'm stuttering, but I don't care. I just need to put some distance between us.

CHAPTER 12

AXEL

*A*rcher's footfalls pound behind me and I slow until we're shoulder to shoulder on the running track.

"You good, Battle Axe?" he asks as we find a rhythm.

There's an edge to his tone, like he really wanted to demand what the hell my damned problem was.

"Why?" I snap my suspicion.

"Simone called asking about you."

Archer stops at my growl, and I pull up short beside him.

"She's got no right to tell you anything. Shit, the guy was an arsehole anyway and someone had to put him in his place. Simone should have kept her mouth shut."

Archer stares at me with huge eyes and I groan at my own stupidity.

"She didn't tell you anything, did she?"

Archer answers with a shake of his head.

"She just asked about you with that...tone. But now I know something is going on, Axe. You're too smart to let me trip you up so easily, you've been spending more time at home and less in random beds, and now you're riled up at work? Come on, man. Is it Flynn? He'll be gone in a couple of months. Or Willow? I've noticed she hovers around you a bit. If it gets too much I can have a word in Rain's ear to get Willow to give you space if you like?"

I frown. I should say yes, but I don't want her to keep away from me.

"No, it's nothing, Frostbite, really. I guess I'm just a bit jaded about finding my way into any more beds. It's pissing me off."

Archer keeps pushing. "So it's not Willow then?"

"No!" I snap. I wish he'd just let it go.

My friend smiles with loaded intent.

"Good." He says. "Then you won't mind spending a bit of time with her then. Rain says Will wants to learn to protect herself, and I said I'd speak to you about it. Can I assume since you don't have issues with her that you'd be happy to teach her a thing or two?"

I clench my jaw and close my eyes. *Spend more time with her?* I ignore the tingles in my stomach at the thought. Being in her company for any longer than is essential is counter-productive to what I actually need. I'm struggling to rediscover a state of peace, and Willow is the cause of its disruption in the first place. But if I explain that to Archer, he'd relentlessly torment me, finding things in my admission that aren't there.

"But you're better than me." I grate. I'm loathe to admit it, even though we know it's true. I just need an excuse to keep my distance. I sigh when I register his smirk that leaves me feeling like he's read my thoughts.

"Yep, I am. But I'm way too busy with the bar to help." He slaps me on the back and airily lengthens his stride. "I'll tell Rain you'll start tomorrow."

* * *

I can hear my own nervous swallow as I round the corner and see her. She's in those loose jeans and a shapeless jumper again, even though the morning is warming up.

"How are you enjoying work?"

She pulls her legs into a hug and smiles warily.

"I love it. I know it's only waitressing, but it's really satisfying. It's ironic, actually, that I once dreamed that I would be the one running a cafe and Rain would be *my* waitress."

"But you don't you feel safe there? Archer told me you wanted to learn self defence."

She fidgets and stares solemnly at her knees for a moment.

"I don't really feel safe anywhere, and it just doesn't sit well knowing I have to trust that someone will have my back when it matters."

Her eyes dull and dart to the ground, heavy with ghosts. I'm so intimate with her reasoning that I feel she's been sitting in my soul running her fingers through my pain. I shiver.

"I understand. Only in the darkest moments do we find out which of our friends will raise their sword against us, and understand that the only person you can trust is yourself."

Her eyes flicker.

"What happened to you?"

I grind my teeth, unwilling to share.

"Come on, Axe, you took a walk over my past, it's only fair you give me a glimpse of yours."

I measure my sigh. I saw how vulnerable she felt knowing I was aware of what she'd been subjected to. My past isn't as traumatic as hers. The resilience she displays in the light of her terror makes my pain seem trivial. I shrug nonchalantly.

"My best friend of twenty years betrayed me."

She frowns.

"Oh, Axel…"

"It's nothing, really. Certainly nothing as horrifying as you had to endure."

She shakes her head vehemently.

"No, Axel. Don't devalue your own pain by comparing it to someone else's."

The sigh that falls between us is loaded with honesty.

"It's my fault, really. Even when we were playing together as kids, Dorian was always competitive. I should have realised he'd set his sights on me when he started turning up at the gym just after I joined. He always wanted what I had. God knows why. When I joined the military, he did, too, even though I know he really wanted to be some bigwig playing the stock market. It was great at first, sharing my experiences with him, but as time passed he changed. He heard my name spoken in some meeting he'd overheard one day, indicating they were considering me for a promotion, and he became hell-bent on ensuring he was chosen over me. He trained harder, paraded his skills at every opportunity, and began bringing up every last, insignificant detail of any time I'd slipped up."

"Ouch." Willow cringes.

"I didn't let it get to me, since I wasn't concerned if I was promoted or not, but Dorian ramped it up, goading me into fights and telling our superiors I had a temper that made me too volatile to be able to depend on me in a higher position. It hurt, but I shrugged it off as Dorian being determined. When I didn't get the promotion, he was overjoyed. But when he didn't get it either, he still needed to win. Prove he could do better than me. So he stole my fiancée."

That old, raw bitterness leaks out.

"Jesus, Axe! He betrayed your trust, and your fiancée broke your heart in one fell swoop. That's brutal."

I nod reluctantly. That was the general gist.

She gasps softly, and I feel it in my spine. "And you were stuck working alongside him, too."

I jab my fingers in my lengthening hair.

"The last time I saw him, he was trying to stop Archer from getting to Rain. I told him no by knocking him unconscious and sending a bullet into his foot. I wanted to plant it between his eyes instead, but he's got a kid. I kind of thought I'd be helping him, shattering his foot. Everyone knew he'd fail the psych test for any promotion, and by giving him an injury it would take him out of that race, but still allow him to be a good soldier."

That isn't the whole story, but I can't continue. The resurfacing sting of betrayal always leaves me fatigued, and I'm resentful of giving the subject another moment of my time. Self-aware, I adjust my posture and exhale the remnants of bitterness from my lungs.

"Thirsty?" I invite.

She unfolds from the bench like a cat, and images of her in that tight uniform showing off her gentle curves parade unwanted in my head.

"That's why you only allow yourself a single night with a woman." She observes as I follow her into the kitchen. "There's no way to get attached in that time."

"Don't go psycho-analysing me, woman, Rain's already trying that one on me!"

There's an element of truth in it, but it's not attachment I'm afraid of. I've never developed strong feelings for any woman. Not even for Janice. I'm just avoiding becoming ensnared. The trap laid out for us by women was Dad's downfall, just as it was mine. He became an empty, hollow vessel in the shape of my father the night Mum loaded her belongings into my English teacher's flash red car. There was no indication there of any dissatisfaction of her marriage before that night. I watched him deteriorate rapidly. They said it was cancer but I knew life can't pump through a man without a heart.

And I liked Janice. I really did, but being drawn into Janice's lair gave her the ultimate control over me to make or break me at her whim. It wasn't that Janice broke my heart when I watched her dance the same dance as Mum did years before, piling her expensive clothes into the back seat of Dorian's car. It was what she did afterwards that left me devastated and shattered.

CHAPTER 13

WILLOW

I pause my hand over the freezer.

"Do you want your water neat or straight up?"

Axel chuckles.

"You're a nightmare, Will. How about however it comes?"

I fill two glasses unceremoniously from the cold tap. Simple banter like this soothes me. There's no uncomfortable silence, there's nothing sinister lurking in the shadows of our conversation. I watch Axel's throat move the water down and sigh. In another life someone like him could have been my normal. Someone who speaks honestly and openly without an ulterior motive. Someone who makes my nerves sizzle like he does. I smirk at the idea of finding love and settling down like Rain and Archer, white picket fence and two point three children. I picture myself being too afraid to hold my own child because I freak out whenever I'm touched.

"A penny for your thoughts?" His eyebrows lift and it's such a familiar expression I slide into a smile.

"I was just thinking that I've been chasing the dream of independence so hard and for so long, and now it's within reach I don't know what other dream I can chase."

"What about this cafe? Don't you want to do that?"

"No. I thought I did, but I think that desire died along with Sarah. I still have to actually achieve financial security and learn to look after myself, but I find it amusing that Rain and I shared a dream of running a cafe, and neither one of us has pursued it. I mean, she's getting married!"

Axel snorts. He sits the empty glass on the table, his biceps working in that mesmerising way that makes me want to touch them.

"Maybe you'll be the one to catch her bouquet."

I choke on my water.

"That's where you and I are the same, my giant friend. Marriage and children don't even enter the realms of possibility."

HIs silver eyes darken and his jaw ticks.

"Don't want kids?" His guarded tone brings a frown to my face.

"It's not even that. It's just the thought of a precious soul being brought into a world full of evil and pain and me being the freak I am; I'm too much of a mess to be able to protect them."

"You're not a freak, Willow." His gaze bites into me, but he doesn't understand. He can't.

"When are you going to let me in on some military defence secrets? Are you going to show me how to wield a knife so I can carve my initials into an enemy's chest with lightning speed?"

Silver eyes narrow to slits.

"You're doing it again, Will. You're deflecting."

Exasperated, I glare at him.

"What do you want from me? I'm an open book. You know more about me that anyone except Rain, and I've only just met you. There is nothing more to me, but you seem to think if you keep poking you'll find something deeper that just isn't there. All that's beyond what you see is scar tissue and ghosts."

"You're already so much more than what you just told me. You go to so much effort staying in the shadows when you should be walking in the light for everyone to see the person you really are.

Why do you think so little of yourself?"

Laughter falls from me like ice.

"Because I was never meant to step out of the darkness. Some people are destined to exist in the shadows, Axel, because it's our place. We need to find aspirations within our lot or we'll go mad seeking something beyond our reach. It's not my opinion, Axel, I know it. My worth has been shown to me over and over again. It's my punishment for wanting more, and so I never forget my place, I was given this to remind me."

My anger emboldens me. I pull aside my jumper and bare the brand that was etched into my flesh on my eleventh birthday.

I hear his steep inhale. He knows about it, but seeing it must make it real.

"It shouldn't define who you are."

I deflate at the challenge in his voice.

"I know, Axel, but it does. It's the red light on the porch that I can't switch off. And I'm so bored from rehashing it. I used to fight it, but just when I think I've risen above, I'm dragged back into another brutal lesson in reality. All I want now is to be able to defend myself and hold down a job. Eventually, I'll find another goal that's not too far out of reach."

I jerk when Axel's fist rattles the table.

"Fine then. Let's fast track it. Then you can see how small your dreams really are, and you can start stepping into the woman you're supposed to be."

* * *

Flynn approaches carefully as I slide my pencil over the paper and highlight with a light smudge.

"Hey." I greet. When he doesn't respond I sneak a glance at him. He's snagged a drawing of Axel and Archer deep in conversation one evening in the living room.

"Willow, these are spectacular! The detail, the emotion in the strokes..."

He stares greedily at me. "Can you do one of me?"

"Uh, sure. I just finished this one. Let me just pull up another sheet."

Flynn is what many would consider classically handsome, his features slightly softer than the hard angles of Archer and Axel. He's the type so symmetrically perfect that adding them into any art is easy.

I stifle a giggle as he stiffens into a pose.

"Okay, shirt off, and lose the pants." I order firmly, tapping my pencil expectantly on my chin. His forehead creases and slowly pulls his shirt over his head with one hand.

I snigger. He's the most naive man I've met, his innocence and trust so angelic that I almost feel a little guilty for stirring him up. Almost. I compare him to the pictures on the internet. He's well-toned, in fact, outside of a couple of nasty looking scars, his body is an absolute work of art. Not as impressively honed as Axel, but a magnificent specimen all the same.

"I was kidding, but thanks for the show."

He smirks and folds his arms over his naked torso, angling his head in a more pronounced pose.

I laugh as he summons a smoldering expression.

"You've been practising that one. You've nailed it."

"What the fuck are you doing, Flynn?" Axel's bulk appears beside me. Tension vibrates off him and he moves towards an unconcerned Flynn.

"She's trying to trick me out of my clothes. Not my fault I fell for it." He chuckles.

Axel flicks his discarded shirt off the floor and thumps it into Flynn's chest.

"Put it on now."

"But I'm posing for a picture. Tell him, Willow." He whines, and I can't hold back my mirth. Axel is a raging thundercloud of frustration, and Flynn is the image of a virtuous angel. Mischief begs to be done.

"It's okay, Axel. I need to get his impressive muscles just

right. His buttocks, too. Come on, Flynn, I said pants off too, remember."

He stands and reaches for his jeans button and Axel drags Flynn's shirt down hard over his head, pinning Flynn's arms to his side with the tight material.

"You damned idiot, Flynn. She's got perfect recall. She doesn't need her vision to be assaulted by your puny excuses for muscles." He growls.

Flynn smirks, fearlessly eyeing off the concrete of Axel's muscles straining against his shirt.

"They're not that much smaller than yours, Battle Axe. You've dropped condition since you've been here. Too much of the easy life, huh? Too many doughnuts on the beat?" Flynn goads.

"Dropped condition? I don't think so." He yanks his own gray shirt over his head as Flynn struggles out of his again.

I'm gasping for breath and clutching my sore stomach as the two men compare biceps.

Rain pokes a bewildered expression around the corner. She sees Axel and Flynn having a flex-off near the fridge, and me doubled over near the counter on the other side of the kitchen and rolls her eyes.

"Why do I get the distinct impression this is your doing, Will?"

I draw the picture and ignore my aching cheeks and erupting chuckles. Flynn and Axel's territorial display dissipates into a heated argument about which of them has greater fighting skills.

I finish and sit back, both heads swiveling towards me.

Axel moves faster and grabs the drawing. He searches it thoroughly before handing it to Flynn, shifting a loaded stare at me. I feel its weight as I hold my breath anxiously for Flynn's reaction. He studies it far too long, his eyes darting over the page. Perhaps it's not to his liking. Instead of drawing the pose he'd shown, I plucked an image from memory, one where he's standing proud and strong as he scans the crowd for threats. He's alert, fierce, and the lighting in The Broken Keg loves him.

I think it's one of my favourite pieces.

"Well? Did I forget to draw you a tongue?" My impatience breaks.

I watch Flynn's bare chest empty.

"Will, it's incredible. Is this how you see me? Is this who I am to you?" He breathes in awe.

My frown digs. It's just a picture of him. I didn't alter the image, not a single hair was added or removed. I shift my confusion to Axel, and his gray eyes glower, his lips pull tight with irritation.

Axel doesn't like my drawing. He glares at it in Flynn's hand, and the air is tangible with a tension I don't understand.

I gather my drawings and pencils in a single swoop and escape into my room.

CHAPTER 14

AXEL

*D*ad leans crestfallen against the verandah post, watching Mum's stiff, silent parade as she carries another load to the car. Mr Bradley stares hard at the ground. Mine are the only wet eyes, but Mum doesn't notice. She just sweeps past me as if I weren't there. I blink the tears away and Willow emerges from the house, her drawings and pencils piled in her arms. I frown at her, and guilt darkens her pretty face. She stops in front of me, her breasts straining against her work uniform, creasing the material around her buttons. She leans in as if to kiss me, and I tilt my face to receive it. She doesn't, though. She sighs.

"I'm sorry we couldn't choose you."

She walks slowly towards the car where Flynn holds the door open for her. Flynn shrugs nonchalantly then calls over to another car.

"It's time to go."

I glance over, and Dorian's victorious smirk is clearly visible over the blonde curls of Janice, whose arms wrap tightly around him, the gentle swell of her belly jutting from the side of Dorian's embrace…

The bed startles noisily as I sit up, gulping air to erase the bitter tang of betrayal.

Mum and Mr Bradley.

Janice and Dorian.

Willow and Flynn.

Third time's a charm.

Not that it matters. I don't want Willow that way, and she's a long way off being ready for a relationship of any kind. Who even knew if Flynn was her type?

But she drew Flynn like he should have wings and a halo and I wanted to tear it up.

* * *

"Hey, Axe." She greets with a small, hesitant voice, and I'm slammed with her complexity. On initial meetings, she's bold. Funny. Then as the surface is slowly scraped away, she switches between timid and sassy. I wonder what comes next, then I frown.

I don't care what comes next.

"Hey Will, are you ready?"

She nods stiffly and I reach a hand out to help her stand, but she glances at my palm reluctantly. I roll my eyes at the motion, realising this will be no simple task, but she narrows her eyes to slits and her posture freezes.

"What was that look for?" She snaps. "You don't have to do this, you know. I'm just as happy to go into town for it."

She thinks I don't want to do this. I don't.

But I do.

I drag my hand down my face.

"No. Will, no. I just realised that everything I need to show you requires me to touch you, and that didn't occur to me until just now. I'm frustrated that I overlooked something so important."

Did I imagine her eyes darkening when I mentioned touching her?

"Oh. Right." She frowns, but I watch the faint tinge of shame crawl up her neck. My chest tightens at the sight.

"It's okay, Will, really. We'll just have to slow it down a bit, is all. Just give me a moment."

I sit at the other end of the bench and mentally sift through all the manoeuvres I know. They all require some degree of physical contact, and I've witnessed how affected she is by it.

"I…want you to touch me." She whispers.

My attention jackknifes to her, my pulse enraged.

She clamps her teeth.

"I mean…I don't want to be afraid anymore. I don't want to be that freak who jumps out of her skin every time someone accidentally bumps into me, or brushes against me."

Her eyes hollow. My chest aches for her. She fears a touch, but she also fears fearing it.

My stomach leaps in selfish delight, and I hate myself for it, but I run with her idea with a sick excitement.

"Okay, Will. That's what we'll do. We will manage your response to contact, and as we progress, I can begin to show you how to defend yourself."

Her shy smile twists my guts. I hand her one of the bottles of water I brought with me, and she fumbles with the cap.

"Listen. At any point, I mean any point, if it gets too much, just tell me to stop. Promise?"

When she merely dips her head, I command her.

"Say it!"

Those blue eyes drift to mine and harden with courage. "I promise."

Without breaking visual contact, I reach out and touch a finger to hers, noting her stiffen. She stares down at the touch and focuses on keeping her hand still. I watch.

"The important thing here, Will, is that if you're going to be in a position where you have to defend yourself, you may not simply be able to pull away. You need to understand that when you ask them to stop, they most likely won't, so you need to find that sweet spot between where you feel discomfort, and before you lose control. I can see how this affects you, now just hold out as long as you can before you tell me to stop."

I watch her shoulders lift to allow her lungs more room and hope she can't see that the touch is affecting me, too. My damned nerves are charged.

"Stop!" Her squeak brings focus back, and I snatch my finger away, measuring her breaths as they gradually settle.

"That was good, Will. Now we'll push a little more." I rest my whole hand gently over her tiny one, feeling the clammy heat blend with mine.

"Stop!" she gasps, and I withdraw. I use the time she takes to calm herself to regain control of my own racing heartbeat. As I watch Willow suck air, I recall the night in the bar when I touched her wrist and she didn't react.

"Will, you didn't pull away when I grabbed your hand at work. Why?

Her eyes widen.

I...I don't know...I started to freak out, but then..."

"Then what, Will? Tell me what stopped you."

I watch her seek the answer. The delicate tilt of her chin and the glint in her pretty eyes as she turns her thoughts inward. The faint evidence of her heartbeat in her elegant neck.

Stop it, Axel. She's just a friend.

She aims her sapphire stare at me with a gasp.

"I started to panic, but then I looked up and saw it was you touching me. And I wasn't afraid."

My lungs were emptied by the unexpected leap in my chest. *Does she trust me?*

With a dry mouth, a plan forms in my mind and I manage to form words amidst the rising guilty pleasure of having her touch me.

"Great, Will. This gives us a base. This time, you're going to look at me, not at what I'm doing, and know it's me touching you."

Something dances behind her expression, but she sets her mouth and bravely nods.

I stare at her face, free to study every tiny centimetre of perfect skin. And she looks right back at me. I show her my control, my determination. Her expression tells me she's afraid, but hopeful. It's as honest as I've ever been, and we're not touching or speaking. When I see her anxiety settle, I glance a finger over hers, maintaining visual contact. Her mouth sags as it registers, and her face floods with emotions. There's fear, front and centre, but surprise and curiosity grow and crowds it out. Slowly, I slide my hand over the back of hers, gradually rubbing my thumb over the back of her wrist. Her breath shortens and shudders, but she holds my gaze and doesn't move. I will my expression to reassure her, and with excruciating caution, I fold my hand around her forearm. I slide my hand languidly up her arm, feeling the prickle of goosebumps rise on the burning satin of her skin.

My hand crawls up, reveling in the texture of her shoulder, the smooth joint that leads towards the curve of her neck.

I need to stop.

Of its own accord, my hand melds to the shape of her neck, and I feel the erratic flutter of her pulse calling out to me. She is silken enticement and sweet invitation, and my hand lifts gently to cup her cheek, my thumb hooked in front of her pretty ear, my little finger seeking out the nape of her neck.

Willow's breath picks up, and mine betrays me by matching it. I'm breathing in her exhales, pulling her scent into my lungs.

From somewhere inside comes a rush of cold awareness. I'm leaning towards her instinctively, my hunger drawing my attention to the lure of her sweet lips. She's tilted towards me, too, her beautiful flesh flushed and fevered from something far away from fear.

Jesus Christ.

I jerk my hand away and leap up, walking away without looking back.

"That will do for today." I manage to rasp.

She utters no sound as I escape into the house. I rip my shirt over my head on my way and don't slow my gait as I snatch up the boxing gloves and slip them on. I land blow after furious blow to the punching bag, grunting and snarling like an animal with the power I put behind each one.

The image of Willow's gorgeous orbs fixed on me and her soft lips built for my hunger challenges my control with every blow.

CHAPTER 15

WILLOW

*H*ow's the training with Axe going?" Rain pokes with a secret glance.

I grimace. "Slow."

Painfully slowly. I know he's reluctant to help out. I thought we made pretty good progress the other day, but Axel stood up all of a sudden and walked away. I thought he'd remembered something he had to do suddenly, but when I came inside later he was working out in the gym. The only thing he had to do was to rid himself of my company.

Rain lands a strange look on me and I clarify.

"We're working on managing my freak-outs when I'm touched. He says if I let panic take hold, I can't think rationally enough to outmanoeuvre an attacker, and it seems to be working…"

"But?" Rain's forehead creases and I my sigh stings of rejection.

"But I get the distinct impression he'd rather be doing anything else."

Rain quirks her eyebrows.

"Every time I feel we're getting somewhere he just cuts the lesson short and goes straight to the gym like it's preferable than spending time helping me. I mean, he tells me he wants to help but his actions tell me otherwise. It's so frustrating."

Rain looks thoughtful for a while, then chooses careful words.

"Will, maybe you can listen to his words, but have a good hard think about his actions as well."

I roll my eyes and groan. "If I wanted cryptic messages, I'd read a whodunnit, Rain!"

* * *

With my mask of eye shadow and rouge firmly in place I spin around the tables. It's fun, learning what my customers want and dishing it up to them. Rain's voice vibrates through the room as I feed the masses and I find that the patrons subconsciously lower their voices to hear her.

I've only had a couple more sessions with Axel, but I'm hyper aware of every touch and brush against me. I feel the initial chill of the connection, but instead of rousing the ball of fear I carry inside, I seem to have gained the ability to push it aside.

I'm almost disappointed that Danny isn't here tonight. I'm feeling brave enough to try out my new spark of 'normal' on him.

As the room empties out, I see Flynn and veer toward his friendly smile.

"Thanks for watching out for me, Flynn. I really appreciate it. You know, it's nice to feel safe in a room full of unpredictable strangers."

I've seen it done before, so I reach out and lay my hand lightly on Flynn's crossed forearms. Nothing happens. I don't feel like I have to pull away, but it's not like Axel's touch, either. While the sensation of Axel's flesh sends ripples of fire through my blood, Flynn's arm just feels…foreign.

He smiles warmly, not even acknowledging my hand.

"It's always a pleasure to ensure no harm comes to anyone."

I keep my hand where it is, my growing boldness delighting me.

"You just like getting paid good money to have a good meal and a show every night."

Flynn's arm shakes free with his laughter, and he drops a pat on my shoulder. I tense but the panic stays away.

"I come for the show, and stay for the snappy waitre-" I hear a growl beside my ear cut Flynn off. Axel steps between Flynn and me, shoving me backwards with his bulk, his venom heavy on his tongue.

"I've told you before, Flynn. Don't go there. You're supposed to be looking out for her, that's all."

He's warned Flynn to keep away from me?

Does Axel think me so dirty that he's warned people away from my filth? Is that why Archer doesn't approach me, or Flynn? I stare hard at his balled fists and feel my stomach ache. He's angry. I know he considers every one of Rain's friends his family, so it stands to reason he wants them protected from me. It must be why Axel has been limiting his time with me.

I spin away and let my feet carry me to the staff bathroom where I find an empty cubicle, pull my knees into my arms on top of the toilet lid and sob. I can't seem to care that there are still tables to be cleaned off.

I don't want to be someone to be avoided. I don't want to be dirty. I just want to be normal.

I've wound down to hiccups when I hear the slow creak of the door. It must be Rain come to check on why I'm not working.

"I'm sorry, Rain," I apologise through shaky breaths before she can speak. "I'll come out in a second. I...I just needed a minute, you know."

She doesn't say a word.

"I just want to feel normal, like I did before...everything. I'm tired of being the freak who jumps at shadows or finds a new level of panic every time someone bumps into me. I'm so exasperated that I'm giving my issues so much airtime because nothing I try seems to take the edge off my anxiety. I appreciate everything you've done for me, but sometimes it's so damned hard that I just don't see the point in constantly fighting it. I never really was the fighter, was I? It was you. You were the brave one, the one who fought and never stopped fighting, and it worked. I don't think I ever told you how grateful I am that you killed Kurt, Rain. I just wish I'd had the guts to do it, but

I couldn't move I was so fucking scared... Maybe if I'd fought harder..."

I swallow and realise.

"That was the moment I met with fear, and I just let it take over, let him hurt me. I felt it all over, Rain. I felt it burn in my stomach, and a stabbing pain in my lungs. But the fear was greater, and even after the agony ended, the fear never did. Maybe Sarah was really the brave one, Rain. In the end she pushed through that fear and won."

I remember the torture and pull my knees in tighter to me and I imagine Rain on the other side of the door, lost in her own bitter memories.

"I want you to know I'm aware that I'm a burden on you all. You guys are all so great, trying to help me. Axel tries, too, but I know he considers me a dirty creature worthy only of pity. Sometimes he's only around for a few minutes before he can't stomach my company anymore. He wants Flynn to keep away, too, like he's worried Flynn will catch my filth."

The tears stream again and I angrily swipe them away.

"Jesus, Rain, half the time he can't even stand to look at me..." My breath shudders and I replay every time Axel turns his grim expression from me and walks away.

Rain doesn't say a word, and I wonder if she's even there still. Maybe she grew tired of listening to my pathetic story and left me to it.

I straighten my clothes, smudge my tears through my makeup and open the door.

Axel sits on the floor of the ladies' bathroom with his elbows on his knees and head buried in his hands.

"Axel?" I gasp. The crown of his head rolls from side to side. Even now he doesn't want to look at me. My body quivers with humiliation that bleeds into anger.

"I can't believe you pretended to be Rain. Jesus, Axel. Do you get some sadistic delight in picking apart my scars? Well now it's out in the open. I don't have to pretend any longer. I know you think I'm trash, and you're right, but I'm not contagious, damn it! I didn't ask for these things to be done to me to turn me into such a freak, but I'm doing my best. You've got no right to warn people away!"

Shame colors his face as he slowly meets my eyes. He stabs his fingers into his hair, as his throat bobs again and again. He appears on the edge of speaking, but no words come from guilty lips.

Resignation dulls my anger to a whisper. "They'll find out themselves fast enough, but please, Axel, can you please just leave it be so I can feel normal for a few moments before they work it out and it all unravels again?"

I blink away another wave of tears, and he's suddenly standing, filling my vision, grabbing my arms. I register his touch. It tingles on the bare skin of my arm, sending sparks deeper until they seep into my bloodstream. I'm not frightened, his pine and musk scent reminding me his touch is safe.

I lift my eyes and catch a glimpse of agony etched into every cell on his face. Is it that hard for him to bring himself to touch me?

Is this a sick game he's playing?

His mouth smothers my gasp of surprise. I stiffen, but my lips open for him. I feel his tongue diving, stroking, possessing me so entirely that my body softens and my head spins.

He's only ever touched my arm and face before, but now I shiver as his palm crawls slowly from my shoulder, curling down behind me, spreading wide over the small of my back. Drawing my body closer to his.

The softness of his lips, the velvet of his tongue, the heat in his breath surrounds me, and I'm kissing him back. With a groan I thread my fingers through his hair, pulling him closer. My blood ignites as his hunger grows. From his heaving chest comes an edge of desperation, and he growls into my mouth.

My answering moan tightens his grip and I can feel every ridge of hard strength ripple beneath his skin.

This comforting light-headedness is a living thing that's

consuming me, anaesthetising my fears and inviting me deeper into its roaring hot promises. And I want it.

Until he crushes my hard body to his and reality slams into me with the thick bulge twitching against my stomach.

The flashbacks curdle in my bowels and I'm a blur of terrified sounds and swinging arms. Even as my panic explodes sideways I feel the frustrated tears prickle my eyes. Strong fingers grip my shoulders, holding me securely away from him. Calming, unintelligible words steeped in regret fill the air but I remain enslaved by my misfiring adrenaline, and yet I know Axel wouldn't hurt me.

Not physically.

I feel him sit me down and release his hold. I shiver violently at the loss of his touch, making it harder to catch my breath. He's still talking, so I try and focus on that, my ears straining through the pounding fog that fills my mind.

"...king sorry, Will. It won't happen again."

That's what this is. A pity kiss, that won't ever happen again because I'm damaged goods and he's embarrassed by my crazy. I can't talk to him. I shut my eyes on the image of him standing there before my panic leaves and brings everything into focus again.

"Just keep away from me, Axel." I whimper.

A few moments later the door announces his departure, and I'm alone again.

Always alone.

CHAPTER 16

AXEL

I glare at the image before me clutching the vanity with white knuckles.

What the fuck is going on? I ask my reflection, but he looks as if he hasn't a clue either.

I'm the man who fought fearlessly in every mission - the way my nerves coil and buzz going into battle was intoxicating. Like a drug, I stepped into my uniform and became untouchable. I took out the enemy with precision and excitement, each new threat calculated, disarmed and annihilated at my hand.

I stare down at my palms. They knew the shudder of a final breath, the slick texture of blood, the sensation of bones losing shape beneath them. Now all they did was drag that damned ballpoint over files and forms all day. There's no rush. No driving passion or knowing I've made a difference.

Three weeks ago I loved it, but now I may as well be a dishwasher for all the satisfaction I'm getting for it. And the only difference between then and now?

Willow.

Willow with her haunting eyes and inner strength she's not even aware of.

Willow who brings me undone with her sass and depth.

She makes my blood shiver and hunger build, and that's never happened to me before, like that day when she allowed me to run my hand over her arm and time melted away in her expression of inquisitive trust. And I felt…what? The answer niggles at the edges of my thoughts and I grind my teeth trying to push it away, but it lingers and reminds me that with the barest of contact, that was the most intimate I've ever been with a woman.

The mirror shatters before I register my fist moving. My lungs rasp as I carefully remove the tiny shards of glass from the split in my knuckle, the pain too fleeting to give me relief. I need to hurt, and I need to be hurt until all I can focus on is that blissful ache that smothers everything else.

Archer looks up from the table and sees destruction on my face. He's on his feet in a heartbeat, making for the door, and I'm right behind him. I slam the door closed just as his first blow slams into the side of my jaw. Skin splits and leaks.

Yeah.

My fist catches him on his shoulder as he ducks away, a blur dissolving into the night. I widen my stance and train my ears, snapping a punch to my left. I connect with warm muscle as Archer grunts before slipping out of view. His next blow catches the back of my head sending stars through my vision. It's a good hit, and I swing into empty air. I miss.

The frustration that's taken root expands until my blood boils, and I do what I've been trained never to do. I see red.

I lose control.

Archer darts into my space with cold composure and calculated blows. Pain explodes on my cheek, my ribs, my kidneys, and I savour the tingle it pushes through my nerves. Within the aches, stings and the taste of blood I find that tiny piece of me that existed when I was in control of my life, and I sprawl on my back, opening myself up to Archer's punishment.

"You let me win." Archer glares at me. Maybe he, too, was after deliverance.

"I'll win next time." I gasp. The adrenaline pulses through me.

That wonderful, life anchoring comfort.

"You know the rules. I win, you talk." Archer pins me with narrow blades of green and crosses his arms.

"She thinks she's filthy."

Archer jerks as if it's the last thing he expected me to say.

"And why are you pissed about it?"

I ball my fist and feel a split on my knuckles widen.

"Because it's me that makes her feel that way." My voice is leaden with guilt, and Archer's eyes widen.

"What? I thought you were getting along well with her, Axe. She thinks so highly of you. She seeks you out whenever you're home. What happened?"

She seeks me out?

I shake my head and groan. "Shit, Frostbite, I don't even know. You know I went to see if she was okay last night? Well, as soon as I walked in, Will thought it was Rain coming to check on her, and she started talking, saying how broken and crazy she was, how their friend Sarah was the strong one and that Willow was nothing but trash trying to be 'normal'. Jesus, she said she was so filthy that even I can't stand to be around her."

It hurt all over again when I voice it, making me want to go another round with Archer's fists.

"That's easy, then. Just spend more time with her, unless you genuinely don't want to. If that's the case, just stay in town longer under the guise of overtime or women and just slowly introduce more space. Just…do it kindly, Axe. Please?"

The back of my skull connects with the tree trunk in bitterness, and I relish the warm throbbing it brings.

"That's just the problem. I do want to spend time with her, but I'm trying to give her space away from me but no matter what I try to do, or how I do it, it seems to be the wrong thing and ends with me feeling guilty and her feeling unworthy."

His face pinches. "Why would spending more time with her be a bad thing…ohh." His features smooth in his epiphany.

"Don't fucking say it, man, or I'll knock your head in!" I snap.

Archer smirks.

"It's a beautiful torture, opening your heart. I say just go with it. You're a good guy, she's a great girl, and you both deserve happiness."

No no no!

"Don't be fucking ridiculous. The last thing I need, or want, is a relationship. You know what happens. They get clingy and then I'm an arsehole for using them. I am not even entertaining that shit. I'll be a friend and spend the next couple of weeks teaching her some self-defence, then I think it's time I left you all and actually do something with my life!"

The words spill from my mouth and taste sour. Archer rears his head back in shock.

That aching knot in my belly doesn't like the idea of leaving, and it never entered my thoughts before I growled it at Archer. My rage ices over and I'm back to feeling again like my sanity is slipping away.

* * *

I steel my resolve and approach Willow with purpose.

"What the hell happened to you, Axel? You're all cut up!"

I huff. I planned out exactly what would happen today, structured, clinical lessons designed to forge a path away from her while honouring my promise to help her. Her concern wasn't part of the design.

"Just blew off a bit of steam with Archer last night." I dismiss, then regain my footing. "Today, I'll teach you some moves that will help you out of most situations. I hope you're feeling strong."

She's curled up on the bench in the sun, her loose pants swimming around her, but when I step close, she hardens with suspicion and her jaw locks.

"I'm not a charity case, Axel. I appreciate your help, but I've enrolled in a class in town. I start next week, so you don't have to come near me anymore."

She returns her attention to her novel, but I see her pain in the way she pulls her knees up, the breath she's holding. The shadow in her eyes. I don't know what to do with it, so I just sigh and fill the space her legs have left on the bench.

She pretends she's reading, but she's wired and tense. The silence stretches. I seek some kind of inspirational comment that will magically fix this, but everything I should say eludes me. I bury my head in my hands and huff my irritation.

"Christ, Will. I'm no good at this."

"At what? Pretending to be my friend?"

"No! Jesus! That's not-"

"Because the joke's over. Go take your intentions to another noble cause and leave me be." Her bitter snark stings more than Archer's punches.

"Willow, please let me-"

I've never seen her angry. The fire flares in her stunning eyes and lights her up. Her courage surges to the surface, shaking loose her skin and unfolding the wings of fury I never knew were there. I stare at her with my adrenaline soaring and can't catch my breath.

"Let you what? Listen to my pitiful dialogue again. Oh, poor me, poor little Willow, the nut job who's trying to be normal, who needs some hero to save me. Find your brownie points elsewhere."

Damn it! She's so infuriating. I'm trying to talk to her and she won't shut up.

My irritation boils as I watch her curled lips move in angry words that don't reach my ears. They need to stop...

The heat of her lips burn mine, and I don't hold back. I scoop her firmly into my lap and register that the vibrations from her voice cease as my tongue explores her mouth. She shivers. Then I gently break the kiss and hold her at arm's length. She sits astride my knees with one hand on my jaw, the other on my chest, a stunned expression hovering on her flushed face.

"Can I talk now?" I growl.

Mouth still parted, wide eyes trapped on mine, she simply nods.

"Like I told you in the bathroom, Will, I'm not keeping away because I think you're an…unworthy person. I'm keeping away because every time I'm near you I want to kiss you, and hold you, just so I can get another whiff of your incredible scent, another spark from your touch, but I stop it, because *you're not ready for it.*"

Her mouth falls open in a delicate gasp.

"You want that? I thought you hated my kiss. You told me it was awful." She frowns her doubt.

"No, Willow. Use that perfect recall of yours. You asked if it always felt like that, and I simply told you it didn't."

"You said it wasn't normally like that, and that generally it's good." She accuses.

I quiver with delight. She's either oblivious to or comfortable with our bodies pressing together. The heat from her thighs burns mine, her hands on me scorching deeper than I've ever felt. My mouth dries and I try and maintain my focus on talking to her, willing my raging erection to behave. The fire radiating from her hovering centre to my tenting jeans is excruciating.

My inhale shudders.

"No, Willow. A 'normal' kiss is good. What I was trying to tell you, while I was attempting to form actual words and failing, was that your kiss was the most breathtaking, incredible kiss I've ever experienced. It wasn't good, Will. It was mind-blowing."

Shock straightens her spine, and I could feel the tilt of her pelvis bring her millimetres closer to me. Still her scent winds through my nostrils, suffocating me in my own desire.

"Why have you been keeping away then? You're barely here five minutes sometimes before I watch your back disappearing through the door again."

Her demand brings my attention back to the straining zipper of my jeans. I zero in on her glimmering sapphires as my jeans jump and I finally make contact with the hot centre of her. Even through layers of clothing I feel the burn.

Her eyes open impossibly wide. She gasps. My erection nudges again.

"Ohhhhh." She breathes.

"You know how I said a man can stop at any time? *I've been stopping.*"

I'm not pinning her in place, my arms forced to my sides so she won't feel trapped, but my self-restraint is holding on by a thread.

CHAPTER 17

WILLOW

*H*e's not holding me or trapping me; he's been showing me I can trust him. I'm in awe of his integrity, his firm grip on his urges. He's wearing that expression again and I've decided I love that dark look of his. On his face it doesn't frighten me.

The huge lump in his pants reaches for me, and instinctively I tilt my hips until his heat presses against mine. A flutter stirs and grows between my legs. I savour the sensation. It starts to throb, and my breath shallows. I press down a little firmer, and the flutter roars into life. The throbbing becomes breathless battering, and a foreign urge washes over me. I flex my hips and delight at the delicious waves of unexplored craving the friction causes.

"Is this how it feels? "I whisper breathlessly into Axel's face. "Because I'm burning up. Inside."

I marvel at every reaction.

He groans his anguish and grasping my arms, plucks me from him as if I were weightless.

"Christ, Will. Don't." He pants, then strides across the courtyard and into the house.

Don't what?

I felt the weight of honesty at his admission. He doesn't think I'm disgusting. I let that warm me for a moment, then realise it still doesn't explain why he'd warn Flynn away from me.

Doubt lurches furiously upward and annoyance flares. If we're being honest with each other, he needs to tell me why he'd do that.

I peer into the gym to find it empty, so I head towards the kitchen, the fire in my core still demanding.

I pass Flynn's bedroom. The door is slightly ajar in that way that only a non-foster can do. I smile. Axel's door is ajar, too.

Yep, it's just us fosters who need the reassurance of a closed door. I step past, but catch a sound escaping that chills me.

Axel makes the sounds that came with the pain of my past, deep from inside his room. Low groans, a harsh grunt.

Does he have someone in there? Someone he's hurting?

I push through the door, oblivious to privacy in my desperation to save a girl from a fate I remember. My lungs leap to my throat as I realise the noises are coming from his bathroom.

I frantically search his room for a weapon and land my grip on a metal weight sitting on the carpet. I could hit him over the head hard enough to free the girl.

With a hard shove, the bathroom door swings inwards, and terror lifts the weight over my head.

Through the curtain of steam, Axel spins his back towards me, head twisting over his shoulder with a flush colouring his face. The shower door is open, a fine spray of water soaking the floor. He's alone.

"What the hell, Will? Get out!" His voice breaks.

I'm locked in confusion, feeling stupid for my intrusion, the heavy disc gaining weight in my up-stretched hands. He was making those noises but didn't have anyone with him.

Realisation dawns too damn slowly on me.

"Oh, Jesus, Axe, I'm so sorry..."

Axel's horror morphs into panic as the adrenaline ebbs the

strength from my arms and the weight slips from my grip.

He swivels with a wet sound, snatching the disc from the air before it strikes the floor, and all I can do is stare.

"Willow!" He strangles out, but I ignore him. Water sluices off those hard mountains on his torso, and I follow the path it takes. The flow hits rapids at his abdominals before it ducks into his tight navel. The water reappears, continuing its descent down the narrow trail of hair below it. It winds through the thicker hair below, and then it abruptly changes course when the flow is interrupted by the long, thick penis jutting out. The water slides off, but my gaze lingers. It makes his long fingers seem small, the mushroomed tip the source of the embers I felt through his jeans. A thick purple vein runs from below the hood to the top of the heavy sack nestled between his legs. The pounding ache returns with a vengeance as I study him. I lick my lips.

"Do it." I whisper.

His growl rumbles from his chest, and his lips are thinned in pain.

"Will-"

"Do it. Please." I don't know why. But that ache inside demands to see.

He keeps his eyes on me as he lowers the weight to the floor. He shifts slightly as if he's debating, then curls his long thick fingers around himself. Entranced, I watch his fist slide in long, slow strokes up and down the shaft, gradually building speed. My attention shifts to the sensuous movements in his wrist. There's something about the fluid motion that tugs at my insides, and I step closer with a low moan.

I curl my fingers around the shower wall and his breath hisses at my nearness. I sneak a look at his face. His eyes are drilling into me, all attention burning on me as he picks up speed. I'm breathlessly watching his face slowly pull into a silent snarl, his eyes wild and hungry.

My hand snakes over the corded lines of his throat to his tight jaw moments before his head drops back and his body coils and jerks, my name on his lips.

When he meets my gaze again, I'm staggered by the intensity of him. Beautiful mouth hanging slack and dark, dark heat in his eyes.

"Willow?" He rumbles in wonder.

* * *

"So why would you tell Flynn to keep away from me?" I challenge. He's wearing jeans and a faint blush, stabbing his fingers through damp hair.

"Christ, Will, I'm still getting my head around you appearing like that and…watching me. Give me a couple of minutes to pull myself together, please."

I huff with an impatience tempered with the residual unsatisfied ache between my legs. Maybe he felt the same, and that's why he relieved himself. I straighten, feeling the plaster against my back and the carpet cushion my legs.

"Why haven't you found yourself a woman, lately, Axe?"

"Jesus, Will. I don't have the need-"

"But you do!" I insist. "Clearly you have the need. Come on, we're friends, right? What is it?"

Axel pushes out an exhale.

"I told you, Will. It's because they all want something more than I want to give."

I frown.

"But *why* don't you want more? I mean, look at Rain and Archer. Don't you want that? One of those women might make you feel like that. Why don't you just think about it? I can see how uncomfortable abstaining makes you."

His adorable blush deepens.

"I can't believe I'm having this conversation with you! I don't want that. I don't want to be at the mercy of someone and hand over the power to crush me when the whim strikes them. I'm not doing that again."

There's that flash of pain, followed by a glimmer I know

intimately.

"You're scared."

"No. Just not interested in a battle of power."

But I catch the tic in his jaw.

"Take it from me, Axe. Being frightened of any type of pain can debilitate you if you let it. Accept that pain exists but don't let it master you. That's the only battle of power that matters. Look at me, jumping at shadows, scanning for enemies every moment. It's exhausting. But it's in the moments where you helped me quiet the terror that I have caught glimpses of a world I never knew existed. In those spaces, I snatch the merest fragments of something beautiful around me and for the first time since I turned eleven, I feel hope knocking ever so quietly. I'm trying to be brave enough to let it in. You can, too."

His shoulders sag.

"Sometimes the pain of betrayal digs deeper inside than you thought possible. When you realise that a simple human could be capable of such evil and inhumane deeds, the hurt never goes."

I hold his eyes, sending what consolation I could.

"I know." I whisper.

There is no need to elaborate. Our own demons strike us in different places, but they leave similar trails of destruction. His eyes wilt with the depth of his secret despair, his expression dim and helpless. For the first time, I see his vulnerability. He's holding his bleeding wounds out to show me, his mask of fierce strength fallen away. He does it without being aware of it, unable somehow to rein in and guard himself. His fragility is the most beautiful thing I've ever seen.

"I won't hurt you."

The words appear from my mouth without warning or knowing why they needed to be spoken, but his eyes widen, face hardens, and he covers his wounds over again with that mask of impenetrability he wears.

Without another word, I stand and return to my room, leaving him to his own reflections. In the bright glow of the afternoon sun, I seek the security of my nest, sinking to the carpet as the walls of blanket fall around me.

Something shifted in that room with Axel, like the air became tangible with some new, indistinguishable emotion, one that settles over me with a subtle yearning for something meaningful, beyond the realms of my own small world.

CHAPTER 18

AXEL

I watch her leave, her long hair falling over her cheek, curtaining her beautiful face and lift a palm to my chest in a feeble attempt to ease the pain inside.

With a brief touch and her insightful wisdom, she reached into the cavity I'd so carefully protected, leaving behind a piece of her that won't dislodge.

I'm not scared. I'm simply arming myself against an attack. Why would I not? If you knew you were going to be run through with a sword, you wouldn't offer your chest. You'd don your armour.

But why her words rang with truth was a dangerous unknown, as if she's the one who wields the sword at me and no armour exists that can protect me.

Telling Archer I was leaving was a spontaneous regret at the time, coming from my ever building mountain of frustration, but as I reflect on Willow, her effect on me, her boldness and honesty, I think it was the right decision. I need to focus on giving Willow the ability to defend herself and then get as far away from her as I can.

* * *

Two speeding fines, a statement taken for a car theft and a simple domestic dispute later, my body vibrates with agitation.

Simone glances up from her paperwork with a sigh as I sink into the leather swivel chair opposite her. She frowns at the light bruising still visible on my chin from Archer's fists.

"You're like a caged animal lately, Axel. You're oozing tension and anger. If you won't tell me what's going on with you, I can't help, and it pains me because up until recently you've been our greatest asset."

I rub the back of my neck. I didn't realise it was so obvious to everyone, or that my work was suffering enough to bring the attention of my superiors as a result.

"I don't know." I lie easily. "I guess I don't find the work as fulfilling as I used to. I'm just a glorified disciplinarian in blue, finger shaking at those who make minor mistakes. I used to make a difference, change the balance of evil in the world, but now I just feel like a shallow hypocrite. It's hard for me to impress the importance of resisting the urge to punch another person when I spent years extinguishing the lives of hundreds without a thought."

"So what do you want?"

"I want a challenge, Simone. I want to be able to exercise all those skills I learned in the military. It's what I'm trained for, and they're all going to waste."

Simone leans her forehead on two fingers.

"Axe, you *are* making a difference. Put your experiences into perspective for a moment. These civilians will never understand the things you have seen. To them, witnessing another's rage and violent act is as traumatic for them as having your team slaughtered in front of you. You're trying to compare two completely different views. I know what you're saying though. It's a much slower pace than you're used to. What do you think might help you find satisfaction again?"

A vision of Willow's soulful expression dances through my mind.

"You could see if there's a way the military might overlook my desertion, or find me a town with higher crime, something edgier that requires me to use my skills."

"You would have to relocate, Axel."

The ache in my chest throbs. Simone watches as I absently rub the feeling away. Opportunity beckons.

"That's fine, Simone. I think I need the change."

As I end my shift, Simone calls me again to her office.

"I made a couple of calls." She watches me carefully. I maintain an empty expression, even though my adrenaline surges and my lungs squeeze.

"There is a town similar to the situation you requested over the other side of the city that might pique your interest. Higher violence rates, gang warfare and illegal weapons more suited to your skill set. The department there is extremely keen for you to transfer."

She leans back in her chair, eyes narrowing as I swallow the dryness away.

"There's more to this, Axel. I can see you're hiding something. And for that reason, I'll not accept your decision for four weeks. Whatever is going on, you need to sort it out. I'm not sending you out with my recommendations to have you take this problem with you and have them question my referrals."

Four weeks. I was hoping for an immediate transfer, but I can work with that. There's tantalising freedom at the end of four weeks, and all I have to do is pack them so full I don't have space to think.

Four weeks to train Willow to defend herself, then that promise is honored. Four weeks to tighten my body into a state of readiness. Four weeks until I can begin to forget all about Willow.

I begin immediately, running through the trees on the edge of twilight, pushing harder.

"You're not seriously leaving, Axe?" Archer's runners pound the path with the same beat as mine.

"It's time, Archer. I need a change of scenery, away from Mountain Plateau. Away from-"

"Willow?" Archer finishes with a sly glance.

"This has got nothing to do with Willow!" I snarl with more venom that I intended. "This is about me finding my place, doing what I enjoy with no complications."

"Complications like Willow?" Archer grins, and my irritation boils over at his smug tone. Without warning, my fist snaps out and catches Archer's cheek. His skin splits but the smile stays as if he expected it.

"Shit, I'm sorry, Frostbite. I'm…just not myself at the moment."

Archer catches his breath with his hands on his thighs. When he looks up at me, his green eyes dance with insight.

"She doesn't know how much she likes you, and certainly doesn't know what to do with it. Besides Rain, she's the most honest and genuine woman out there. Why won't you give it a chance? You both deserve happiness, you know. Love isn't available to everyone. It's to be snapped up and held tight when it shows itself, because if you let it go, it's gone forever."

"I don't fucking love her so stop talking shit and looking for something that isn't there! Snapped up and held tight? I watched how my father loved my mother, and took particular notice of how that worked out for him when Mum walked out. It's not worth it."

"It doesn't all end like that."

"Really? Because then I had the pleasure of watching my fianceé do the same thing. Seems to be a pretty consistent pattern there."

"That's just bad fucking luck, Axe. Look at Rain and me, how amazing it is. My father beat my mother to death as I watched, but if I held onto that as a picture of what a relationship was supposed to be, I'd have missed out on feeling this."

I snort cynically.

"You forget I knew you when you thought you lost her. You existed in that hollow limbo in a half-life for months. What would have happened if she was dead, Archer? From what I recall you were ready to join her. Why would I want to become that? I'm not relationship material, Archer. I don't know why everyone keeps insisting that I am! I've already decided. In four weeks, I'm relocating to Diamond Valley."

* * *

"A hard knee to the groin will drop any man like stone. Go on, give it a try."

Willow's eyes widen.

"I'm not kneeing you in the balls!"

"I'm not going to actually let you. I'm going to block it, but you need to show me you can."

She rolls her eyes but widens her stance. I make a show of attacking her, grabbing her securely to me. Her warm body pressed against me immediately tests the limits of rationality. She squirms tortuously in my arms, trying to free herself without having to retaliate, and my jeans tighten uncomfortably, pressing like a traitor against her belly. She stills the moment she becomes aware of it, her hair falling away from her eyes as she melts against me.

Jesus help me. My attention falls to her lips, parted with the exertion of escape. They tighten slightly, but I'm too distracted to realise her intention. She brings her knee upwards, gently, but with enough force for the explosion of pain to blind me.

I drop to the ground, the pain still somehow spreading and mounting, even though she's nowhere near me. I groan and cup the source of my agony.

"What the hell happened, Will?" Archer's voice intrudes on my blinding torment.

"He asked me to knee him in the balls, so I did."

"He asked you to...holy hell, Axe, you've just had your arse handed to you!" He roars his delight, and all the cuss words I can imagine never make it to my mouth.

Instead I struggle desperately for air and try and keep my

stomach from erupting.

CHAPTER 19

WILLOW

*W*ith Axel's lessons, my confidence has begun to make an appearance. Thankfully, he never again invited me to test out a knee to the testicles. Even though I felt guilty, it was amazing to see how a simple move could allow me instant freedom.

After the mortifying bathroom incident he's been overly guarded whenever we're together. He exercises more and avoids me every other moment. At first, I thought I was imagining it, but a sick understanding curdled my stomach when he came into the kitchen, saw me at the sink, and quickly left with a frown.

Until then, I didn't understand how important he'd become to me, how much I missed him when he wasn't around. When he sought me out for defence lessons, he did so clinically. His instructions were brief and direct. If it weren't for the darkness looming in his hooded gaze, I'd think Axel had simply disengaged from me. He can control everything but his body's reaction to me.

* * *

Danny comes in on the busiest nights, securing his secluded table in the far corner under the dimmest lights. Little by little I've learned to master that feeling of dread that squirms in my belly whenever his eyes darken on me.

I collapse into the empty seat next to him.

"Busy night?" He smiles.

"Yeah, I like the theory that keeping busy makes the time pass faster, but if it were any busier, it would be tomorrow already and I'd have to do this all over again."

I roll my neck, attempting to dislodge the crick there.

He lays his hand on my arm with a sympathetic smirk. I'm accustomed to his touch. It still makes my skin crawl, but it's become less of a crawl and more of an unpleasant prickle.

"Take a breather with me, Willow. The crowd's thinning, and some night air might be just what you need to dump some of that tension."

It sounds so inviting I actually groan. "Sure. I'll just let someone know I'm ducking outside for a bit."

I dump the cloth on the counter and call across the bar to Archer.

"I'll be back in a bit. I'm just taking five."

He looks up from the glass he's polishing, nods, and stuffs his cloth into another one.

Danny's already outside when I step into the night, drawing the clean air deep into my lungs.

"That's the antidote, right there." I sigh away all the tension in one go.

Danny watches me, his eyes twinkling in the reflection of the distant fluorescents. For a while he's silent.

"Willow, can I ask you something?" His voice lowers into a calming timbre.

"Sure" I shrug, my stomach tightening.

"Well, I've been coming to see you for what, a couple of months now, and when I first came in, you would barely speak to me. Now I like to think we're friends."

I confirm with a careful nod.

"But I like you as more than a friend. I'd like to start meeting you outside of work, have lunch with me sometimes. I think we have fun together..." Danny breathes a lungful of night and lowers his voice. "What I would like to do right now is kiss you."

"Oh." I exhale. That familiar uncertainty returns, but I suppress it. He asked. He didn't just take. He's gently seeking permission, and waiting patiently.

I'm nervous, but I know how to kiss now. Axel taught me, and I've been quietly disappointed he hasn't kissed me again, despite saying that he wants to. I enjoyed kissing him. Perhaps Danny's lips will bring that overwhelming tingling sensation back.

"Um...okay."

Danny steps closer, his hands tentatively snaking around my waist. I feel his breath on my face, and his head filling my view.

His lips glance over mine, hot and careful. I move my mouth against his, waiting for the rapturous explosions of excitement to dance through my blood, but nothing comes. It's nice though, even if he tastes of beer and chips.

His tongue sneaks into my mouth, and I kiss him back, eager to find that elusive spark. He groans into my mouth and the faint stirrings of alarm being born in my stomach. I want to back away, but instead I think of Axel, encouraging me to hold out to discover the moment after discomfort, and before panic. So I do just that, allowing his tongue to dive deeper, feeling his hold on me tighten.

"Stop." I pull away, and his hands drop. I fill my lungs, but it's a breathlessness that stems from anxiety, not desire.

He reaches forward and plants a chaste kiss on my cheek, smiling as he steps backwards.

"That was better than I imagined, Willow. I hope you'll allow me to kiss you again soon."

I nod stiffly, but inside I'm leaping for joy. I allowed a man to touch me, hold me and kiss me without responding like a freak. I want to do it again, just to prove to myself that I can, like everybody else. Just not tonight. I need to go slowly.

* * *

"A well-placed punch to the throat will render an attacker as useless as a knee to the groin does. But use this move with caution. Aimed right, it is entirely possible to kill a person, and although you may think it's the only option, you need to consider all possible consequences."

I listen intently but struggle to focus. His mouth dances as he speaks, and it's very distracting. I'm fascinated by the difference between Axel's kiss and Danny's. My mind wanders as I step out the instructions, jabbing a fist at his throat, feeling the tingle of my skin as his palm catches my blow.

"Okay, that will do today." He announces, his back towards me, his feet already taking him away.

"Wait." I call. He stops but doesn't turn.

"Can I ask a question, Axel, as a friend?"

I watch his jaw lock as he turns slowly, reluctantly.

"What is it, Willow?"

I fall to the bench, drawing my knees up.

"I feel awkward asking you, actually. Just forget it."

Axel takes a few tentative paces, lowering himself beside me, an odd pain emanating from him.

"I told you once you can ask me anything, Will. I keep my promises. Are you okay?"

I chew my lip for a moment, drawing courage. I close my eyes.

"Axel, you said that not all kisses feel the same. That some are better than others. Is it the same with sex? Is that all different, too?"

The muscle in his jaw flexes.

"What do you mean?" There's a warning in his tone.

"Well, when I kissed you, my entire nervous system caught fire. If it's not always like that, then I...err...can assume that if I experienced another kiss, from a different person, that it might not feel the same. Is it the same principal with sex? Can you feel that good sometimes, but with another person that sensation isn't present?"

His swallow is loud and hard.

"What is this, Willow? Are you trying to play with me? Make me jealous? Because it won't work. I told you I can't give you more than I am."

I huff out a laugh. "Oh, Jesus no, Axel. I'm asking because you're my friend and you said I could ask. I know you don't want me, because you said you've wanted to kiss me and you haven't. I'm not playing with you. Rain's been so busy lately that I haven't been able to talk to her, so there's only you. If you'd rather me not speak to you, let me know and I won't bother you again."

He studies me for a while, a touch of ice visible in the flames of his eyes.

"No, Willow. It's different. Every person is a different experience and no two are the same."

What a relief. It was perfectly normal to feel nothing with Danny after all. I smile, comforted.

"Thanks, Axe. I really appreciate it."

I leave him on the bench and hit the shower.

I stare at my body in the mirror as I towel dry my hair and quiver in excitement.

I'm an average girl with a normal job and an ordinary home. I kissed a man, just like other regular people and now I want to start dressing like a normal person, too. I'd become used to my uniform, no longer bothered by my exposed legs and clothes that didn't hide my shape, and nothing bad had happened.

As the sun grows hotter, I begin thinking of shorts and shirts instead of stifling baggy jeans and jumpers. I still don't feel brave enough to go into town alone, but asked Rain to set aside some time to take me shopping. Two days later, she squeaks with delight as the bus pulls slowly from the curb, half empty.

"I'm so excited, Will. What made you want to change your look?" She asks.

"It's too hot for jumpers." I mutter, a deep blush burning my face.

She squints at me through the harsh morning glare.

"There's another reason, too. Isn't there?"

I sigh. No thought or intention was sacred around the astute regard of Rain.

"Maybe." I allow the barest smile.

"I knew it! I can't say I'm surprised. It was only a matter of time. I've watched you bloom the last few weeks into the beautiful, brave woman you always were. I'm so happy for you, Will. He's a lovely guy."

"You know Danny?"

Her smile falters and slips.

"Danny? No. Oh…sorry Will, I thought you meant…someone else."

"Axel's a friend, Rain. Nothing more. He's made that quite clear and has given me no reason to assume otherwise."

"But…" I can see the confusion dull her excitement, and momentarily my own heart sinks. I think the world of Axel, but he knows how damaged I am and is hyper aware of all the work I am just to be able to exhibit the illusion of normalcy. I've watched him, the frustration, the wrestle-with-patience expression he wears on his face every time we're together. That dark heat that overcomes him every moment we're in the same room hangs heavy over him, and I long for the tingling burn of his mouth on mine. But it seems he's decided to not give in to it obviously seeing that the effort he has to put in initially isn't worth it. I'm not like his other women who come to him without a war, women he doesn't have to dance on eggshells just to be able to touch. Women that aren't used and damaged. I carry the shame of it, keeping my distance almost as much as he's kept his lately. It pains me, though. He's become my best friend, but once the novelty of me wears off, he'll discard me too. It's the routine that's followed me ever since I could remember; Off to a new foster home, sometimes without knowing I'm leaving until I finish school and notice my case next to the front door. No time for goodbyes. I wonder if Axel will even care to say goodbye when our time comes to an end.

Rain watches me in the reflection of the bus window, and I blink my misery away. With the well-rehearsed grace of an inconsequential foster child, I push the weight of my thoughts aside and bury them beneath a genuine looking grin.

"I'm so excited, Rain!"

CHAPTER 20

AXEL

That smell, embedded in the upholstery of every pursuit car. The faded odour of two cops who remembered the way it felt to believe they could make a difference. Almost undetectable now, too saturated by the bitterness of disillusionment and futility.

The portable crackles as dispatch makes contact.

"VKC to Hawker 307?"

Dane shoots me a frown, spine rigid as he answers the call.

"Hawker 307 to VKC. Go ahead"

"Hawker 307, we have a welfare check at Eight Huntley court. Neighbours report screaming and indications of property damage and advise there is concern for a child at the residence who may be exposed."

I exhale and crinkle my forehead at Dane who replies with a curt nod. I turn the engine and the car growls urgently as it picks up speed.

"Received. Enroute."

"VKC to Hawker 307, I'll run some location checks and get back to you."

"Roger, Hawker received."

The car swings into the court and we know immediately which

house it is. A tipped rubbish bin is barely visible amongst the long weeds on the front yard, and the two concrete lengths that form the driveway are scattered with sun bleached children's toys and the haphazard sprawl of a garden hose. A battered red sedan sits with its bonnet up under the carport, the engine block sleeping on the ground on a blanket of oil. The white fairings of a dirt bike are the only maintained items about the place.

A commission house, no doubt. We are attending another cliché. I pull up in the street.

Dane announces our arrival to dispatch.

"Code 5 at your last in Huntley Court."

"Copy that, just an update when you can."

Dane and I switch our portable radios to life.

In my periphery a dozen different curtains reveal the edges of wide eyes, and the court is deathly quiet. Dane moves past me, stepping up to the door. He raps his knuckles twice, firmly and waits, turning to me with a frown. There's no yelling, no screaming. No sound at all. Dane moves to knock again and my attention is caught by the frantic movement of the neighbour's curtain. The curtain falls back and exposes the frightened man's fist, his thumb and two fingers extended.

My heart leaps to my chest.

As the doorknob rattles from the inside, I slam a hand on Dane's shoulder and yank him to the ground.

"Gun! Gun!" My warning roars through the air the same instant the door flies open and the gun barks, biting into my ballistic vest and throwing me off balance.

I clench my teeth, but the wiry offender takes advantage and slips past, landing on the bike and in the same motion, kicking it to life.

Dane rolls to his side, and I hear his urgent vocals alert dispatch.

"Code 9. Shots fired!"

The air explodes into radio madness, dispatch hounding us for updates, issuing orders for all available units to render assistance, but it's nothing more than the crackling theme to the action movie playing out around us.

Dane scrambles to his feet as I lunge at the wild-eyed offender, but he opens the throttle and the bike lurches to obey, yanking him out of my reach. I twist aside as he points the gun over his shoulder and empties two rounds.

The sting of chipped brick burrows into my neck.

A cry of shock sinks Dane to the ground, and I unholster my own weapon.

My military training automatically kicks in and I harness my adrenaline, breathing out a measured breath as the steady barrel of my Smith and Wesson pistol follows the bike. He slides the back wheel out and almost lays it down avoiding the patrol car, but when he reappears, I squeeze the trigger.

I'm running at him almost before the bullet strikes, desperate to disarm him. Right beside him as the bike tips, I wrench him roughly off the toppling machine and grind his face a little too roughly into the bitumen. His weapon clatters to the road and I snarl into the side of his face. He sobs like a baby as I fasten the cuffs and roar his rights at him. Behind me, the bike chokes, floods and loses life.

I fist his collar and ignore his screams of pain.

"It's just a scratch, you piece of shit!" I spit at him, wishing I'd have shot him in the head instead of the shoulder, and I fight the urge to snap his neck.

Dane's voice wavers through the portable.

"Hawker 307 to VKC, one male in custody. He has a gunshot wound to the right shoulder. He's conscious and breathing, approximately 30 years of age. We will need an ambulance ASAP. You can slow down other units."

I walk him to the car and scan for Dane. He's doubled over against the brick wall, a crimson stain visible where his hands clutch his thigh. I release a breath, relieved to see the trajectory of the bullet missed his major artery.

I snatch the portable and bark my command.

"VKC, we have a member down. I repeat, my offsider has been shot. We need an ambulance *now*!"

Dane grimaces, his pallor faded and pinched, his breath hissing with the fire roaring through his leg. It's not a serious injury, but my stomach churns with what it could have been if I hadn't caught the warning from the window. He catches my eye and nods with tight lips; it's a reassurance and forgiveness in a single movement, but this time it falls short, my guilt too heavy to shake.

"VKC received. Ambulance has been dispatched."

After ensuring the assailant isn't armed, I shove him roughly into the back of the patrol wagon. I advise dispatch of my intention to investigate the premises to the tune of his pathetic whimpers and moans.

The house remains suspiciously quiet as I approach the door. I hear Dane's shuddering groans. He acknowledges my silent query with another stiff nod, his teeth clenched so hard his jaw pops.

I hope the ambulance arrives soon.

Curling my head around the door, I'm met with the same palpable silence that waited for us in the street. It's the quiet that comes with impending horror, and I mentally ready myself. The neighbour knew there was a gun involved so I can assume a few rounds were emptied somewhere in the house.

Most of the windows are darkened, the stained curtains the same filthy brown of the carpets. Mismatched chairs and dented coffee table decorate the room.

Through the crack of another door, the glimpse of an elbow resting against the tacky green linoleum of the kitchen floor hones my senses. The door gives way soundlessly.

My lungs empty slowly. I know that mottled look, the odd blue tinge that paints the skin as the heart beats one last time. Crouching to check the pulse is simply a trained response. The red stain on her chest already answers that question. I step over her carefully, check the laundry, the bathroom. The master bedroom reeks of human waste. A tiny blue dummy in the doorway sends my heart into overdrive. I hear my own footsteps now, unable to remain silent with the urgency of searching the last room.

A wooden cot is centred in the room like a tiny monument, the solid sides and shining paint the newest item in the home. The shelves are lined with blue teddies and brightly coloured picture books. A frame has pride of place above the back wall, tiny balled fists and bent toes frozen forever in pewter.

My stomach twists and becomes lead. Instinct, training, experience. It all assaults me with its dark theories, but I have to look. It's my job. My head pounds as I step forward. A tiny leg shaped lump changes the landscape of the neatly tucked blanket. Another step. A tiny hand, limp as if in sleep rests its knuckles against the wooden rails.

When the flat white pillow comes into view my lungs seize. It's one of those pillows that contours to the baby's small head without an abundance of stuffing that might gather around the child's nose. But this pillow is a dome, the edges still displaying an indent on either side.

And the baby's head is beneath it.

With blurred sight my pistol clatters to the floor and I rip the pillow away, and the light spattering of dark fuzz shuffles in its wake. Tiny eyelashes rest on chubby cheeks, the blue lips slack.

The past, carefully buried in the darkest depths of my soul comes crashing out around me. The force of it makes my head spin.

"Thomas?" I whisper, carefully scooping the small cold body to me. His head falls back and I catch it before it falls too far. I pull the limp bundle close to my chest and stroke his soft skin. I murmur, hoping that somehow, he might hear me.

"Thomas? I'm so fucking sorry. Daddy's got you, baby boy."

* * *

Archer and Rain won't be home yet, but that's irrelevant. My feet carry me automatically to Willow's room, tears still making it difficult to see. I knock softly, grief rolling down my cheeks as I wait. When she doesn't answer I pause, forehead resting against the door.

I don't know what I'd say to her. I don't know why I'm even here, but I just know that this is the only place I can be right now. Being with her will ease the pain a little. Make it manageable for a while.

I turn the handle and step inside, and I'm instantly aware she's not here. I drag at the back of my neck, the ache in my throat making it painful to swallow.

The room smells of her, the frangipani and lime a balm for my pain.

"Willow?" My rasping whisper expects no response.

I need to see her. She's always here. But somehow, not today. I groan when I realise I don't even know her mobile number. I hesitate to seek it now from Rain. She texts entire conversations that I'm in no state to entertain. I can wait. I sit on the bed and pull the pillow against me, desperate for her scent.

Her pillow doesn't smell like her at all. It reeks of dust and fresh stuffing, and it's clear she's never used it. Baffled, I search around, my anguish still hitching my chest.

In the corner of the room, tucked away from view behind the open door is a pile of blankets. I shove the door closed to expose it, that exquisite scent thickening as I move closer.

Without understanding why, I step into the middle of the blankets and pull them around me, her fragrance surrounding me. I relish the feeling of security as I burrow into its comfort breathing Willow deeply as I close my eyes.

"Willow?" I whisper to the empty room. "I need you right now. I need you to tell me it's okay, to kiss me and make me forget the pain for a minute or two. The baby boy, Willow, he could have been Thomas, with his hair dark like mine. But I couldn't save him. I couldn't save Thomas either. Everyone I love goes away in the end. You just wait and see. You will too."

Straining me ears, I listen for her wisdom in the silence. I just keep listening.

CHAPTER 21

WILLOW

I shove through my bedroom door, dumping the armful of paper bags and boxes unceremoniously on the bed. I even bought new underwear, the kind that isn't gray from washing and still has elastic. I open the pack of bra and panties, the red that the shop attendant assured me would suit the colour of my hair. I strip off excitedly, discarding my old sensible bra, and shiver with excitement as the lace lovingly strokes my skin. It feels so decadent and sinful, like the time Rain and I crept into that shop with the expensive evening gowns and tried some on. We were discovered quickly, of course, but just the quality fabric against our skins made us feel like princesses deserving of such finery.

The bathroom mirror reflects a woman worthy of a matching underwear set, and I grin as I stare. I imagine I'm in a mansion, my pale chest of drawers transformed by my imagination into a thing of hand-crafted oak, my bed a four poster with...

The pillow has been moved. How had I not noticed that immediately?

I'm suddenly aware that there's someone else in my room. My nest is overflowing.

Axel!

He's so deeply asleep that the racket I made didn't rouse him.

I'm on the brink of raging at him, demanding why he thought

he was entitled to enter my room when I see it. A dried path of tears staining his cheeks.

I look past the man, the body of steel and unbreakable mettle, and get the sensation that I'm seeing him for the first time. He's the result of a merger between two separate beings. The impenetrable facade of a soldier, and the vulnerable little boy that sleeps before me now. Somewhere along the line the distinction between the two blurred, bringing him here.

A sensation blooms inside me, one that burns with an intrinsic need to soothe his sadness. It doesn't stem from my stomach, although I feel a hunger for him there, too. It's not the cry of my body wanting to feel his touch, and it's not the quickening of my heart when I think of him. It's an unfurling of my soul, an ache to connect with his and understand the intricate quirks that fuel him.

His breath shudders, his eyes darting behind closed lids.

"Thomas?" He breathes tightly, an agonised sound.

Who is Thomas?

I kneel before him, instinctively pulling the blankets away, and tuck in against him, arms gathering him to me like I would a precious thing. So much contact, my skin against his shirt, the contours of his muscles hard against my chest. His scent blending with mine. Unsure if it's because we're in my safe place, or if it's simply Axel, I marvel at my steady pulse. So much of me touching so much of him, but I don't feel the slightest bit anxious.

The warmth of Axel's body has me almost drawn into the arms of sleep when he stirs.

"Willow?" His anguished whimper empties his chest beneath my arm.

"I'm here, Axe. I'm here." My mouth moves against the nape of his neck.

"Willow!" With a low growl his tone changes, and I'm suddenly wide awake.

His eyes open black and dangerous, the dried tracks a reminder of his vulnerability as he angles his face towards me.

"I need you." His eyes shimmer again and my blood hums.

I trap his earlobe between my teeth, my body catching fire as his inhale hisses. I grow bolder, my hands slipping beneath his shirt, my nerve endings fizzing no matter where I touch. His stomach contracts as he shifts over me, his hot breaths singe my neck.

"Oh, Jesus!" His chest explodes into heaving waves as he skids his eyes hungrily over my body. I remember I'm virtually naked before him.

I stare into that ebony abyss as he looms above me.

"Tell me to stop, Will. Now." I've never heard his tone so low and tight at the same time.

I contemplate. *Do I want this?* Every fibre in his body is taut and coiled. He holds me in a firm but gentle grip, like he would a precious stone. He won't move a muscle until I respond. I trust that he'll look after me. My mouth falls open as I watch the animal inside of him straining at his chain, but carefully held in check.

I trust him.

"Don't stop, Axel. Please."

His pupils blow out as his lips devour mine, ferocious with the weight of his desire, and my pulse thunders. Strong hands discover me with skill and care, the ticklish bit that clenches my stomach, the sensitive spot that makes me gasp into his mouth. I kiss him back, my head against the carpet, his mouth holding me in place. It's a situation that should have me clawing for air, fighting for space, but my hands bring him ever closer. I break the kiss to slide his shirt over his head, and his eyes never break from mine. He studies me intensely, noting how I react to his caresses, slowing down, speeding up again as if he's taking direction from my body.

I moan when I feel the crush of his body shifting over me, and arc towards him.

"You're so damned responsive, my Willow. More than I've dreamed."

I cry out as he grazes my neck with his teeth, sending a flood of electrical pulses through my veins, and an unbearable throb between my legs. His skin is satin sliding down my body as he rains light kisses on my chest, lips exploring the red lace. I expect him to take it off, but he simply continues his trail to my waist.

Wide hands run down either side and stop at my hips and he pulls back to stare at them before he finds my eyes again.

"Fucking perfect, Will." He wears an expression of torture, but I can't think past my burning skin and my rasping lungs. I fumble for his jeans, moaning as the furnace behind his zip jumps at my touch. My mouth dries out.

"I need…oh, please?" I groan.

"Say my name, Will." He grates.

"Axel." I gasp.

He moves then, feeling me tense up as he reaches the delicate lace that matches my bra.

"Do you trust me, Will?"

"Yes." And the lace slides down my thighs. His hands push them off my feet with languid patience, then retrace their path. I feel his touch burn in that forbidden place and I freeze. He stops before I say the word, locking his gaze on me. He watches me relax and lowers his head until all I can see above my stomach are his incredible eyes. They burn with something I can't define.

"Do you trust me Willow?" He asks again, softly, seductively, a dare.

"Yes."

"Then say my name."

I suck air as his head drops.

The word becomes a forceful cry of ecstasy as he swipes his tongue through the secret centre of me. Violent euphoria detonates over me in an unexpected wave that ignites every nerve in my body.

It's as if I've existed in a state of anaesthesia and Axel just injected liquid fire into my bloodstream. My skin, a dormant housing for my thoughts suddenly a living thing, responding with waves of rapture at the briefest touch. I never knew such pleasure existed! My fingers clutch desperately at his hair, unsure of what they want, but needing more. He brings me to the brink again, over and over, and I writhe in torment.

"Axel." I whimper my plea, my skin a sheen of sweat. I helplessly kneed his thick shoulders, frantic in my desperation to touch him. He brings me to the edge once more, the tremors held at bay by Axel's cruel skill.

He shifts up over me and my spine arches upwards.

He kisses me again, the musky flavour on his tongue sending me crazy.

I can taste me on him.

My lungs lock as every nerve is alerted to what's happening now. At some point, Axel discarded the rest of his clothes. We're skin to skin, nothing between us, and his massive erection is nudging between my legs, hot and hard.

"Will? You okay?" He hovers, his stomach hard on mine with every breath. His focus is strained. I feel the stirrings of panic creep in and I clutch him desperately. I want him. I want him to show me more of how wonderful this can be, but my lungs squeeze.

With a tenderness that I feel in my soul, he smiles gently down at me. His lips graze mine.

Tears well in my eyes. He's giving me all the power. I can tell him to stop and he will. He's still poised at my entrance, waiting patiently for me to decide.

A bolt of utter clarity strikes me breathless. This mountain of strength, muscles straining with control, hovers awaiting my command. He's giving me the lead in this beautiful dance, shelving ego and offering himself to my desires. In that moment, I realise with undeniable certainty that I love him.

Any misgivings I had moments ago become null and void, my heart and soul open completely, helplessly to him.

The tears stream down my cheeks, his thumb tenderly

interrupting their path.

"Don't stop, Axel."

He holds my eyes, whispering "Don't take your eyes off me, Will. I need you to know it's me holding you."

I nod, but realise he's waiting for my words.

"Show me how good it's supposed to be, Axel."

The explosion of pleasure as he presses into me drops my head back, but Axel stops, fists my hair and holds my head.

"Eyes on me, beautiful." He pants.

He eases in slowly, keeping his incredible eyes on mine, watching every gasp, every writhing groan as my fingers dig urgently into his back.

An exquisite burn radiates through me from where he's seated inside me, stretching me until I feel like he fills my entire body. I tilt my head, in awe of the sight. Both our chests heave and surge with desire, their erratic rhythms too fast under the layer of sweat. Between my legs, I see Axel lodged deep inside me, the sight of our bodies connected in such an intimate way tears an incredulous moan from me.

"You ready, Will?" He rasps, his gaze flaring so hot I can almost feel their burn.

"Yes, Axel, I need more, please!" I moan.

He doesn't obey my command immediately, his appraisal sliding over every inch of me as if to savour the moment.

Then his body moves, his hips pulling back. I whimper and scratch a canyon of demand into his shoulders as I feel him withdraw from me, then he fills me again slowly, a torturous grunting sigh plumes in my face. I gasp it in.

"More." I plead, the crescendo boiling in my veins needing escape. Relief floods his expression and his locked jaw slackens as if all his restraint lay there.

Our hips snap together, hands sliding over skin, digging in, kneading. Our breaths keep pace with the building friction, his animalisic growls responding to my own groans and gasps.

My head drops back as my nerves bunch and sizzle, and Axel's fist closes in my hair.

"Eyes. On. Me. Will" He rasps, his other hand diving under my buttocks to deepen his pounding thrusts.

How I keep them open when my body explodes in bucking waves of rapture is beyond me, but Axel's name smashes into mine as his expression is wonder colliding with untamed fury, and his body stills, then ruptures. The pressure of his release deep inside my soul announces he's found his own peak.

In the panting reality that follows, my mood sobers. One night is all I have with him. It's all he is capable of offering. A tiny moan springs from my throat as invisible strands of barbed wire bite into my heart, and silent tears slide as he pulls me against his chest.

We slip into sleep naturally with the alien familiarity of each other, and when I wake in the darkness some time later, the ache for a connection unwelcome in his future is so bitter, I weep silently. He stirs against my back, his arms wrapped protectively around my waist in sleep.

I turn in his embrace, urging him awake with my lips and hands to remind me how making love should feel. I tell him with my caresses how much he means to me because it's the only way I can, and his groans of desire once again entwine with mine.

Then, as sated sleep steals his attention from me a second time I stare into the darkness. Axel found and exposed a secret place inside me, a dying ember he tenderly urged to life, setting me alight with this new sensation. Is it normal to feel so vulnerable?

I love him.

My chest burns as I acknowledge this craving I hold for him is one he avoids. Resents. To think of his expression closing down as the sun rises, when he takes the warmth of his body from mine when the vision of desire is carved so deeply in my mind, claws at my chest. I can't watch his eyes dim and turn away. Not from me. I'm accustomed to rejection, but his will break me.

I slip from his arms carefully, climb from my nest and sneak into my clothes.

And I walk out.

CHAPTER 22

AXEL

*S*he creeps into my dreams, her helpless surrender, her mouth forming an astonished O of pleasure. Her perfect body reaching for mine, the exquisite smell of her arousal merging with that frangipani and lime scent that sends my mind into overload.

It wasn't just sex. It was a joining of souls, the silent understanding passing between us in the puffs of our labouring lungs, and the starving thrusts of our bodies; a divine connection with the ethereal sylph sent to me from beyond the stars. I fell asleep in sated bliss before I could ensure she was okay, but like a goddess of dreams she reached for me again, her own hunger matching mine, her sweet voice sighing my name, showing me just how good she felt.

I sense daylight hovering before my closed lids and a satisfied smile curls my lips. I give a sleepy, nonsensical murmur as a warning of my lust and reach for her, chasing her scent.

It's not only the first time I've fallen asleep with a woman since Janice, but the first time I've not been driven away by that sensation of regret. I could never regret Willow.

My eyes snap open when my hand falls on cold, empty blankets.

She's gone.

Like a physical blow I wince, scanning the room. That red lace set lays discarded on the carpet, her drawers left ajar to reduce the noise she made as she left.

Instantly sobered and awake, I question my own memory. That gleam in her eyes told me of emotions stirring and waking. I watched their birth with my image in their reflection. That look that in other women made distaste bloom, in the delicately stunning face of Willow had my heart soaring.

I swallow the cold emptiness that crawls into my throat.

Sure, I'd planned to feed her the same mantra I always used the following morning.

'Thanks for a great time, have a nice life. I might see you around.'

Gentler words for Willow, but the gist was the same. But first I'd wanted to have her again.

I climb from her nest slowly, reassured that I can have another taste when she inevitably seeks that dreaded 'more' from me.

But then what? What if, after a second helping of Willow, I crave another one? And another one? Her surrender reached me, awed me in a way I never thought possible. I push aside that niggling tug and set my jaw. She will come back, and we will have another night before we're done.

* * *

We debrief in the hospital once Dane is out of surgery. We are both asked to give statements and agree to appear as witnesses when the case goes to court. After battling severe depression, the woman stopped taking her medication and smothered her three-month-old boy. She was shot in unpremeditated rage and grief, but he's still up for manslaughter, possession of an illegal firearm, assaulting an officer of the law causing bodily harm, among other charges.

The loathing I'd felt for the man melts into painful empathy.

That could have been me.

The standard calls from our senior sergeant and police welfare were received with a carefully measured amount of shock and confusion, enough for them to believe I had dealt with it.

Enough so they can pat themselves on the back for helping me through a rough patch and stop calling me. Simone's call was the toughest one to take. Her concern was genuine and I forced myself to swallow my grief, only giving in to my tears when the call had terminated and I knew the wind in my helmet would blow them away.

Thomas. The image I summon is a creation of my imagination alone. *Would he have been like me if he'd still been alive?*

I sink into the familiar bitterness that never stops hurting.

The reluctance of an awkward conversation is overridden by an unfamiliar compulsion to seek her company. I find Willow at the kitchen table, drawings strewn across the surface in an overlapping collage of talent.

"Hey Axe, you're home early." She smiles casually, as if greeting an acquaintance instead of a lover. I frown, uncertain. This is new territory for me.

"Hey Will, how are you this afternoon?" I'm digging for that response, seeking her acknowledgement that last night happened.

She blinks at me, her expression carefully curious.

"I'm good. You?"

I flinch. She's acting as if the universe wasn't blown off its axis. I fill a glass with water, suddenly needing to sooth my arid mouth.

"Oh, Axe, about last night…" She begins cautiously.

Here it comes. I quiver with an anticipation I'm unsure what to do with.

"Why did you come to see me? What upset you?"

My breath whooshes out. I didn't know I was holding it. Her shining eyes rest on me, full of concern for me. But nothing more. Not the glossy dazed look of lust or adoration, and its absence slices out a chunk of lung.

"Just a shit day at work, is all."

She frowns softly, and unbidden my mouth keeps moving, hoping that soon it will lead the conversation back to last night.

"There was a domestic disturbance yesterday. A depressed mother smothered her kid. The father lost his mind and killed her, then lodged a shot in Dane's leg." Did she detect that tremble in my voice?

"Oh, Axel, that's heartbreaking. I'm sure you've seen your share of violence over the years, but…" her tone wavers, "… domestic violence would be on a completely different level. Is Dane okay?"

"Yeah, took the lead out last night and he's on the mend. Shook us both up, but it was closer to home for him. He's got a kid and wife."

Her ghosts gather in her face. My chest begins pounding again as I watch her, aching with the need to comfort her and… something else.

"I'm going to see Dane tomorrow morning. Did you want to come?"

I have no idea what made me ask her, but I'm certain I look as surprised as she is.

She blinks at me. Twice.

"Sure."

"Have you been on a motorbike before? Otherwise I can use Archer's car, or Flynn's."

Suddenly the invitation is becoming complicated, but she laughs softly, that high, sweet cascade of sunshine that warms me.

"Actually, I've been feeling braver lately. I'd love to try your bike."

"I have a couple of spare helmets you should probably try on, then."

Her eyes sparkle, but I only see excitement.

I wait on my bed, a couple of dusty helmets beside me, palms sticky with nerves.

What the hell, Axel, it's just Willow. I remind myself. Even so, my breath snags when she opens the door. She lifts the first helmet, the lilt in her tone suggesting she'd uttered a smart quip, but I don't hear the words for the chaos in my mind.

She looks at me expectantly, her eyes narrowed. She'd asked me a question.

"Umm, yeah?" I mutter, unable to shift my attention from the perfect shape of her mouth.

Willow's laughter clears my head and she shoves my shoulder.

"You're not even listening, Axe. I asked if I should be worried about your driving. Apparently, I do. What's got you so distracted so suddenly?"

"I'm uh, I'm thinking about-" And I can't help myself. I swoop in for a taste of Willow's sweet mouth, groaning as I find myself once again sampling her heavenly flavour.

She grunts in shock, but so quickly does she melt into me that all my senses ignite. I wrap my hands around her tiny waist, pulling her hard against me, knowing she'll feel the stab of my erection in her belly.

She moans into my mouth and my body shudders its response, tingling with anticipation like I'd never had her before.

There's no hesitation this time, her hunger matches mine, her arms and legs ropes binding me to her. When I press into that slick, tight tunnel to heaven, her head falls back, mouth and eyes wide open in utter awe. It's that look, that penetrating expression that touches my soul and brands her name on my heart.

Just for tonight.

She's braver than last time, meeting me thrust for thrust, the friction sending me insane with need, crazy with lust. I keep her attention, convincing myself it's only so she doesn't get scared, but all her expressions are so raw. I need them. I need her eyes on me, my name on her sweet lips.

For a while I'm sated. She's pulled against me, catching her breath. A pretty little melody of bliss. There are no words, nothing we say that can't be conveyed with the touch of our skin.

I'm drifting into sleep when she turns, and her mouth lands on my chest. She takes her time, savouring my body as I did hers, the tickle of her fingers, the smooth touch of her hand, her hair caressing the places she's already kissed.

Her mouth closes around my rejuvenated erection and I growl in desire. Her swirling and swiping tongue bobbing with hot strokes, has me seeing stars. Then I do speak.

"Come here, Will. I have to have you."

She slips her mouth off with a victorious grin. Then she's on her back and I'm screaming her name.

With Willow enveloped in my arms, I slide into sleep.

* * *

Again, she comes to me in my dreams, but when I crack my eyes to reach for her, Willow is gone.

I lie on my side, the space in front of me where Willow should be, cold and empty, my arms wrapped possessively around air.

I watch my hand crush the sheet into a fist. A hollowness sits in my chest, that ache that I'm beginning to associate with Willow. I sigh heavily. I should be happy. No next morning awkwardness to deal with.

But I sure wish I'd woken to her warmth.

CHAPTER 23

WILLOW

*T*his time the light had crept up the walls by the time I'd woken. Axel's breathing was that of a man still cradled in the embrace of deep sleep, but it wouldn't be long before he woke. I lay there for longer this time, reluctant to break away from the warm security of his chest, the tickle of his breath on my neck. It was even better than last time, if that was possible. And that expression on his face, that tender gentleness that never strayed from me.

If only he could love me.

I snort with disgust. I'm only a convenience for him, but even as it hurts my heart I know I can't refuse him. I don't want to. I want to take whatever he's willing to give me for as long as my heart can hold out.

But I can't bear to wake naked beside him and watch his face harden when he tells me to leave.

I shower, finding some joy in choosing warm weather clothes from my new selection.

White shorts and a light top should be cool enough today. I'll ask Axel if this is suitable for a bike ride.

A scruffy haired Flynn is slumped over a morning coffee when I get to the kitchen.

"Top up?"

Lifting his head sleepily, he shoots me a grateful look and holds out his mug. Almost every night now I hear the volume of his nightmares, note the thickening bruising beneath his bloodshot eyes.

I make up three cups, then put on bacon and eggs for the three of us. Archer and Rain will be asleep for a few more hours yet, and Axel usually wakes up about now.

"Big night last night?"

He nods, swigs a mouthful of coffee and stares into it.

"How is it that you always make it taste better?"

"It's the spit she adds." Axel emerges, grinning at me.

Lifting his eyebrows, Flynn takes another swallow.

"Mmm, that must be it. Delicious. Simone called last night. She's finally had the list of compounds released to her, so now she's selecting her team for the operation. I know I seem ungrateful, but the delays are sending me mad when all I want is Amelia home."

Amelia is Flynn's sister. When he was at boarding school, his father sold her into a child trafficking ring. Since Rain bust it open with the help of Archer and Axel, Flynn has been searching for her with single minded determination.

'Oh, well that's great news, right?" I ask as I slide his breakfast in front of him.

"Yeah, but…I'm so scared, Will. I don't trust that this is real anymore. I've had so many false starts I don't even know what I'd do if one of them actually led to her. Then the next issue…I know she'll be different, but will I even recognise her, or will she be completely lost in the nightmare, and I'll be left with a shell where my sister should be?"

I wrap my arm around his shoulder and plant a kiss on his head. Axel watches with hard eyes.

"I know it's frightening, but nobody's going to know how she is until she gets here. She might be like…Rain." I was going to suggest myself then, but I don't need to remind him Amelia might be as messed up as me.

"If there's anything we can do, mate, just say the word." Axel lays a comforting hand on Flynn's shoulder, then looks at me.

"Ready?"

I nod quickly, half expecting that he would have changed his mind about me coming with him.

"Is this okay to wear?"

I can feel his eyes, running over the parts he'd explored last night with his mouth and hands, and my face burns. Flynn's gaze flicks between Axel and me with alert interest, amusement ghosting his lips.

Axel clears his throat. "Let's go."

He hands me a protective jacket, ripping the price tag off it with a frown, and I wonder who it was meant for who never had a chance to wear it.

His face flushes.

"I hope it fits."

Axel zips into his own jacket, the thick material making him seem broader, taller. He's all muscle and testosterone and seeing him looking so magnificent now crashes with the image of him last night. My breath quickens. He mistakes it for nerves.

"You'll be fine. Just hold on tight around my waist, and lean with me into the curves, not against me. You'll have foot pegs to rest your feet on, but if you want me to stop, just tap me, or squeeze me, okay?"

"Lean against the curves and scream. I got it."

He chuckles and plants a quick, soft kiss on my lips, throwing his leg over the bike.

He kissed me. Subconsciously, spontaneously, kissed me!

I twist my hair up under the helmet to keep it from knotting, and take a few precious seconds to contemplate just what I am to him now.

* * *

"This is Willow. Willow, my partner, Dane."

Dane's perched in an armed hospital chair, a shirt informing the world 'I'm the good cop', his bandaged leg lifted on a stool.

His eyes widen and he shakes my hand.

"Oh, hello, Willow. Axe here speaks of you often. He tells me you're learning some of his moves." He gives a mischievous smirk, and Axel glares back at him.

"I'll bet. I guess he told you how he was gracious enough to show me exactly how a man is disabled with a swift knee to the groin then?"

"He let you knee him in the jewels?" Dane's eyes shimmer.

"Oh, he didn't let me, it's just that my skills are far greater than his and I bested him." I smirk.

We both laugh at Axel's dark growl.

"She caught me off guard once, and I'll never live it down." He mutters.

I lay a hand on his arm. "Sweetheart, it's okay not to be exceptional at everything. You don't have to make excuses, we understand that you just met your match with me."

Dane's laughter echoes. Axel's lip quirks up as he stares at me.

"Oh, Axe, you gotta keep this one!"

And with Dane's comment, Axel's expression chills, and I have to look away.

An unexpected, queasy frost rolls around my insides. One I have to swallow hard to contain. Perhaps with the bitterness of Axel's reaction needs to be neutralised with a bit of sugar.

"Uh, how about I grab us some drinks? You'd be pretty over water and juice by now. Want something with flavour?"

"Thanks, Willow, that'd be great."

Axel is quiet as we leave the hospital, a solemn frown on

his face. I'd left the two men to chat, hunching over my own soft drink before bringing them theirs. They were deep in conversation when I returned, their sentences cut short the moment my footsteps sounded too close.

I zip up the jacket and Axel hands me my helmet, drilling his gaze into me. His eyes darken on me and he watches my lips part as my body responds instantly. He holds the helmet a few seconds too long before releasing it.

We don't head straight home and I barely notice. The rumble of the powerful engine and the tensing and shifting muscles as he leans into each bend is hypnotic. I'm hyper aware of how closely I'm pressed against him, yearning but resisting the urge to rest my head against the flat of his back. My arms loosen and drop relaxed into his lap. Even with the wind buffering against me I can feel the heat from his jeans burn my hand, and I'm suddenly aware of the bulge twitching beneath my wrist. I hold my breath. Should I be bold and touch him? Will he shut me down and condemn me for wanting more?

I wriggle against him, pretending I'm seeking comfort, and in doing so, I brush the lump in his jeans again. I rest my thumb against him, carefully rubbing in a way I can deny innocently if I need to.

Axel gears down suddenly, gravity pressing me hard against his back as he steers the bike down a dirt track.

Once stopped, he kills the engine and spins on me. His eyes are an inky inferno of lust, and my blood races as he flicks off his helmet and tears mine away. His mouth devours mine at that awkward angle, dipping, tasting each other with a merging of tongues and insatiable desire. Without breaking contact, he lifts me around in front of him, side saddle with my left buttock resting against the handlebars.

He fumbles desperately, working my shorts and panties down my legs while I breathlessly release his zipper. He springs free and my fingers wrap around his girth, but he knocks my hand away. In the next instant, he manoeuvres me so I face him, straddling the bike backwards. With a grunt and a smooth motion, he slides deep inside me, my head falling back as I savour that exquisite burn and stretch.

"Axel!" I gasp, but he's hungrier than I've ever seen him. His animalistic grunts and wild growls as he thrusts hard and deep have me screaming in pleasure. My nerves vibrate. His breaths chop at the air, and I bend to taste them. One arm around my waist, the other on my shoulder pulling me into his pounding thrusts, he focuses on me, the flare in his eyes hinting at a secret pain inside him, a flash of fear.

Shock waves rattle my bones at the same time he roars my name into the trees.

I watch him come down, the silver slowly returning to his eyes, his chest losing speed. I pull his lip into my mouth, breathing in his exhales, running the tip of my tongue over it.

When I pull back, I'm shocked by the look of utter defeat in his expression. He's raw and vulnerable in a way I can't grasp, so I merely hold him.

"Stay with me tonight, Will?" He asks in a fractured whisper.

"Yes." I breathe back, and we just sit there, Axel still lodged within me, our arms around each other like we're both afraid the moment will break.

CHAPTER 24

AXEL

amn it. I used to own this godforsaken world. All my enemies would fall away because I attacked with fearlessness and focus. It was simple.

Now it seems like I'm second guessing myself. Take my bike, for instance. I race the wind on this machine, feel it dance on the bitumen as it struggles to hold on to the corners I won't slow for. Feel my knees brush against the panels of cars as I weave through the narrow gaps in traffic. But now? I wonder what obstacle could appear on the road that could unseat me, throw Willow off. Hurt her. I slow down, sit behind a queue of cars at the lights, double check in both directions.

And why?

I think I'm addicted to Willow.

It makes sense, I surmise. I've avoided the women in town lately, so it stands to reason that I'd latch onto a woman conveniently near to me who meets my needs. And that she does. Now that I've woken her beast, the hunger resides in her eyes. By the time I thirst for her, she's already reaching for me.

I convince myself of this, even though when the night comes we simply lie beside each other and talk for hours, falling asleep only when the dawn begins brightening the world.

When I rouse, I note something is different. A heaviness that

I never knew existed has leaked away overnight, and I'm more relaxed and refreshed than I've ever been. Willow, as promised, is curled up against my chest, her hand clasping the arm I've draped over her in sleep. The blankets reveal the barest swell of her breast, her golden skin flawless and delicate against my charcoal sheets. Her mouth is slack and bent out of shape from her pillow squashed cheek. I watch her pulse tick calmly in her neck, the heady aroma of frangipani and lime as I breathe it in. I simply stare at her, remembering how every cell felt beneath me, how she arched and reached and gave it all to me willingly. The ache that's carried her name is absent, and I feel invincible in her arms. I feel complete.

I've been waiting for the perfect bubble to burst. At some point, she's going to want more of me. They always do. But I've been searching every nuance, seeking subliminal evidence that she's getting clingy, but besides that expression she saves for me, the one that shakes my world when I first breach her body, there is nothing.

"Why don't you want anything from me, Willow? Am I not enough for you?" I breathe into her hair.

So accustomed to women throwing themselves at me, the idea that I found one who doesn't want me is messing with my head. Had I not asked her, I'm sure my bed would be empty again this morning.

"Mmm…" The sleepy siren murmurs, and I smile.

"Not a morning person?"

Without opening her eyes, she mumbles in a voice thick with sleep; "I'm actually an evil demon who devours anyone within reach as soon as I open my eyes. The only way to avoid it is to immediately drink a cup of double strength coffee, otherwise I'll be trapped in demon form forever."

I chuckle, nipping her neck.

"Since I don't have a coffee machine in here, or a slave, I'm going to have to defend myself against this demon instead."

She shows all her teeth.

"Don't say I didn't warn you!" She giggles, and she's moving before her eyes open, pushing me onto my back where she spends the next hour wrecking me.

* * *

Dane irritates me with his smug smile. Until right now, I thought having Dane back in the office, even if just to wade through paperwork, was wonderful progress. He moves the swivel chair to face me, careful not to knock over the crutches leaning against his desk.

"Considering staying on after all?" He quips.

For a moment I'm stunned. I'd forgotten about that. Willow spends most nights in my arms, and after work I make my way into The Broken Keg to give her a ride home.

It's a comfortable routine, but one that brings an entirely different ache with it. Besides the bedroom, she never initiates contact with me, and never mentions or questions the whatever-it-is we have going on.

"You're still rejecting the idea of a relationship then?" He asks, his head shaking.

"It wouldn't work. I'm not relationship material."

"So what is it that you two have right now?"

I consider carefully.

"An unspoken agreement?"

"Seriously, Axel, when are you going to man up and do something before you wake one day and she's in another man's arms?" He huffs.

I hadn't thought about that. I hadn't thought about where her kisses and sweet smiles would fall after me. After me. Would someone else get to see that euphoric expression that renders me helpless?

"You're a complete idiot, Axe. You're too wrapped up in fear that you can't see the good thing you have going with her. Think about it, man. Sleeping together is one thing, seeking out her company is another thing entirely. How many deep and meaningful conversations have you had with, well, anyone you've bedded?"

I frown. My thoughts flick through the faces I barely recall. Nope. The lengthiest conversation I'd had with any of them was that day after mantra as I'm backing out the door. Even Janice... we never really had much to say to each other. The biggest conversation we'd ever had was the one where she explained how she'd found whatever was missing from our relationship in the bed of Dorian.

"Yep, thought so. So what's the problem?" Dane crosses his arm and waits, demanding more than guilty silence for once.

"It's Willow. She doesn't want anything more from me."

Dane's eyebrows escape into his hairline.

"And you know that, *how*?" His tone sharpens.

My shoulders drop with my sigh.

"She says nothing. Absolutely no indication or reference to whatever we have going on. She doesn't hold on to me longer than she should, she doesn't seek me out, she doesn't flirt with me. Nothing. If I had no memory of her in my bed I'd assume we're just friends."

By the time I've finished, my hands are balled in fists.

"Maybe you're too busy looking for excuses as to why it wouldn't work to see the signs that are there. You seem hell-bent on finding a reason why you shouldn't be with her, why you shouldn't be in love with her."

"I'm not in love with her." I snap, but my words lose venom, sounding more like a whine.

"So you admit you're looking for a fault. A deal breaker to hold onto so you don't have to lose your heart and feel vulnerable. Keep looking, Axe, I'm sure you'll find some obscure, trivial thing at some point you can wield like a weapon so you don't have to be weak enough to admit you love her!"

With a final glare, he turns his attention to his paperwork, frustration radiating from him.

* * *

"Are you certain this is what you want?"

Simone narrows her eyes at me as if she's impatient for me to be gone. It's been three and a half weeks since I found heaven in Willow's body, and I've been floating in a cloud of satisfaction ever since. The problem is that when I'm working, or Willow is out for the day, a tiny nibble of self-loathing persistently reminds me that I miss her company. I try to convince myself I feel nothing for her, but there remains a lingering ache in my chest that intensifies when I think of her. Which is too often.

"Yes." I deadpan. I know violence. I know I can drown myself in the adrenaline and distract myself with the focus required to tackle the harder criminals of Diamond Valley; the town where guns outnumber the population and drugs are prevalent.

Simone purses her lips.

"I thought you might. You have an interview and psych test tomorrow, oh eight hundred hours. Oh, and Axel?" She drops the paperwork she's clasping on its end, neatening the pages.

I wing my eyebrow.

"If you're running away from something, the psych will pick it up. I'm hoping for your sake Diamond Valley are too desperate for a cop that they ignore the bullshit you try to feed us."

* * *

Dane is bending over the paperwork on his desk with pen hovering above. He sighs and leans back in his chair as I approach, moving his crutches from the chair to sit beside him.

"Simone said you're officially leaving us. Tail between your legs, I see. I hope you manage to outrun your heart while I'm left to find a new partner."

I rub my forehead.

"Sorry, man. After you put in your request to be on permanent admin duties, I figured there's nobody else I want to be partnered with here."

"Bullshit, Axe. You forget I know you better than that. I know a half-truth when I hear it from you. It's that girl of yours. She's got you all tied up and you're wasting all your energy trying to fight it. Everyone can see it except for you. You're so determined to sabotage your own happiness that you don't see how much it's impacting the rest of your life."

"Are you suggesting that I allowed you to get shot because I'm supposed to admit I love her?" I accuse and his face boils.

"See! This is what I'm talking about. You've lost your head! I wasn't talking about that day at all, but you choose to warp what happened and hold on to a misguided belief that I'm attacking you, or blaming you."

His ire takes the heat out of my own. I stab my fingers through my hair, agitated by the vortex of conflicting emotions caged in my skull.

"I don't think you're attacking me, Dane." I mutter, but he's not deterred.

"You're making a pretty good impression of it, then! This anger and irrationality isn't you, Axel. You're using it as a defence to shield you from the truth. As long as you're allocating yourself some imaginary blame for allowing actual feelings for Willow, or dreaming up some underlying evil in her that you've made your mission to protect yourself from, you feel safe. It's much easier to feel angry than vulnerable, so you just go ahead and do that; take the easy path."

He doesn't understand. I huff impatiently.

"You're my *partner*, Dane. I was *supposed* to protect you, but instead I let thoughts of her interfere with my duty. If it wasn't for her, I could have stopped you from being hurt, Dane. That's not love, or whatever you imagine I feel for Willow, it's manipulation. It's what women do, Dane. They make you feel good, then, when you're all secure and contented, they find all your secret wounds and rip them open while you watch. Don't you understand? If it wasn't for Willow in my head, you wouldn't have had to explain that bullet hole to your wife!"

Breath rasps from my constricted throat, the words hissing through my teeth.

Dane slams his pen down with a temper I'd never seen before.

"You're so blinded by your need to lay blame on Willow that you choose to forget *you saved my life.* If you hadn't shoved me aside…"

His eyes close and he draws a sobering breath. "Did you see where the bullet lodged in your vest, Axe? If you're too messed up to have noticed yourself, it was at the *exact* height and location as where my head had been seconds before you shoved me aside."

Stunned, I think of the bullet impact point. No, I didn't notice.

Dane stabs a blazing glare at me.

"You're so fucked up that you couldn't see the evidence? I'm pissed that you didn't tell me you were leaving, and I'm disappointed that you aren't brave enough to face your fears and tell the girl you love her. I looked up to you, man."

I punch a dent into my locker, relishing the fire that races up my arm. Damn Dane for his ridiculous theories. Damn Willow for the way she makes me crave her.

But there mere thought of her skin beneath my fingers brings a peaceful quiet to my soul, and my shoulders hang in defeat. She's bewitched me.

I hope Simone's right and Diamond Valley overlooks my demons.

CHAPTER 25

WILLOW

*a*n ocean couldn't penetrate the dryness of my mouth. My hand shakes and loses strength and the tiny stick drops to my lap.

The thick blue lines are the answer to why I've been so exhausted. Dread burns in the back of my throat and a wave of nausea rises. I breathe through it.

I can't believe it never occurred to me. An offhanded comment from Rain got me thinking, and I'd asked Danny if he could pick a test up for me.

He'd wanted to kiss me again, but after I was honest about my feelings for Axel he backed off. But only his romantic advances. It was eerie how he not only seemed to accept my revelation, but that strange light dancing across his features as he enthusiastically offered his support had my stomach curdling. Maybe I'm over-thinking it. For the last week I found myself reading into every word anyone spoke and perhaps in the same fashion, my heightened suspicion is merely a byproduct of my nausea.

He'd brought me two tests, and only when I saw the result reiterated by the second did I begin to accept it.

I'm pregnant.

I'm damaged and broken. I can't do this. I can't bring a life into this world when all I can offer is jaded views and broken dreams.

I suck in a shaky lungful of sickly sweet lavender stench of the cafe's bathroom deodoriser.

"Well?" Danny whispers impatiently, eyes flashing with something darker.

I thin my lips as an answer.

"I…I need to be alone, Danny. Please, can you take me to work now?"

He squeezes my arm, and it makes my skin retract. I shrug off the sensation. Damn hormones.

I grab my backpack and wait by his car for him to drive me to work. I'm numb, even after I arrive at The Broken Keg and head to the bathroom, going through the motions of pulling on my work uniform as if my life hadn't just been turned upside down all over again.

* * *

My heart pounds in my head as I curl into the fading scent of Axel lingering in my nest and stare wide-eyed into the dark.

My hand flutters gently over the flat plain of my abdomen, as if anything more than the slightest touch might hurt the baby.

The baby. A tiny creation of Axel and me. A life created in one of our mind-blowing nights.

He won't want this. His life is structured. Work hard, play hard. No distractions.

Except since I've been here, he hasn't been playing.

I know because instead, he's been playing with me. And just sometimes I allow myself to fancy I'm more than a simple plaything for him.

But I can't do that to myself. I drew a picture of him. A snapshot from my memory, his beautiful face full of everything I dare not dream I could ever deserve. If I look at him now and meet the empty stare of a man moved on from me would tear me wide open. Because I know I'd beg for just one more night. And I know how he'd have to break my heart, regretting that it came to this.

But it's different now, because I'm pregnant.

And I can't do this alone.

Oh, God! What will Axel say? We did this together and I need him beside me for this decision. Tears slide down my cheeks as I press myself into the blankets that hold the reminder of his touch. I can't be with him tonight.

Axel sits on the wooden bench seat, so lost in thought that he snaps his head towards me when I'm almost beside him. His shock quickly sinks into that warm smile, like I'm everything to him, and it's all I can do not to run away.

"Hey. I missed you last night." His smile stretches with his words and my lungs constrict at the velvet rumble of his voice.

"Hey Axe, have you got a few minutes?"

Suspicion clouds his careful nod.

I swallow, not knowing where to begin, listening to his silence scream at me. As the minutes pass me by, the urge to escape builds. It's now or never.

"I'm pregnant." I whisper.

The chair jolts as Axel's spine welds, and I can't look at him. If I had any tears left, the raw emotion strangling his breath right now would have drawn them out.

His knuckles whiten on the edge of the seat.

"What are you going to do?"

There's an edge to his tone, almost accusatory, but that's not what rips my heart from my chest.

What are you going to do? You. Not us. I know then. He's had his fun with me, and now I'm just another message from an unsaved number in his phone to delete without reading.

I'm afraid that if I speak louder than a whisper, I'll unravel before him, an ugly mess of romantic designs and lacerated scars.

"I don't know."

His body tenses as he drags a palm down his face. It's an unconscious gesture of anger and hurt.

"Shit." His voice is threadbare, and I cringe, instinctively curling my arms around my stomach.

"Shit, shit shit." He stands suddenly.

"Axel?" I brave a glimpse at him, and everything I feared I'd see is on display for me to feast upon. His lips curl in distaste, his face hard concrete of detached bitterness, and he's not even looking at me. He stares past me, through me, with betrayal and loathing radiating off his entire demeanour. Every smile, every laugh and caress we shared are all erased in a split second filled with ice.

He holds up a hand, daring me to speak, then turns his unseeing glare on me.

And walks away.

I'm on my own.

* * *

I'm staring at my pitiful reflection with its terrified eyes barely ten minutes later when Axel bursts into my room. He's returned with an army of fury, if the storm in his eyes and the stone of his face is anything to go by.

"Tell me what you're planning to do about it." He rages, fists clenched and teeth clamped.

A knife in my heart would have hurt less. This man before me is a creature I've never met. He's a furious soldier of cold judgment.

"I didn't do this alone, you know. Why is it up to me to decide?" I snarl back.

"Because no matter what the man says, it's always comes down to a woman's decision in the end. What I think will have no importance whatsoever" He glares at me coldly.

"Jesus, Axel. I've never been in this situation before, how can you condemn me for a decision I haven't made yet?"

"Because." Dry ice sharpens his words. "You women are all the same. It's only ever meant to be a single night, but you women always want more."

My heart shatters and bleeds and I sink boneless to my bed. It's ironic that all my agony has ever occurred on a bed. But it's the first time it's happened on mine. I'm just like the others? No. I can't be. I'm not like every other normal woman, because there's nothing normal about me.

Clarity fills my lungs as I stare at the stranger before me. He's an impenetrable tower of ice, but at its core, a scared little boy stares out from his prison.

Axel's playing the victim because it's safer than the unforged pain of whatever truth he's running from, a safer pain than confronting the root of his fears. Fury fills my skin, my rage making me feel as tall as him.

"How dare you, Axel! You're as much a part of this as I am, but you're holding a shield of old bruises and you won't let me through. I know I'm not like everyone else, because that's all I've ever wanted to be. And no matter how hard I try, I'm not, so you can stick that accusation up your arse! This is about you and your fear that has you keeping people at arm's length, and boy do I know about fear! I used to think we had something in common, that you were damaged but I was broken, but as it turns out, I'm not the one who needs saving. I'm so fucked up, Axel, but at least I'm strong enough to face my fears. You just keep holding onto your pain without realising it's eating you up, without noticing that the shadows you're trying to protect yourself from has been you all along. It's terrifying, facing the things that wound you, Axel. I know that more than most. But when I face them head on and find the strength to battle them I find the courage to face my next demon. You need to grow up and do the same."

My lungs are burning with my rage.

"You're wrong, Axel. I know now more than ever that I don't want anything from you. Absolutely nothing. You can forget about this whole thing, let it fade away into that trench you've built around the fortress of your own denial. I'll deal with this,

Axel. You need never think on it again."

The gentle features that once reached into my heart with such sweet tenderness now contort with the poison that falls from his lips, and in the midst of my ire, I bleed with the certainty that this is where Axel and I finish.

"You're trying to trap me, then when I try to do the right thing, you'll destroy me with it." His accusation is gravel and hostility, shaking with barely contained control.

Axel's expression is full of loathing.

I square my shoulders indignantly, and as my chin lifts, I catch a glimpse of his ghosts. He's not seeing me at all, just some past life that he's trapped in.

"Fuck you, Axel. I don't deserve this, and I certainly don't need you."

With head held high I give him a hard shove out my door. When I return to the bathroom mirror, a new woman stares back at me. She's bold, defiant and glows with a strength no longer dormant.

CHAPTER 26

AXEL

I fold over the basin, lungs heaving with the poison of her deceit.

I knew it! She's trying to fucking trap me! She lured me in, manipulating me into caring for her, and now like a worn out recording, it's happening all over again.

She's shoved it in my face and tore any possibility of hope from me with her cold, empty condemnation. *"I'll deal with this, Axel. You need never think on it again."*

She never cared for me. That truth is a razor in my heart.

I can't look at her. The vicious vessel that holds a new life from my seed. Such precious cargo in an evil wrapping.

Thomas.

My fist passes through glass, tiles and plaster and comes to rest with a thunk on the wooden stud behind.

Seven years bad luck, I think as shards of my image fall into the basin. I stare at them as my wound begins to weep. The fragments warp my reflection, my nose not quite meeting up with my mouth. An eye is missing and I wonder if perhaps this is one of the truest images of myself I've been shown. I'm shattered.

I'm the fool who didn't see it coming. I could put Janice down to the naivety of youth, but Willow...

I fist my hair as I fall to my bed, stabs of pain jolting in my chest at her scent on my pillow.

My rage melts into helpless grief. I let the tears fall unashamedly.

Well, Thomas, you'll get to meet your brother or sister soon. Tell them Daddy loves you both.

I can't. I just can't. Everything here reminds me of Willow. Willow's scent, Willow's laughter. Willow's expression of ecstasy beneath me. Willow's deceit.

I'll bet she's laughing now, just because I was weak enough to give in to my desire to have her one more time.

Why did I do that? I knew the risk and didn't use protection. That in itself is so unlike me. She's a drug. That's why. I was so hooked on her, even before I'd laid a hand on her, I lost my damned mind.

I can't stay and face her. I can't see her again, because if I do, there's a real danger that with one flash of her eyes I'll forget her deceit and fall to my knees at her feet, offering my chest to the poisoned blade she wields.

With a clarity that pulls back the curtain of agony, I check my watch. Another hour before she goes to work. I find an old backpack, one large enough for my requirements and get to work.

By the time everyone leaves, all my worldly possessions are zipped up in the one bulging bag.

On a whim, I quietly open Willow's door and shuffle through a pile of her drawings. My gut seizes. There's a picture of me, the expression of a fool in love plastered all over my face.

Fuck it! I rip it in half and drop the pieces to the carpet. As I reach the door again I hesitate. Her scent, that alluring ambrosia that empties my head is all around me. Resentment blurs my vision, but it's for myself. She's cruel, but if she were here I don't doubt that I would fall back into her arms in a heartbeat. I retrace my steps and grab a handful of drawings from the bottom of the pile. They won't take up much room.

I veer into her bathroom, not for a purpose, but because my feet simply take me there. Her top drawer is cracked open. It slides out easily.

I recognise those sticks from Janice. The two ominous lengths of white plastic with tiny windows glare up at me with their silent confirmation.

She checked twice.

I take one, needing something concrete to prove that once upon a time, there existed a tiny part of me that was brave enough to become more.

* * *

The heavy emptiness follows me no matter how hard I twist the throttle. It's neither ache nor burn, but a crippling combination of both. The speedometer needle points angrily into the red but I keep accelerating. I weave around cars so fast it's like they're parked. The faster I go, the more my adrenaline smothers the pain so I just keep pushing. The pre-twilight dim wakes up the streetlights as I fly past and the evening chill makes my wrists throb. I see the glowing dome of the next town as the rumble of my bike stutters, yanking me from my numb stupor. Flicking the fuel to my reserve tank, my bike regains its rhythm and I pull into the next petrol station.

As I fuel up, my adrenaline subsides enough for that pain to return with a vengeance.

"You alright man?" the female attendant steps deeper into the security of the counter with wide eyes.

I remain mute, sliding my card over the counter. A shaking hand snatches it away and swipes it, shoving it back at me before the payment processes. With a sick satisfaction I hold her gaze until she's pressed against the wall, colour draining from her face, and only then do I slowly turn away. I listen to her catch her breath as the automatic doors slide apart and suck me into the night.

An hour later I check into the motel. It's a cheap one. Your standard double bed with the hideous cover pattern of odd pastel coloured rectangles, a kettle and those tiny capsules of milk in the fridge.

I consider room service but I'm sick of being trapped in my own head.

I place my order in the quiet pub with a nervous waitress, wearing the scowl that keeps people from approaching me. She stutters my order back to me.

Women. My sneer reaches my face. Acting vulnerable until their tiny hooks have taken hold.

I take a table with a good vantage point. An elderly couple sits at the next one along, the bald man wearing suit pants too flash for a place like this, the snowy haired woman in a floral dress and purple brooch.

A swarm of five men laugh and hoot obnoxiously to my left. The elderly couple lean stiffly forward, straining to hear each other. The woman says something, and the man smiles with his whole face, his wrinkled fingers resting over the age spots on her arms.

A scrawny young waiter, having drawn the short straw, deposits my steak in front of me and wrings his hands.

"I hope you enjoy the meal, sir." That wobble in his tone tells me how much he hopes I like it.

No spit in this meal.

Damn Willow.

The waiter flees.

The table of men are in an uproar. They smash their glasses together and howl in laughter. I grind my teeth. I watch the old man say something, but his companion sadly shakes her head. She can't hear him over the din.

I stand slowly, noiselessly, but a hush falls over the room as if the air itself quivers with my intention. Five sets of huge eyes watch me approach. They lean back when I rest my fists on the table.

"Do you think you could keep it down? There are other people here trying to enjoy a meal."

One mouth gapes, the lot of them are a scattered wave of nods.

Only when I'm seated with a forkful of steak in my mouth does the talking start again. The men are too afraid to raise their voices and the elderly couple find a more comfortable posture and resume their conversation.

I'm nearly finished when the seat beside me fills. The white-haired lady peers sadly into my face.

"I wanted to thank you, sir. My husband and I have been married for sixty years tonight and we don't go out often. It's nice that those young boys were having a good time, but we couldn't hear each other."

Her skin is crumpled paper, loose where the meat has fled her bones and her eyes are watery blue. But they seem to penetrate, the way Willow's did. I swallow.

"You know, I've seen you before. I don't mean you personally, but I'd recognise your kind of pain anywhere. It's a particular pinch, or sting on the soul that shines in your eyes for everyone to see."

I firm my lips.

"You're wrong. I'm perfectly fine, thank you." I growl low intending to scare her away, but she laughs. It's a soft sound but her whole body shakes with it.

"Phooey. You don't scare me, son, and you can't lie to me either. I've been around too long. But I remember how it hurts. I remember the feel of barbed wire being pulled tight around your chest, and you've got a big chest. Big chest, big heart, big pain."

She pauses in thought, staring deep inside me as if she can see where it hurts, then her eyes widen.

"She's not scared of you either. She cares for you." It's a statement.

I sigh, reluctantly playing along.

"I thought she cared for me, but it was all a charade to hurt me." The woman is wrong.

Her face lifts and her too bright dentures shine at me.

"Was it? We women are strange creatures, but often incapable of devising intricate plots to destroy someone for no reason. What I do know after all these years is that men and women are rarely present on the same wavelength, and thus misinterpret each other. I've wasted too many years holding on to a pain that existed only in my mind. Harold and I have had our share of misunderstandings, believe me. Some have been close to tearing us apart, others have been smaller but spanned the decades and did just as much damage. But here we are, sixty years down and the only thing I'd wish for is another sixty with my husband. One lifetime is simply not enough."

Her creased eyes soften and land on Harold.

"I'd better get back to him. He misses me when I leave him too long. We need each other, just like you and your lady need each other. I can feel it here." Her knobbly fingers rest against her skeletal chest.

She uses the table to heave her frail bones up. As she pauses to catch her breath, she gives Harold a smile.

"Isn't he handsome? When you find the right one, son, you'll know. You'll know because that ache won't fade or go away. It'll remain just as excruciating as it is now. It will be the same for her, too until you're back where you belong, because only when a heart is whole can it beat properly."

"She says I'm too afraid." My whisper trembles and breaks.

"We all are, son. It's what makes us human. You look like a brave lad to me. Someone not afraid to fight a little fear."

Her eyes light on Harold and she shuffles towards him.

I'm a little more subdued when I pay the bill, and theirs, too. Then I order two of each dessert for them and leave, taking my ache to bed.

CHAPTER 27

WILLOW

*Y*ou look like you're going to be ill. What's happened?" Danny's face is full of concern.

I sigh and thump into the plastic cafe chair.

"I told him."

A spark flicks to life in his eyes.

"And?" He leans forward.

"And he didn't take it well. He says I did it on purpose to trap him. He was brutal, demanding to know what I intend to do about it. I know he's shocked, but I gather he's not interested in a child. He…he didn't come home last night, so I haven't had a chance to talk to him about it, but I'm hoping he'll be over the shock soon."

Danny frowns. "Really? I thought he'd be happy."

I snort. "You haven't even met him, Danny, how could you think that? Anyway, I didn't handle it well either. After he started yelling at me that it was all up to me, I relieved him of all fatherly duties. Told him to forget this even happened."

Danny's eyes flicker, but he buries it quickly under a frown.

"So you've decided you won't go through with it then? It's probably for the best, really. I mean a single mother who's a waitress? It's a bit cliche don't you think? Bringing up a kid is hard enough even when you don't have your own issues."

I swallow my shock. Does Danny not believe me capable of bringing up a child on my own? Will my own issues do that much damage to a child?

"I…I think I need to talk to Rain." I mumble.

"You haven't told her? Well that's one good thing at least. You really need to think about what's best for you before you involve anybody else. The last thing you need right now is someone trying to manipulate your thoughts based on their own interests."

I bite my lip. He's right. It's still early in the pregnancy and I need to know I'm making the right decision.

"Besides," he adds with a bright grin. "You have plenty of time to make up your mind, that way you can think about it as long as you need to and nobody has to know until you start to show."

I gape at him. "Start to show? I hope to Christ I've well and truly decided before then!"

Suddenly far removed from the caring friend I thought I knew, he straightens.

"It's okay, I know a doctor who can look after you up until twenty weeks."

I scramble from the chair in horror and make for the door.

Danny appears silently beside me as I suck the cool night air into my lungs, heart clattering.

He snakes a hand over my shoulder. "Sorry Willow. I didn't mean to scare you, I just wanted to reassure you that you didn't have to rush your decision."

His very presence is claustrophobic, and I fight the urge to shake him off. Lifting a palm, I gasp for breath. *Everything feels so wrong.* My saliva thickens and that old familiar dread settles over me as my shoulders heave with the effort to draw air.

"Willow?" Danny leans into me, wrapping the too tight ropes of his arms around me. Too close, his touch too unwelcome, I instantly become a whirling flurry of nails and arms.

"Jesus, Willow! What's *wrong* with you?" Danny gasps as he hastily retreats, crimson beading on his face and arms.

I fold inward, the hard concrete catching my slump. Danny stares down at me with that confused horror I'm too accustomed to, but instead of walking away he stands aside and waits for my anxiety to subside.

Tears bloom. I have no more control over myself now than I did when I arrived, despite the self-defence lessons. I'm still a freak. Always have been. Always will be.

Danny sinks to a crouch, cautious space between us.

"You know I think a great deal of you, Willow. But I urge you to have a hard look at what is best for you and the baby. What happens if you're caring for it and you do this? You know me. You've kissed me, but you blanked out and attacked me. Would you do that to the baby?"

* * *

The doctor presses firmly into my abdomen, spreading the cold jelly over my warm skin, nodding her approval as Danny gathers my hand in his.

"It's lovely to see such support. It's a pretty exciting thing; creating life. Are you the friend or the father?" She asks, pressing a device into the gel and sliding it carefully.

"I'm the father." Danny grins at her, and my blood chills.

I snap my attention to him, but he's watching the moving images on the greyscale television on my left as though his blatant, unnecessary lie was never uttered.

"See my cursor?" She monotones, then continues without waiting for an answer.

"This is the abdominal wall here, but see this spot here? That's where it's all happening. The dark area is the amniotic fluid, and this right here..." She shakes the cursor over a lighter, mottled patch.

"This is your baby."

My lungs deflate. She keeps talking but her words fade into

nonsensical sounds. That tiny spot is a tiny person, growing inside my body! A tiny human made of splitting cells, selecting without hesitation elements of both Axel and me. Steeling my breath with the utter wonder of it, I stare at the indistinct picture, afraid to blink lest I lose sight of this incredible creature.

The image shifts with the slide of the implement on my stomach.

"That's better. Now you can see in more detail. You can actually see the head here, and evidence of arms and legs forming there and there. Those darker bits here are the eyes."

The eyes! Would it have the silver eyes of its father? His beautiful, thick head of hair?

"Now, we'll turn on the sound to check the heartbeat."

The cursor freezes and the room is filled with the soft swish swish.

"Is that…?" I ask.

"No, Miss Zimms, that's the sound of your blood travelling through the placenta. If you focus, it sounds more like tiny galloping horses, or some patients say, a tiny train. It's pretty early and faint, but it's there. It appears you are well on track with a normal, healthy pregnancy."

I can't speak. A *normal* pregnancy. Her flippant phrase trumps the heartbeat I can't seem to hear. Normal. From the ruins of my soul, a tiny person comes into being quietly, without fuss, perfectly normal despite my failings.

I flick my glance to the man at my side, and that burning ache roars its disappointment.

He's not Axel. It's been over two months since he'd left. There was no warning, no notice. The conversation I needed to have with him sits unattended on the tip of my tongue. He transferred and asked Simone not to tell us, escaping the trap he accused me of attempting to ensnare him in the day I told him.

I tried to reach him. The letters I wrote and handed to Simone were returned unopened. The last one, a blue envelope, sits at the top of the pile in my bedside drawer as my closure.

I knew by then he wouldn't open it, so instead I let my heart bleed out in blue ink, telling him about the very moment I fell in love with him. It was almost a relief when it, too, was returned. I sought closure by saying goodbye to my heart along with him without feeling his rejection again, not knowing why the tears continue to fall on the edge of sleep each night.

Rain watches me carefully, but I held my emotions in tight reign for so many years, I'm satisfied she can't detect the real reason for my grief. She just questions me gently about the emptiness she sees inside me that grows. I took advice from Danny, keeping the secret until I decide, but the more I consider my situation, the harder it is to find a clear answer.

* * *

I change in my room and survey my bed. Axel once showed me a bed can be a safe and beautiful place. A place of comfort and pleasure. I move slowly, alert. I stroke the soft pillow. Nothing happens. I run my hand over the covers and shiver at the softness. No memories come.

I hook a careful finger and oh so slowly the white sheet beneath is revealed. My breath locks as I reveal a span of exposed sheet. I gingerly slide my hand so it rests tentatively on the bright linen.

Flashes of sneering men and cruelty tumble through my head. I snatch my hand away, cradling it against my chest as if burned.

* * *

The storm dissuades the usual crowd from venturing out and the slower night drags out way too long. It's too quiet for Danny to come. It's odd how he seems to choose the busiest days to come in for a meal, instead of turning up when it's quiet enough for us to actually talk in between orders. Most days now I walk down the street and meet him in the park, sitting beneath the trees and watching the days pass before work. If the weather isn't great, we pass the time in the tiny cafe until it's time to drive me to work.

Piling up an armful of plates, I glance up at a commotion a

few tables over.

A woman bends over a small toddler, a baby balanced awkwardly on her hip. She's attempting to embrace the wailing boy with one arm as he sags to the floor.

I've dumped the plates back down and am at her side in a heartbeat.

"Can I help?"

Gratitude and relief swarms into her smile and the next second I'm holding the baby, and she's gathering the older boy into her lap, consoling him with soothing tones and loving arms.

I'm aware of the warm, alien weight of the child in my stiff arms. I've never held a baby before and I'm terrified I'll drop it, or it will cry, declaring to the world with its high-pitched squall that I'm lacking.

Dressed in blue, he curiously watches his mother and brother with huge, clear eyes. His soft, fat cheeks are so round I wonder if they're swollen. His tiny breaths are unconscious reactions, the hot little fingers gently pinching my flesh like they're continuously investigating their surroundings. The tiny hand is strong, opening and closing as he gazes openly at his big brother, now soothed into quiet hiccups and lung spasms.

If innocence has a smell, this is it. Seeping from the light layer of blonde down on his head, the warm, milky aroma sails into my nostrils, urging me to draw the child closer.

I must have twitched, because his huge brown orbs blink up at me, the same fearless curiosity as before.

I hold my breath, waiting for the imminent rejection. The tiny fist stops flexing on my arm, coming to rest boldly on my cheek.

Then he grins.

A toothless, saliva brightened grin with tiny pink gums and his whole heart. His fat cheeks scrunch, his perfect little lips stretched and his eyes sparkling with honesty. Eyes that stare with utter faith that I won't let him fall. Eyes that see absolutely everything. Eyes that see past my scars and see me as whole.

I know in that moment that I would lay down my life for my

baby.

I taste my decision over the next few weeks, mentally decorating my room with a cot, bright toys and tiny shoes. I search the backyard for dangers lurking where none used to exist.

I scan the internet, absorbing all the things I need to know, making a list of everything required to welcome a tiny being into existence.

I now have a plan, a shopping list and a bank account healthy enough to support it.

But my mounting excitement is tarnished by the dull ache that bears Axel's name. It burst into existence the day I found Axel's room empty and refuses to fade.

CHAPTER 28

AXEL

*T*he city breathes with evil. Around every corner it seems there is a theft in progress, or someone screaming for help.

I take a bite from my apple as I punch in the entry code for the old sandstone buildings that house the Diamond Valley Police headquarters.

"Hey, partner! Another exciting day of taking inventory in another break and enter. I'm taking bets on the business partner being behind it. What say you?"

The stunning blonde in protective blues strides towards me with all her teeth showing and every male head in the station following her path. In another life, I'd be salivating like the rest of the boys, but in this life, Angie is my work colleague and new friend only.

I shrug, playing along. "I smell a rat. My money's on the guy that called it in."

Her eyebrows dart up, and she turns her thoughts inward while I don the necessary body armour to survive the notorious Diamond Valley battle ground.

There's a constant struggle to keep up with the demand; the call-outs come through faster than we can clear them. I recall that first day, when Angie and I hit the ground running. Plastic wrapped uniforms were pushed into my chest and Angie and I exchanged greetings as we were shunted into our vehicle. Then off to intercept a couple of youths involved in a hit and run.

I'd made the decision to ram the offenders, and before the tires even stopped Angie was out, slamming the driver's face into the bonnet as she whipped the cuffs on.

We'd led the two teenagers into the holding cells without a single query as to the state of our vehicle or the blood from the kid's busted nose.

Angie shrugged. "Treat 'em mean, turn 'em clean."

For a slip of a thing, Angie has proven herself to be fearless in the field. She engages in hand to hand combat as readily as draw a weapon, and what she lacks in stature she makes up for in ferocity.

* * *

With crime so prevalent, there's little time to sit in my own head. I embrace the calamity of Diamond Valley. It's exactly what I need to get my head on straight, but every morning when I pass the pigeon-holes, I automatically scan mine for a letter.

The first one arrives via internal mail in my first week, Willow finally realising I wasn't coming home and sending it through Simone when she can't find me. Then another a couple of days later. Then another.

Every time it took all my strength not to tear it open, to read the words she never said. *I love you, Axel.* But it's a delusion I need to let go of. There is nothing she can write that won't make me bleed all over again, yet every time I held one in my hand, the image of her the night she looked at me like I was her whole world speared through me, and I fought the need to drive right back to her.

Now, weeks later, I try to remain nonchalant as I pass the empty box, even though my chest squeezes painfully.

She's moved on. It's for the best.

But that final one almost tore through the walls of my

resistance. The neat, blue envelope with the water stain that I know didn't come from rain, but I couldn't weaken. I knew what it would say. The same message Janice sent with different words.

I decided I couldn't.

It would cause too much disruption in my life.

After carefully considering how the change would impact me, I've made the decision to terminate.

I couldn't read those words again.

Now I didn't have to. Since that last one, the weeks pass without further attempts.

She got the hint and forgot about me, as easy as that.

Archer sends letters sometimes. General information about the possible expansion of the pub, Flynn's slow progress with finding his sister and his growing concern about how it's affecting him. News that their wedding will be put on hold until next year while they grow the business and Rain finishes her psychology degree. He even mentioned Heather and Simone a couple of times, but absolutely no news of Willow.

It's a contradicting kaleidoscope of relief and frustration. *Is she well? Is she still working at The Broken Keg?* I seek any titbit between the lines, try and detect a tone that would suggest peace or tension within the household, but there's nothing, so I head to the gym and make another futile attempt to forget.

* * *

My team turn their faces towards me.

"To Battle Axe!"

I smile and raise my glass. This is where I'm supposed to be, in the company of my team, contented in the celebrations of another successful month of crime fighting, but instead of the satisfaction I'm supposed to feel, my heart weighs heavy.

A familiar face appears beside me with a sly grin and open hand.

"I knew it was you. There's only one mountain of a man in this country with the skill to take down some of Diamond Valley's most elite criminals"

"Haydn, my brother. Great to see another capable body among us here! What made you quit the military and don the blues?"

I pull him into a hug, remembering the wars we fought together, slapping him hard on the back.

"Who's the piece?" He rolls his head towards Angie, barely tolerating the usual crowd of men vying for her attention in the corner.

"My friend and field partner, Angie." I reply with a shrug.

He whistles low and long, pulling up a seat. "Just a friend and partner? What's up with you, Battle? You used to be such a player... Oh my god, you're not married, are you?!"

"Shit no! Just...in a different place right now."

My dull tone lifts Haydn's eyebrows and dilutes his smile. Haydn can see there is a story in the silence I wasn't ready to delve into quite yet. Maybe I'd never be ready to let it out. That pathetic, pitiful story of how Willow broke my heart and stripped every reminder of me from her body the moment we argued. Just like Janice had before her.

Haydn used to be my brother in the military, and the connection and understanding forged in battle stops the questions he yearns to ask.

I raise a finger to the waitress to bring another round, and Hayden tactfully diverts our conversation to military days.

As the empty glasses pile up around our memories, the mood sobers, and we reminisce those no longer with us.

"Whatever happened to Frostbite? After you two went AWOL he was wiped off the map. We were all pretty anxious about the possibility of him switching alliances and us having to engage with him. He would have snapped us in half without a thought. That guy was born without emotion." Haydn reflects.

My belly laugh rises over the chatter, drawing curious stares from the far corners of the bar.

"Would you believe he's engaged to be married and running a pub in a small country town?" My laughter softens at the thought of him and Rain.

"No shit? I didn't see that coming. How do you know?"

I grin at Haydn.

"Because I was living with him until I transferred to the Valley. He's my best mate."

Shock registers, then understanding softens his features.

"Makes sense. I'm surprised it didn't occur to me there was a woman involved. When they all came back without Archer they were instructed not to disclose any details, but I just assumed he'd escaped and we weren't supposed to know about it."

I nod, the alcohol warming my stomach, loosening my tongue.

"Well I wasn't issued such instruction. He'd been told his girl been killed, and he did an exceptional job of exacting revenge."

"No." Haydn frowned. "I think it was more than that. Perhaps he was the perfect soldier because without his girl he may as well be dead, too. That could explain why he acted without the normal caution natural to us to instinctively preserve our lives."

I quirk an eyebrow.

"You're an expert now?" I smirk dubiously, but Haydn doesn't take the bait.

"You know, my wife...years ago now, before we had kids, she got really sick. We'd just argued, which we did a lot while we were getting to know each other. It was something so trivial I could never recall after what made me so angry, but I slammed the door when I left, yelled through the door that we were over. I walked for hours, but I always knew I'd end up at home. When I got back, the front door was unlocked, which was weird, since she always was big on security. I found her collapsed on the floor. She must have fallen seconds after I slammed the door.

"Anyway, she was in a coma for almost a month. Turns out she had meningitis and the swelling in her brain triggered off her collapse.

"It was the longest four weeks of my life, and all I could think about was how my last words to her were telling her I didn't want her.

"When the first week came and went without improvement, my body went into shock, like it was suddenly missing a vital organ. By the second week I was completely empty, and I knew that if I couldn't go through life with her, I...I just couldn't. I wasn't suicidal or anything. I never sought to harm myself or end my life, but I...just kind of hollowed out and invited death in. Quietly sat beside her bed, just waiting for an out. I simply didn't care. The day before she woke up I was crossing the street to go home when a truck lost control and pushed through the traffic heading straight towards me. I remember feeling a complete absence of fear, and made an effort to smile at the driver so he knew I was ready. I remember thinking, 'oh, thank god'. Someone pulled me out of its path, and I brushed myself off and returned, a little disappointed by the outcome but otherwise unaffected, to my wife's side.

"There's a single moment when time just stops, and it occurs to you that every war we fought together, every victory that made the world a better place; it was all just fleeting and trivial. I view my years in the military as nothing more than a way to pass the time until I met my wife."

* * *

Eyes glued to the dilapidated weatherboard just visible behind the old gnarled peppercorn tree we're parked behind, Angie passes the packet and I pull out a fistful of chips.

"Damn, Ange. Salt and vinegar is disgusting! It's like seawater mixed with cleaning products!" I let my handful spill onto the ground and rinse out my mouth with water.

"Hmm, tough guy can't handle strong flavours?" Angie smirks.

I huff a laugh. "For someone determined to become a detective, you should have already worked that out when I refused to eat the potato cakes you'd soaked in the stuff last week."

She wriggles down into the seat with a smirk.

"Maybe it's because you're the mystery I can't seem to solve."

I quirk an eyebrow as I fish in the bottom of my bag for a stray muesli bar. My fist closes around it and Angie giggles at my triumphant whoop.

"There's no mystery here, Ange. I'm an open file. Started in the military, donned the blues in Hawker Ridge and transferred here. Oh, and I hate salt and vinegar chips. Add that to the list."

Angie snorts. "That's not all, Axe. You're closed off. You love the challenge of Diamond Valley, but even when you're out getting the bad guys your thoughts are elsewhere, and not in the way other guys thoughts are elsewhere either. That's another thing that's off. Every other cop in this damned place has tried to hit on me. Everyone but you. Why is that?"

I shrug. "I don't shit where I sleep? Not my type? I don't know. Pick one."

"Pfft! I'm everyone's type. Just like you are. There's not a girl around with a pulse that would kick you out of bed."

For the first time, I take my attention off the house and take Angie in. She's right. With legs for miles, perfect breasts, and that face that doesn't need cosmetics, she's stunning.

But she's not Willow. Willow whose beauty isn't as obvious but is somehow so much...bigger. Willow whose strength is so much greater than Angie's fearless combat abilities.

Willow whose honesty and openness cuts through every defence I built.

Willow who tore out my heart and crushed it beneath her feet.

I swallow down the pain and blink away the uninvited image of her face, the way it looked when I claimed her for the first time.

My eyes find Angie's, and my words taste foreign as they tumble out.

"Would you like me to fuck you?"

CHAPTER 29

WILLOW

*D*anny pats my hand.

"Just relax, we'll find out everything in a few moments."

After I announced I was keeping my baby, Danny became terse, like my choice angered him. I avoided him for a while, but eventually we started hanging out again, although it was never the same. He continued making attempts to influence my decisions, but I'd found that once my mind was made up, I was able to move towards my goal with a determination I never knew existed inside me.

I relented, though, to his suggestion to change to another doctor. After I'd bled, I was scheduled for an ultrasound every two weeks, but Danny insisted on changing to a specialist a few towns over.

The other thing I allowed him was my silence. He was adamant that it stay between us for just a little longer, although he never really gave me a reason. Rain asked repeatedly in the beginning if I was falling ill or if work was too much since I always seemed so tired, but after a couple of months she stopped.

We are here today because at twenty weeks, I don't actually look pregnant. There's no swell, no thickening, no bump. And I'm terrified.

The nurse indicates the bed, and the cold jelly raises

goosebumps on my arms.

While she slides the handheld instrument through the jelly, she reassures me.

"It's natural to be concerned, and hyper aware of any changes that take place, but most of the time it's nothing to worry about. Have you experienced the quickening?"

I blink at her.

"You know, can you feel movement?"

"Oh, yes. When I'm about to sleep, the little gem gets restless, but not so much during the day. It's not that that's the problem. I'm not showing and I'm worried it isn't growing properly."

The truth is that I'm so terrified that my mental issues will be transferred to my baby that I'm panicking about every tiny change in activity. If I have a day with little movement I stress, if I feel a little more tired than normal I worry.

"Let's have a look then...Ahh! I see. I'll be back in a moment."

I dart a frantic look at Danny. It never stops hurting that it's not Axel with my hand in his.

But Axel doesn't want me.

I wish I could erase him, as he seemed to do effortlessly with me, but my damned perfect recall won't allow it and I have a thousand identical drawings of his beautiful face scattered throughout my room.

The nurse returns with two doctors and an intern in tow. My heart stops and my elbows lift me off the bed. *What could be so wrong that all these people would need to be involved?*

Dread drags bile into my throat.

"What's wrong with my baby?" My voice quivers.

The nurse smiles excitedly.

"Wrong? Nothing is wrong Mrs. Zimms, in fact, baby Zimms is a strong little thing and is just perfect in all aspects. I took the liberty in bringing these fine people to see a one in 2,500 pregnancy where the positioning of the baby is just so that in most cases, the mother isn't even aware she's pregnant until the first stages of labour commence."

I must have seemed concerned, because the older doctor smiles warmly.

"It means that all visual symptoms, such as a swelling belly as the baby grows, will be absent. It's called a cryptic pregnancy, and is unusual, although perfectly fine in all other aspects. Now, would you like to know the sex of your baby?"

Danny's eyes gleam.

* * *

"Do I want to know if you're a boy or girl, little gem, or wait for the surprise?" I spread my palm over my stomach. Danny sulks.

"Why do you girls always talk to your belly? It's weird."

I shrug. "What harm can it do? Besides, I think it's incredible that there's a tiny human inside my body. Don't you?"

He sneers.

"I think it's disgusting, to be honest. It's a parasite invading your body. Even the body thinks it's a germ, that's what morning sickness is - the body trying to rid itself of the parasite that alters it's hormones for the sole purpose of living off the nutrients of its mother. Like an infestation of intestinal worms. Ugh!" He shudders.

"I think it's safe to assume you don't want kids then?" I snap, irritated by his negativity.

"Oh, I've got a kid. I just don't see it."

"It? You don't even know what your wife had? That's awful. I'm so sorry." My turbulent hormones turn my agitation immediately into empathy.

"Pfft, don't be sorry. She had a boy, he's three next week, but she took off a year ago with him, and I haven't seen him since. I'm better off without her, anyway. Besides, she cheated on her ex to be with me, so there's no way I could ever trust her."

A wave of ice crashes through me.

"But Danny, he's your son-"

He silences me with a warning glare.

We fall into a chill silence. There's a feeling that persistently grows and flourishes that Danny is not all that he seems. But he's been a consistent presence through my pregnancy. Not an entirely supportive one, but the only one I have.

I hold my secret tighter, understanding that the more time passes, the more difficult it is to reveal to my friends. Shutting them out of this part of my life hurts, and the countless hours I've spent trying to find a way to come clean never resulted in an answer. I sometimes hope I will wake one day with a distended belly and be done with the weight of hiding this undisclosed miracle.

"Well, little gem." I whisper to my flat stomach. "If your Mummy's going to be a big girl, she's going to have to sleep in a big girl bed. I can't have you growing up thinking a pile of blankets in the corner is normal…"

I slide my hand over the exposed sheet that's been taunting me for weeks. I shiver. I measure my breaths and slide the covers back some more. As my adrenaline spikes I focus, calling on memories of Axel lying on sheets similar to these, of the way they felt against my bare skin as they gave and cradled my body. I recall his pupils, blown out with desire, his gentle smile and the way I melted into bliss beneath his touch.

Oh, Axel. Why did I have to fall in love with you?

I fix on Axel and pleasure, and ignore the tears that rain down my cheeks as I sit on my bed, hugging my knees. Facing my fear.

It's another few days before I can lay for any stretch of time on the bed, and even then it is only possible after I crept into Axel's old room to retrieve the pillow that contained the lingering scent of raw pine and musk.

Then one morning, the tears having run dry with the memories of Axel's touch, I wake with my head on my pillow and my body stretched out beneath the blankets.

* * *

The rich smell of bacon and freshly brewed coffee entices me into the kitchen. Rain's smile is fringed with sadness. I pull her into my arms, her tears escaping.

"Rain, honey. What's happened?" I whisper.

"Oh, Will, I just want things to go back to the way they were before. My family was so happy, but now I fear we're broken. Flynn is fading away before our eyes and he won't let me in any more. Even Archer's having sleepless nights worrying about him. Axel is gone, and you...I don't even see you anymore. But when I do, it's like you're existing in a limbo, like you're locked away in a place I can't reach. But what cuts the deepest is that you've stopped talking to me."

The truth pauses on the tip of my tongue. Here's the opening I need to let it all out. Keeping my pregnancy a secret from the sister of my heart hurts me, but when I open my mouth to say the words aloud, Danny's scowl fills my head. He explicitly told me to keep it from her. Against every instinct, I choke the words back down, because Danny has a plan, and he'd be disappointed in me for ruining it. Instead of the truth, I offer Rain a non-lie.

"I'm learning independence, Rain. I'm growing and making decisions. Adjusting to that is much harder than I thought, is all. I'll be fine, Once Flynn finds his sister his nightmares will stop, and Axel," My voice slips, and I hide it beneath a tight shrug. "Well, Axel is exactly where he wants to be."

"You're right." She sighs a shallow huff that tells me she doesn't believe me.

I miss Rain.

I pull her into a hug, seeking the comfort I've always found in her embrace. "I'm so proud of you, little sis. Just look at the beautiful world you have carved out for yourself, surrounded by such wonderful people, too. Before I came here I thought happiness was something set aside for the exclusive few who were born into an environment where they were wanted and loved, not meant for the likes of us. We were the discarded, the unwanted; chosen to bear the cruelty of man as punishment for being found unworthy."

Rain draws back, tears shimmering as she grips my hands.

"But we're *not*, Will. We are the *strong* ones, don't you see? Do you think those with charmed lives would be able to face what we have and be able to fight back? No. They couldn't. I've carried my tattoo with shame for so long I couldn't see it's really a badge of strength. We've seen things that children should never be exposed to. We have had to step into the adult world at a time when we were supposed to be playing with dolls. But here we are at the other side of it, still able to experience joy and laughter in spite of everything. It's empowering, knowing that no matter what obstacles show themselves, we will survive it."

I savour her words, then break the silence with my own truth.

"They leave us with soul deep scars, though. Our wounds change us into something we were never supposed to be. We overcome one agony, just to meet with another. Yes, we will survive. Of that we of all people can be certain of, but the pieces that have been damaged never ever come back, and that is a strange grief we carry always. I've always felt like a caterpillar put to the task of spinning a cocoon with spoiled silk. I'm trying to do what should come naturally to me but it's never quite right, and I don't understand why. So I try harder and all I manage to do is make a more obvious mess of it, hanging like a brightly coloured blemish of my inadequacies. It's exhausting, Rain."

She squeezes my fingers, her tone abnormally tight.

"Don't think like that, Will. You focus so hard on the cocoon that you forget that the butterfly is forming."

I snort. "What kind of horrific monster will emerge after so long in a corrupted cradle? It's impossible to expect a normal outcome when vital components are absent. I have mourned so many parts of me I wonder if there are any original pieces left."

I find it strange that of all the physical pain I've experienced, all the times people have destroyed parts of me and left me hollow, the greatest pain, the one that persists, was borne from the most beautiful and pure of intentions.

Rain's eyes bore into me. She burrows through my walls in the way only she is capable of.

"You love him, don't you?" She murmurs in rhetorical epiphany.

I look away, hardening my expression. That's my pain, not a wound to be shared with anyone else.

"As if I even understand what that means! Besides, it doesn't matter what I imagine I feel, Rain. He made his intentions clear in the beginning and it never altered. Any opinion I may have in the matter is irrelevant."

CHAPTER 30

AXEL

*A*ngie throws her head back and roars with laughter, and I feel the corners of my lips twitch, not even remotely embarrassed.

"Jesus, Axel! If I thought for a second you would go through with that I'd have you right here before you changed your mind."

I smirk and return my attention to the stake out while her amusement slowly ebbs away.

Then softly she murmurs; "She must be pretty amazing."

I land a hard glare on her.

"Nope. I thought she was, but I was wrong. She was supposed to be different but in the end they all want the same thing." Even as the words tumble free they don't ring true.

"A happily ever after with Battle Axe beside them?" Angie smirks, and my blood runs cold.

Because Willow didn't want that. Every other girl I'd been with wanted more, but never Willow. I'd laid myself bare at her feet and she'd trampled over me with her nonchalance. The wound she left still bleeds. But Angie is looking at me, sympathy flooding her face.

"The only one who *didn't* want that, huh?"

Hesitantly, I give the barest nod.

"She's an idiot then."

I clench my jaw. She's sweet and brave and so damned clever, and it grates me to have her labeled like that. Especially by someone who doesn't know her.

Angie's mouth drops as she straightens in the seat, her full attention on me. I watch her suspiciously as her brain ticks over.

"You love her. She hurt you, so you tucked tail and tried to escape your pain in Diamond Valley!"

"I *don't* love her! Would everyone just stop accusing me of that, damn it?" I snarl.

"Don't give me that bullshit, Axel! People keep accusing you because it's obvious to everyone else on the planet but you! What did she do, Axel, for you to be so scared to face her you had to run away? Cheat on you? Lie to you? Started demanding too much of you? What makes big, bad Battle Axe afraid?"

Willow's face fills my head, the fierce courage in the angles of her jaw telling me I need to face my fears. She's so vivid I could almost touch her. My teeth clench on the vision.

"I've told you before, Willow! I'm not afraid!" I grind.

Angie narrows her eyes on me as my words echo in the silence, slowly dawning on me. I growl and drag my hand over the nape of my neck.

"Damn you, Angie." I murmur.

"What did she do?"

"She betrayed me, Ange, and I can't ever forgive her for it. Now can you just drop it?"

The silence she granted me did nothing to keep the waves of memories from crashing around me. She came to me fearing a touch, and when I left her, there wasn't a single part of her body she hadn't wanted me to touch. I was the first man she gave herself willingly to, so full of trust and faith that it brought me to my knees. That moment when she decided that her need for me was something more powerful than the fear that consumed her…that was everything to me.

But it just didn't make sense. I knew her soul. I knew the

colour of her ghosts and the feel of her heart, and somehow it just didn't match up with someone who wanted to be rid of the life I planted inside her.

"Axe! Look!" Angie hisses and she's out the door before I even notice the group of men dragging a struggling figure into the house.

Leaning hard up against the wall, I roll my head stealthily to the side. The oily smell of the gun barrel hovers under my nose as the scene slides silently into view.

Two men in the centre of the lounge room grip the arms of their captive, a slight young man with wide eyes and a blade against his throat. I frown at Angie and flash my palm open twice, silently asking if she can see anyone else. Head nodding, she begins to lift a hand when her eyes suddenly widen.

They're ready for us!

Pain explodes in my head as the weight connects, knocking me to my back and the gun from my grip. Protecting my face I zero in on one body, stabbing a leg out and knocking him to the ground. Just like in training, I default to a detached state, striking with deadly accuracy, blood pumping strength through my body as knuckles connect and bodies drop before me.

Too easily I disable my attackers, barely breathing heavily before the pile of twelve moaning and defeated bodies.

"Grab the zip ties in the glove box!" I bark my command, and moments later Angie shakily hands me a bunch.

"Holy shit, Axel! Now I know why they call you Battle Axe!" She breathes in awe as I secure arms behind backs.

I step away, and stare down with a heavy feeling. Because it dawns on me that everyone is right. I'm trying to run from her, but here I stand, a thousand miles away, and Willow is still with me, pulsing through my veins, dwelling in my heart. Every one of my victories belongs to her.

* * *

She doesn't fade away. The months apart have diffused my anger into hurt betrayal, but the ache that is the absence of Willow remains as insistent as ever. Just like that old woman told me it would.

With trepidation I retrieve my backpack from beneath my bed. I finger the zip hesitantly. Am I just torturing myself, wanting to reopen old wounds? Perhaps I was mistaken when I thought she felt something for me. Perhaps that expression was no deeper than a picture of how I made her body feel. I'm sure of it. That's why she wanted nothing more from me other than to use me for her own pleasure and then rip my heart out.

My fingers take on a life of their own, and the zip exposes the corners of the dozen pages I'd snagged from Willow's desk.

My chest throbs when I run my fingers over the first. Rain, her mouth open and eyes shining, lost in the song that the pencil tells me she's singing. I'd forgotten just how talented Willow is.

The next one is of Flynn, and I glare at it. She likes him. I can see it in every line that she feels safe with him. Here's me thinking I was the only one who made her feel like that.

I grit my teeth and wonder if she's moved on with him. Will he know the touch of her skin? The way her body burns with desire?

Even before I glance at the next image I know it's of me. My stomach flutters and pulse springs alert as I peel back the paper.

I swallow hard. I know when she drew this. The first night together when she allowed me in her pile of blankets, and she proceeded to effortlessly break down every wall I'd built. I'm asleep, the pencil so tenderly applied that my heart cries. I look sated and completely contented. A smile is faintly evident, like I've just learned a happy secret. There are shadows of sadness around it, and I understand suddenly that it's the way she feels about me. She looked down upon me with…what? Tenderness? Desire?

Love?

Am I just looking for things that aren't there?

The next one is me again, the moment before I took her, when she'd been so afraid of what came next, where I watched her wrestle the impulse to stop, and bravely step into the unknown with me.

There's a heaviness in my throat that burns. *Did I really look like that? Did I really look at her like I loved her?*

The page escapes my loosened grip, the next picture sending ice through my veins and shards of jagged glass through every muscle I tense.

Dorian.

Burning pain ricochets along my spine, every bone and tendon over-tightened. Momentarily disorientated, the cold fist in my stomach collides with the need to damage and the page crumples beneath white knuckles as I fight for breath.

Jesus! How long has he been around? *How could I not know?*

Willow never goes anywhere outside of The Broken Keg. She must have met him at work.

The pencil strokes tell more of the story. I can feel the care she's taken in the lines, ones drawn with wariness and confusion. She's not sure what she thinks of him.

A blinding flash shatters my thoughts. Willow announcing she's pregnant then telling me I can forget the baby ever existed.

How could I have missed a threat like Dorian? It's just like him to be seeking some kind of revenge using Willow as the bait. And it worked. Completely blindsided by him yet again, only this time it stings like it never did with Janice.

That's because I never loved Janice.

I don't love Willow.

Do I?

I wish I knew what went wrong with Dorian. Or perhaps he was always unbalanced and I never noticed. No, I think I must have always known, but refused to see. I can still picture that odd gleam in his eyes when I told him Janice was pregnant, remember how my blood chilled at it, how I dismissed it as we toasted the baby. I remember because I closed my mouth after that and didn't tell him the rest. I never mentioned I'd told Janice I wanted to break up. I didn't love her, and she deserved to find someone who did. Then she sobbed into her hands and told me she was pregnant.

I liked her well enough, and although I was too young to consider a family yet, the idea of a miracle created from my body made my heart soar. She accepted my proposal with a sadness that I could never shake, and I vowed that although I couldn't love her, I'd do my best to make her happy. She was my family.

As the months progressed, though, Janice became more and more withdrawn. I assumed it was the pregnancy hormones, but when friendship becomes bitterness, everyone feels the sting of its blade.

I'm trained to detect subtleties, to measure up an enemy and predict their attack. But I underestimated the both of them and never saw the ambush unfolding before me.

I shiver with resentment. I know Dorian's moves.

I growl through the burst of pain in my chest as I open my drawer and power up my phone.

There is one medical centre in Mountain Plateau, and like salt in my wound I just know he'd make sure she went there.

"Welcome to Dr Henry's office, how can I help you?"

I fight to keep my voice light and casual.

"Yes, It's Dorian Zimms, just double checking on our next appointment for Willow."

"Sorry? Oh! *Danny* Zimms, sorry, the line dropped out for a second. How's Willow going? I haven't seen her in a while. Let me see. No. No more appointments scheduled, but you're overdue. Your wife missed her appointment at twenty weeks and hasn't been back since. Is she alright?"

Danny? Willow mentioned Danny several times, and I never made the connection.

My chest empties and I cancel the call without another word. I'd thought Willow had made her decision the day she'd told me, but it seems Dorian is a creature of cruel habit.

The trembling starts with a shudder, but consumes my entire body with tormented convulsions within seconds.

CHAPTER 31

WILLOW

I stare at the slight rounding of my belly and I feel my smile deepen as I run my hand over it. Seven and a half months, and there's finally a hint of evidence that I have a baby growing inside me. My little gem pokes out a knee or an elbow and I grin as my flesh moves with it.

"Hey baby. You awake too? Are you craving bacon and eggs like I am?"

Another odd sensation flowers inside my womb and my thoughts drift into a heavy melancholy. I stroke the gentle ripple of movement beneath my skin, whispering a prayer to the life inside.

"Will you be like your daddy, little one? Big and strong? I hope so. Please just be stronger and braver than I am. That's all I ask."

The baby rolls as if in answer, that other-worldly sensation of an entity coming into being that never fails to invoke a smile from me.

As with every other morning, Axel's eyes linger in my head like the ghost of my heart. When tears threaten I throw back the covers and rub my eyes, trying to dislodge the ache that never lets up.

I've plated the bacon and eggs as Flynn staggers, groggy from another night of elusive sleep, into the kitchen, and I slide his plate onto the table.

"You're priceless, Will. What would we do without you?" He murmurs appreciatively and digs in while I get the coffee ready.

The strong smell of coffee summons Rain and Archer to the table soon after. My gaze lingers sadly on the one chair that sits empty as a constant reminder that I meant nothing. I know I shouldn't be surprised, or still nursing the rejection, but I can't shake it. I wasn't good enough. I wasn't worthy.

I swallow the lump in my throat with a mouthful of orange juice. Well, I'm going to do my damnedest to be enough for my son or daughter, no matter what I have to do to give them a better life than I've had.

"Gone off coffee, Will?" Archer's casual remark startles me, green eyes burning a hole through my train of thought.

Rain's eyes narrow on my glass and I shovel a mouthful in before she sees inside me.

The suddenly tasteless food covers the waver I know is in my voice.

"I sniff so much of the stuff at work that I'm afraid that if I actually drink any I'll never sleep again!"

Flynn ghosts a smile and Archer's head tips, but Rain doesn't shift her curiosity from me.

By the way she doesn't move in her chair when the boys finish up, I know she wants to talk. She's silent while I clean the dishes and put them away.

"Well, I'll see you later R-"

"What's going on Will?" Rain snaps off my escape.

My pulse races and my baby moves restlessly. Even though I know she can't see anything, I drop into the chair opposite and hide my belly below the table.

"I told you, Rain. It's nothing. Just getting used to this new life I'm in."

"Rubbish! You forget I know you better than that. There's something going on and the others are starting to notice it too, and it hurts that you don't trust me enough to talk to me about it."

Her tone is firm, but her sorrow makes her eyes heavy.

I turn my attention on the table, stomach churning. Not telling Rain goes against every instinct inside me. It's on the tip of my tongue, but I clamp my mouth closed.

"We may not be blood, but you are the sister of my soul, and no matter what it is, I'll be here for you. You know that. Nothing can be so big or bad that the two of us can't conquer."

I blow out my frustration.

"Your love means everything to me, Rain. It's the only thing that's carried me through to this point, and I'm so afraid you'll think less of me, or find me unworthy. I just couldn't handle that. Not from you."

I let the tears slide free and feel Rain's hand cover mine. So warm, but so much smaller than Axel's.

"Honey, there is nothing on this planet that can ever make me think anything but how strong and courageous you are. There is no part of you that is unworthy. You are so much more than you believe yourself to be, and there's not a person alive who thinks otherwise. Our customers love you, Heather and Simone love you. And your family loves you; Flynn, Archer, Axel and me. We adore you because you are one of the most amazing people we know. No matter what it is, Will, I will always love you."

But the tears won't stop, because Axel never did love me, and that lie slid off her tongue as easily as the one about me being worthy. She doesn't know that I know that, but it shows me the truth. What Danny has been saying all along rings true, though. I'm making a mistake by bringing a child into this world with all my issues etched into its DNA, and deluding myself I can offer it a good life.

"I can't Rain. I'm sorry." I sob and make for the door.

I bury my head in my pillow until my tears dry and my throat burns. Then I send a text to Danny.

Can I see you?

Sure. When?

I can meet you out the front if you're free now?

I'll see you in ten.

The car rumbles to a stop and I climb in. Danny's eyes gleam and his lip twitches up like he's annoyed and my heart sinks. At least Danny doesn't pretend I'm something I'm not.

"What's the problem, Will?" He cuts to the chase as if I've interrupted his valuable time.

Suspicion holds tight to my words, but desperation to talk to anyone sets them free.

"What have I done, Danny? I'm not fit to be a mother. How can I give a child the life I want for them when I have absolutely no idea what that entails. And what if they're born with all my issues? What then? I can't even help them, because I haven't been able to find those answers myself!"

Danny's eyes are so cold my tears freeze.

"I told you, Willow, didn't I? I tried to get that through to you months ago, before it was too late, and you thought I was being an arsehole. But you see I'm right now, don't you?"

My guts are churning, my instincts telling me to get out of the car, but the car keeps moving and my bones turn to rubber.

"I knew you'd eventually see clearly, but it took longer than I expected, and now you're stuck in this…situation."

Through a dry mouth, I respond.

"I know I deserve this, Danny, but I don't need to be reminded how badly I fucked up. I need some help to work out what I'm going to do going forward."

Oh, why didn't I give this more thought? Was it the pregnancy hormones that made me feel like I could actually do this like a normal person?

"Maybe-" I begin but Danny cuts me off with his hand.

"Shoosh. I'm thinking." He snaps, and I sink inside myself.

I'm a piece of trash who didn't have the intelligence not to get knocked up, and no matter what I do to fight for my independence, I find myself running to someone for help.

"Okay, Willow. How about this? We can start the process to

have the baby adopted out as soon as it's born. There's families out there who might want it, and then you can forget this whole mess."

I feel sick. "No, Danny. This baby is a part of me. I can't have it think I don't love it. I know what that does to a person. No. I'll never do that."

He glares at me, then something flashes in his eyes. Excitement? I shudder. I hope not. Then his tone warms and smoothes out as he delivers my second option.

"You can marry me, Willow. It's not ideal, but I don't see you having any other option. We can bring this kid up as if we were a real family, and I can give it everything you can't."

Bile rises in my throat.

"No, Danny! You can't do that! You already have a son you don't see. Think how this will affect him? And my baby isn't even yours. It would ruin your life!"

He stomps on the brakes so hard the seatbelt cuts into me and my hand flies down to soothe my precious baby.

"Jesus, Willow! You ask for my help but you reject my suggestions. How about you come up with a solution then?"

I recoil at his tone, but he's right. I've got nothing. I can't do this on my own, and Danny is the only person who can help me, now I can't trust Rain to tell me the truth.

Only once have I ever felt more of a captive than this, and I feel the familiar tightening of my chest and squeezing of my lungs as my panic attack threatens.

Danny's lips curl in disgust, and with it comes an expression so cold a shudder grips me.

"See, Willow? This is why you need me. What if you were holding the kid when you flip out like this? You'd drop it."

My fingertips tingle and I know what he says is true.

I struggle to fill my lungs and cringe when I feel his hand on my back until I manage to fight off my urge to shake free of him, and concentrate on filling my lungs again.

Danny reaches into his glove compartment and pulls out a tiny box. The ring inside is a tiny sapphire, dulled by someone else's finger.

"It's my ex's" he explains, devoid of emotion. "If we're to avoid making it obvious that we're doing this for the baby, we should at least navigate the proper avenues."

It's a little snug, but Danny forces it on. The entire time my stomach rolls in dread that might not be entirely from the remains of my panic attack.

I glance up at him and see the oddest expression dancing there, then his face quickly clears.

CHAPTER 32

AXEL

*M*y knuckles split apart on the cheekbone of the guy I have pinned beneath me, and I growl triumphantly as the pain buries the sting of Willow and Dorian. I pull back my arm again and again, blind in my need to anaesthetise.

"I said that's *enough!*" Angie's voice stabs into my ears as she shoves me off him.

I shake my head clear, my rage hissing through my teeth and I realise the guy is unconscious.

"Shit!" I stab my fingers through my hair and slam my palm into a tree trunk.

When I turn back, the woman stands beside Angie with mouth open, her one good eye wide in horror, the other swollen closed at the sight of her boyfriend, bloodied and limp in her front yard.

That look on her face, that timid, defeated expression is one I know well. With a single stride I pull the woman against my chest, and my voice rough with emotion I tell her.

"Sweetheart, don't let anyone raise a hand to you. They try to do it because your worth is greater than you believe and they don't want you to see that, because they don't want you to realise *they're* not good enough for *you*. You are stronger than you know, so don't ever be afraid to stand up for yourself."

***

"Two things, Battle Axe. One: That was the sweetest thing I've seen anyone do for another person. I think you just gave her the fuel she needed to get her life together. And two. What the fuck were you thinking? I'm not saying the guy didn't deserve it, but you nearly killed him in front of her! Whatever you've got bouncing around that great skull of yours is making you volatile!"

My sharp exhale falls between us, and I avert my gaze, flattening my lips in silence.

"Fine. Don't tell me then, but I have to tell our superiors. I need to be able to trust you to maintain control, and I'm starting to doubt that I can."

My thoughts jump to Simone when she told me in no uncertain terms that if I didn't deal with my shit it would keep coming up. She'd see I'm in no state to be a cop anymore, and I need this. I need a job that is exciting enough to keep my mind off Willow, otherwise I know it will send me mad.

"Please don't." I whisper.

She flicks her gaze to me and sighs.

"In the couple of months we've worked together, I've come to count you as a friend. A pig-headed, opinionated friend, but still a friend, and I can see you being dragged into a place that will eat you alive if you let it. I have a proposal. I've been on the beat without a break for four years, and I have months of leave up my sleeve. How about we both take some time off and we can sort this shit out back home?"

The hollow ache starts up again. Is it better to get closure, or will it make me worse? It seems the only thing that can burrow through my defences and break me is Willow.

"I don't know if I want to find out. What about you? What would you do if we took time off?"

Angie rolls her eyes. "I'm coming to support a friend, you big idiot!"

Against my better judgement I consider it. With Angie there, at least I won't be alone and trapped in my head. And if I find Willow has chosen Dorian, at least I will know, and I can have a stunning blonde at my side to prove to them all that I've moved on and never loved Willow in the first place.

"Really?" I ask, and she pats my thigh.

"Absolutely, big guy. I have no life, and all I'd be missing out on is a few weeks of daytime soap operas."

* * *

I disconnect the call with the oddest sensation that I'm having an affair. I've booked a bed and breakfast between Hawker Ridge and Mountain Plateau. It's a cute little three bedroom cottage so we can still have our own rooms, but making sleeping arrangements with another woman just seems...wrong. So does pulling my rental car up in front of Angie's house and loading her suitcase into the boot next to mine.

"So, are you going to tell me what's actually going on, or do I just sit back and watch the drama unfold?"

I scrub my hand over my face. I didn't consider that I'd have to tell her anything. I fill my lungs and let the air out slowly, trying to explain what's happened in easy terms.

"Willow betrayed me, but now I find she's become good friends with an enemy of mine, and I'm worried about her."

"Wow. That tells me less than nothing. If she betrayed you, why don't you just let her go? Clearly she's not the one for you if she treated you so badly. And a nasty piece of work if she's got herself mixed up with someone you don't trust!"

"No. It's...not like that. I don't know why I can't get her out of my head after she...did what she did, but she has no idea this guy is a bad guy. He gave her a different name. Calls himself Danny, and I think she's been spending time with him. A lot of time."

"Come on, Axe! This is like pulling teeth! I'm going to need more than this. Is she sleeping with him? How do you know it's actually him, and not some random guy whose name really is Danny?"

"Okay, okay...I don't think she's sleeping with him. Her past is...troubled...and she finds it hard to trust anyone enough to physically touch her. As for if I really know Danny is really Dorian, this is how I know!"

I fish in the backpack I threw in the back seat and grab a handful of Willow's drawings. The top one is her picture of Dorian.

"Did Willow do these, Axel? They're incredible! So much detail. Oh, and the emotion!"

While Angie flicks through the drawings, I revisit every memory I can access of the occasions I went to see Willow at The Broken Keg. Vague shadowy images of a man's outline slumped in the darkness beside Willow's upright figure. Hiding, lurking. Plotting.

Fuck.

And despite my training, Dorian slipped under my radar once more.

"Shit, Ange. I even saw him. He was right under my nose and I had no idea..."

She glances up, expression soft.

"Axe, you couldn't have guessed. There was no way you would be expecting him in your own backyard, so there was no need for vigilance. Stop being so hard on yourself."

While the drawings have stopped Angie's questions, it stirs up an inexplicable feeling that I'm baring my soul to Angie. Within those images is the truth of how I feel about Willow, and I'm not ready to analyse that yet.

It's too late to take them back. Angie flips through them and gasps, gripping the pile tightly.

"Oh, Axel. I can see how much you love her!" Crimson crawls up my face because I know she's holding the one of me, that look on my face like I've just handed her my heart.

"And I can see just how much she loves you, too."

I grip the wheel, feeling the weight of Angie's comment. If only she knew how wrong she was. Willow didn't love me. She never wanted something more with me. I cringe when I remember how I virtually begged her to stay with me just so I could wake up with her in my arms.

* * *

"Thanks, Ange. I really appreciate you doing this for me. Remember, Archer's at the bar, Flynn is security, Rain is singing and Willow is waitressing. At least she was the only waitress last time I was here. I need you to look out for Dorian. Be careful and don't let anyone know you're connected to me in any way, because if Archer sees Dorian he'd recognise him immediately, and I don't want Dorian to know I'm onto him yet."

"Sure thing." Angie smiles. She truly is beautiful in a long, figure hugging dress and her hair in an elegant style off her face. I pull her into a grateful hug and she sighs into my chest.

"You really feel nothing for me, do you?" Her breath warms my chest, and for a moment the same remorse that followed me for so long from the beds of faceless women finds me again.

Then in a flash, it dissipates. I have nothing to regret. I didn't give her false hope, or use her attraction to me for my own gain. It's only empathy I feel.

"I'm sorry, Ange." I breathe into her hair.

She steps back and brushes her hand lightly over her perfect hair.

"Well, I can't wait to meet her, I must admit. And your family, they sound pretty special, too."

I walk her to the car, then settle in for the most excruciating wait of my life.

* * *

I'm waiting in the driveway as Angie pulls in. Finally.

"How did you go?" I ask with more impatience than I intend, because Angie's face is so damned pale I know it's not great news.

She steps into the hallway and her face smooths out like I've seen so many times before, right before we knock on the door to tell a mother, or father that the accident we attended resulted in the loss of their child.

"I saw them all, Axel. Archer, Flynn, Rain…" She swallows loudly. "And I saw Willow and Dorian."

I sink into the couch, digging the heel of my palm into my eye sockets. The pain that is Willow spreads until I can't catch my breath.

"I'll skip the rest for now, but Dorian was there for most of the night. He sat on his own in a corner where nobody would see his face if they looked over, but I knew it was him. Willow kept flitting anxiously over to him. Never touching him, but she didn't look comfortable at all. She looked very much as dejected and withdrawn as that woman last week whose boyfriend you nearly beat to death. She looked as if she didn't want to be around him, but she was compelled by what seemed to be expectation anyway."

What has Dorian done to her? She was so much stronger before I left her.

I left her. I didn't want to, but I had to, and now she's been dragged down by whatever Dorian is doing to her.

"What about Flynn?"

Angie frowns.

"Flynn kept watching her, but I guess he had no reason to think she was in any danger. Dorian only tried to touch her once. He reached out, but Willow backed away as if his touch would burn her. Flynn reacted, then, but as soon as Willow put distance between them, Flynn just went back to watching."

Angie fell silent while I processed her report, then I felt the couch move as she sat beside me, her hand rubbing my back.

"Because nobody knew me and the place was packed, I asked Dorian if I could sit at his table with him. He agreed, and I struck up a conversation with him, pretending to be an interested tourist passing through for a while, then I asked him about Willow. I'm so sorry, Axel, but he said Willow is his fiancée, and she was wearing his ring."

I barely made it to the bathroom before I emptied the contents of my stomach, and the rest of my heart in the toilet.

CHAPTER 33

WILLOW

When the blonde left my anxiety returned. She was an absolute stunner, so out of place in a remote uneventful town like Mountain Plateau. She could easily have been a model, had she been graced with a couple more inches, and she was lovely. A kind smile and easy small talk, I'd wished she'd have stayed. She would have been good to make friends with, if only for the night, and it would buy me some time before Danny got me alone.

Whatever friendship I'd felt for Danny in the past had disintegrated the moment he stuck the ring on my finger.

"We're engaged now, Willow. You have to kiss me now, otherwise people won't believe we're a couple."

As the crowd dwindles, Danny claims the need for fresh air and ducks out the back door. He lands an expression on me that has me second guessing his expectations, so I regularly check in on him until the last patrons leave. I fill my lungs with the night air and lean my spine against the cool brick wall. The moment I do, Danny's moves are instant. He has me caged in, hands splayed either side of my head beneath the streetlights, the smoke on his breath choking me.

Without warning, Danny drops his head and crashes his mouth so hard against mine that I feel my lip split. I gasp in pain and try to shove him away, but his tongue intrudes rudely into my mouth. He tastes of stale smoke and I swear I feel a morsel from his dinner pushed into my mouth. My arms rope with pressure, struggling harder. His tongue in my mouth makes me gag, but he presses his body against the length of mine. My pulse trips in terror, and as Danny nudges his erection into my stomach, that switch in my head flicks, and I'm a panicking flurry of nails and screams muffled by his relentless mouth. He catches my hands and pins them between us as my tears fall freely. All my memories dance before me, every unwanted touch, every violation inflicted upon me. I'm right back in that room with the chilling horror on Rain's face and Kurt's fetid breath on the back of my neck.

And then it all falls away.

*　*　*

I drag air into my lungs, choking on a leaf I manage to inhale off the grass beneath my cheek. Danny stares down at me, his lips curled in a cruel shape.

"You're so damaged, Willow. Thank god you agreed to marry me, otherwise this kid will have no hope."

"I don't care what people think, Danny. Maybe we should call this engagement thing off. It's turning me into a mess and you into a monster."

He offers me a hand, and I reluctantly take it. The world still spins, but he holds my waist tight until it evens out. He gives me a little squeeze and lets me go.

"Will you look at that, Willow? No freak out that time. Maybe Axel was too soft on you. Maybe what you really need is to be pushed harder to make progress."

My exhale shudders. Hearing Axel's name reminds me that I'm somebody to discard, but the chill in Danny's face is replaced by crumbs of unexpected kindness, that I cling to desperately.

I'm frightened, alone, worthless, but Danny just held my waist for almost two minutes without a single reaction, so maybe I'll be alright. It didn't feel good, but I didn't freak out so maybe it could work. Perhaps I'm being too hasty pushing Danny away. I'm pregnant to a man who doesn't want me, and here Danny is, offering to support me and the baby, when nobody else will.

* * *

"I'm not letting you go until you talk to me!"

It's the genuine concern in Rain's eyes that has me recoiling. I'm unable to meet her gaze. She's always found me so easy to read that I'm afraid she'll see my secret if I look directly at her.

"Will, something's going on and I wish you would tell me. You've found your power since you came here, but now you've become a shadow of yourself, and I don't understand what has happened to change it. Please? Is it this guy you've been spending so much time with?"

Her tone is gentle, but the panic hiding inside it causes that knot that sits with a constant heaviness in my gut to tighten. I'm not worth her concern. If I tell her, she'll expect me to stand and fight, and there's no energy left inside me for a battle. I'd just let her down, and I couldn't survive seeing her disappointment. Maybe that's why Danny insisted I don't tell Rain about the baby. He was right to suggest it, but I have to give her something.

"Danny is helping me cope with physical contact. It's working, but it takes a bit out of me sometimes. It's fine, really." I assure her when she frowns.

"Will, don't you think it's strange that you've been friends with this guy for months, yet none of us has met him yet?"

I feel my blood pump and moisten my mouth. I can't put my finger on it, but there's something so wrong with the idea of Danny meeting my family. I manage a stiff shrug.

"How about I come and say hello next time he's around? Would that be okay?" She asks too gently.

I nod at my shoes, then shuffle away, mumbling about getting ready for work.

* * *

I'm relieved when the table Danny usually occupies remains empty. I'm even more relieved when the blonde woman from the other night takes a seat at the table, positioning herself so that she takes in the whole pub.

"Welcome back to the Broken Keg. I'm Willow, your waitress. If there's anything you need, just give me a wave and I'll be right with you. I remember you from last night. Did you get a chance to have a look at this exciting town?"

Her laughter is clear and crisp. "Actually, no. I'm staying with a friend and we didn't get a chance to get out yesterday, but I've been here. Does that count?"

"Oh, well in that case, you have just seen everything this beautiful town has to offer." I beam at her and she chuckles.

"It is a beautiful little town when you've come down from Diamond Valley," she says.

"Oh, that place is meant to be pretty rough. I never would have imagined you're from there. You seem way too…untouched by the things I've heard go on there."

She shrugs, her blonde waves bouncing prettily on her shoulders, then she leans forward conspiratorially and lowers her voice.

"I might not look it, Willow, but I'm pretty tough when I need to be. Much like yourself, actually. You strike me as someone who's not afraid to enter the battlefield."

I feel my smile slide away.

"Maybe once I was. Before I learned that you can't win a war when your army doesn't believe you're worth fighting for."

Her eyebrow leaps.

"Maybe your soldier was so used to fighting on a losing side that he was afraid to stand with you because the possibility of winning was somehow more terrifying." she whispers, and I feel sadness well up. I fill my lungs, and blow it out as I seek her eyes.

"I'm never the winning side." I summon a weak smile. "Now, what can I get you to drink?"

I'm shaken by the time I place her order. I feel like so much more was discussed than our words, but I get nothing but a good feeling from her. I'm always interested in a new face in the bar, especially a fascinating woman from the bowels of Diamond Valley. She's everything I wish I was. Confident, interesting and not afraid to be here on her own.

At the end of the night, when the tables are cleared, she waves me over.

"Willow, if it's not too much to ask, will you sit with me for a while? I've had a lovely night, but I need some good conversation now."

I frown, and her smile falters. "It's okay, Willow, if you don't want to, I just thought it would be nice."

I shake my head and sit with a sigh. "It's not that. It's that I'm not great at conversation. I am great at meaningless small talk, but there's really nothing more to me, so I don't know if I can give you what you're after."

The woman's mouth drops. I search for evidence she's mocking me, but see none.

"You're kidding me, Willow! You're one of the most fascinating creatures I've ever met. I've been keen to chat all night."

Eyeing her suspiciously, I lean back in my chair.

"See. That's fascinating. You're looking at me as if you doubt what I say. Let me put you at ease by telling you a bit about myself, and I apologise in advance if I'm too confronting. I can't handle surface conversations. I'm more interested in talking about the meatier topics. My name is Angela, but my friends call me Angie. I grew up in Thornvale, not far from Diamond Valley, but almost as rough. When I was twelve, my mother ran off and Dad got himself a girlfriend who hated me so I took off. I lived on the streets from age fourteen to sixteen, then decided to pull my life together and do something worthwhile, so I delivered food for a Chinese restaurant in the evenings and put myself through school. I joined the police force and have been working as a cop, making a difference ever since."

"You're a cop? That's a noble career. I'm good friends with a detective...and I was close to someone who worked in Hawker Ridge as an officer too. They were...are good people."

"Oh, you're not still friends with the officer then? That's a shame."

My lungs constrict and I shake my head slowly.

"He decided that he didn't want to be around me anymore, so he left."

Her scrutiny darts between my eyes and I feel myself withdrawing.

"Ahh, boyfriend, was he? Well, it seems you've moved on from that. Danny seems…nice."

"He's helping me. You see, my childhood was pretty different to yours. I spent a lot of time in foster homes until I moved in with Rain. She sings here. But some of the homes weren't nice, and it kind of messed with my head. Danny is all I have now. I need him."

I can't continue. Discussing Axel and Danny brings up memories I don't want to deal with.

Angie sends me a hard look. "No, Willow. You don't need him. You don't need anyone. I see it inside you, buried deep, but it's there. You have this incredible strength, resilience and independence, and you have people around you who love you."

It hurts too much, and my blood surges, demanding I leave.

"You're wrong, Angie. People like me weren't meant to be loved. We're tolerated, used and discarded. And that shit you imagine you see in me? It's all gone. The time for strength has passed."

I leave her to her wine and finish wiping down the tables.

Images of Axel race through my mind, the pain so raw I feel like it's happening now instead of months ago. I curse my perfect recall when my memories of Axel's patience when he laid his hands on me for the first time, and carefully gauged my reactions to make sure I felt safe.

I discreetly wipe away the tears that escape.

I reach the table Angie had occupied and arranged the vacated chairs, clearing away the empty wine glass.

It's fifteen minutes til knock off time when I crave fresh air. I wonder if my baby can feel how hollowed out my heart is, or if it's safely oblivious to the mess its mother is in.

I slip outside, close to the wall so I don't trigger the sensor light. I need the intimacy of darkness to lose myself in, but even the moon betrays me. The clouds shift and the concrete glows with moonlight. I lean my head against the wall, listening to the crickets, and the faint rustling as the breeze pushes the leaves around. Around the corner I hear a voice and recognise the pretty tone of Angie.

"Thanks for picking me up. I don't know why you didn't come tonight, but it gave me a chance to talk to her."

My ears strained. She's talking to someone about me. A low, deep voice rumbles without distinguishable words.

"Yeah, I'll tell you everything when we get home. I don't know about you, but I'm dying to get to bed. Oh, yeah, that's just what I need, Axe."

My head swings towards the voices and I see Angie in the tight embrace of the man I'd know anywhere, His tall, muscular frame large enough for his shadow to touch my feet.

I'd sought the comfort of his images so many times in the last few months, pitiful attempts to recapture the way his skin felt, and the way his incredible scent drove all other thoughts from my mind. Now he's here, in the flesh, and not a single fantasy of mine could have prepared me for the sting of seeing another woman in his arms where I'd once imagined I belonged. My heart shatters, and the pain tears a sound from me.

Axel jerks his head, glimmering pewter finding me in the shadows.

"Willow!" He rasps.

How I've longed to hear him call for me, but it's a cry filled with guilt. He found happiness in the arms of someone superior to me in every way, and got her to spy on me.

I stumble inside and with shaky fingers, flick the lock.

CHAPTER 34

AXEL

S hit! Willow?"

I shove Angie from me and run towards Willow, knowing already she's locked me out. The look on her face…I'll never be able to tear that from my memory. She looked utterly defeated. Broken. My heart twists and doesn't ease when I rub it.

I throw an agonised glance towards Angie.

"I'll be fine, Axe. I'll take a taxi. Go get your girl."

My heart thunders. After all this time, the first she sees of me is when I'm holding Angie. I know what she would have thought, damn it, and it couldn't be further from the truth.

I obliterate the door lock with a practised twist and drop the components to the floor as I push through it.

Archer's eyebrows leap off his head when he spots me, but I don't have time for him. He's over the bar before I take another step.

"What did you do to Willow?" He thunders.

I scan the pub wildly for her, but all I see is Flynn coming towards me, too, a hard glare locked on me.

"I need to see her. Where is she?"

"You need to tell me first why she tore through here like the hounds of hell were after her!" Archer growls, his stance loose.

He's prepared to fight me.

"I'll explain later, Frost. I just need to see Willow." I need to explain and stop the pain I caused her.

Archer's palm presses my chest. "You'll tell me now. We don't hear from you or see you in months and suddenly you're here, and you've already upset Willow. Otherwise, mate or not, I will remove you from my pub!"

"She was outside and saw me hugging...a friend. It startled her. I'm coming to make sure she's okay. Now will you let me see her?"

It's Rain's soft voice that gets through to Archer and unlocks his frame. She slides a hand over his back and lands a soft expression on me.

"Archer, let him speak to Will. She's in the bathroom, Axe."

His eyes narrow, furious green on me, but he steps aside with a growl, allowing me to pass. I make it in two strides, slamming into the ladies bathroom, but as soon as I hit the tiles I'm taken back to when she'd bared her soul to me, thinking it was Rain. I stuffed that up, too. I hear the sound of her heart breaking, the sorrow echoing softly around the dimly lit room.

"What do you want, Axel?" The bitter venom in her voice makes the ache in my chest pound.

"I just want to talk to you." I whisper, because I'm so close to her I could just open the cubical door and touch her, and holding back is damned excruciating.

A metallic *click* cuts the air and she slowly appears. I have to force myself not to go to her. The sapphire of her eyes appears first, but now they house a thousand new ghosts and my exhale falters. What happened to her?

Her skin is paler than it used to be, and her lips seem to default to a thin hard line. She's lost some weight, too, her beautiful eyes sunk a little deeper into her face. But within the sadness, all the feelings I had for her come flooding back in like an avalanche that steals my breath.

I love her.

I love her light and I love her darkness. I love every fractured piece of this girl with all that I am. So powerful it is that my back thumps against the wall and I slide to the ground at her feet.

But her beautiful face is twisted in rage.

"You want to *talk*? What about when I wanted to talk to you, Axel? When I needed to talk to you, and you left me to make the biggest decision of my life all alone? Now suddenly you want to talk and you expect me to just obey and listen? Maybe you wanted to tell me all about Angie? You've come a long way from meaningless romps, I see. You've finally found someone you aren't embarrassed to be seen with. I don't need you dangling your happily ever after in front of me. Now you can leave."

Her fury is more stunning than I remember, but it's also stronger, adding concrete to the walls she's built up to keep me out.

"Willow, it's Danny. I needed to warn you about him. He's-"

"*He's* the only one willing to help me out, Axel. What is your problem? You wanted nothing to do with me, but suddenly it's of great importance that you travel from wherever you ran away to, coming to tell me that the only person that's been there for me is someone you feel you need to warn me about. Why do you even pretend to care?"

I want to tell her everything. I want to tell her that I love her, that I'm sorry, and that I want to fix it, but my mouth refuses to work. She steps so close I can feel the warmth of her body. I can smell her, and it's sending me crazy.

"I can't trust you anymore." Her voice loses venom then, and the calm finality of that breaks me.

"I've never lied to you, Will." I manage.

"Trust is not just words. It's your actions that broke it. I needed to feel I wasn't alone in a scary situation that could change my life, and in the end the only thing you showed me was that when the going got tough, I wasn't worth the effort. Danny was kind enough to take your place and offer the only solution I had left."

The knife twists in my guts.

Her face crumples and her voice flattens out, the life dwindling from her tone.

"Danny convinced me that I'm too broken and damaged to be able to care for a baby, but it wasn't supposed to be him that told me that. It was supposed to be you. You don't need to waste any more time on me. Go to Angie. She's a strong and brave woman, everything I wish I could have been for you. Goodbye, Axel."

I bleed helplessly as she walks out the door. I can't let her leave. I can't let her just disappear out of my life. I have to find some way to make her stay, some way to apologise for walking away and leaving her to be poisoned into destroying our baby without me there to stop it.

"I love you Willow." I moan, and her knuckles whiten on the door.

A ghost of a smile haunts her lips as she looks on me with an expression full of broken dreams.

"No you don't, Axel. But *I* loved *you*, once, and you would have known that if you'd read my letters. But you didn't care enough to, and that's how I know you're lying."

*　*　*

I hear the distinct footfalls of Rain.

"Axel, honey, what happened?"

My head is still cradled in my hands, the queasy dread lurching about unpredictably through my guts. Rain slides to the floor beside me.

"I ruined everything, Rain. I let Willow down and she won't forgive me."

Her slender hand soothes my arm.

"There's nothing you could have done that would stop her from forgiving you, Axe. She loves you just as much as you love her, and there's little in this world that can trump the heart in the war of love."

I huff. I saw Willow's pain, but it irritates the hell out of me that Rain is being so blasé about what Willow would have gone through. Most of Willow's scars are by my hand. I'll admit that, but Rain was meant to be her confidant. Rain let her down, too, so she deserves to share my guilt.

"You're pretty nonchalant about the whole thing? I thought you and Willow were close, but you left her to find Danny because he was the only one who offered to help her? Just shrug her off to someone else? Is that why you expect she'll come around if I just apologise to her for running away when she told me she was pregnant and I left her to deal with it on her own?"

Rain sucks air.

"*What?*"

Her hand disappears from my arm and I look into her shocked face. My heart sinks into my bowels.

"She didn't tell you?" I groan.

Her palm presses hard against her mouth, her nails digging into her face.

"Oh my god, Axel. She never said a word. She just kind of retreated into herself. Jesus. How could you do that to her?"

The regret I've been holding at bay for so long comes out in a bone shattering roar. My body quakes with it. It resonates with the same old pattern.

Mum and my teacher.

Janice and Dorian.

Willow and Dorian.

The only difference is that this time it was me that broke it.

CHAPTER 35

WILLOW

*H*e's happy with Angie, she's perfect for him, and she's not damaged. The way he held her told of an intimacy, a comfortable, natural bond built over time. He must have found her as soon as he left me. The blinding pain I'd buried with anger seeps back like a stealthy tsunami. Every inch of skin hurts with it.

Rain's eyes don't leave me the whole car ride home, and as soon as we pull into the driveway, she starts.

"Willow, I want to talk to you."

I'm done with people trying to talk to me tonight. I just want to curl into a ball and shut out the world.

"I'm really tired, Rain. I just want to go to bed."

But the moment I look into her face I blanch. Her eyes shimmer with helplessness and right now I just want to tell her to erase that pain from her. But I press my lips closed. Just one more day where she thinks I haven't disappointed her. She nods her head reluctantly, her lip quivering.

I breathe out despair and clutch her hand.

"I promise, Rain, I'll come to you when I'm ready to talk. I'm okay, though. You know us girls, Rain. We're tough enough for anything this world throws at us."

A single tear slides down her cheek and I hurry to my room.

I spend ages staring at my reflection. I see what Rain saw in the car; has been seeing for months. I'm a husk, empty and useless when there was a time not long ago when I felt strong. My hand finds my belly and my baby kicks.

"I wish I could be strong for you, little gem. I wish I were someone you can be proud of, someone who can show you that when life beats you up, you don't cower, you damn well fight back. But I can show you how to survive, if you can be patient with me when I freak out. And I'll have to teach you the things your daddy won't be around to show you, and to do that, I'm going to need to make a few changes. But I need you to hold on and believe in me, because It's likely to be a bumpy ride."

I was so furious at Axel. He left me, refused to read my letters, but continued to spy on me? That's just sick. For some unfathomable reason he doesn't want me to find happiness.

Happiness?

I snort at the mirror. I don't get to do happy, but I can fight for tolerable. Lately it seems as if Danny has been dictating more and more about how my baby is to be brought up, when he doesn't even like kids.

My ring catches the light like a beacon of captivity. It's ugly, so tight my flesh puckers and reddens around the band. Twisting and tugging, I manipulate the tiny manacle from my finger, flexing blood flow through my swollen flesh. I hate everything about it, everything it represents, but my stomach rolls and lurches because Danny would be angry at me if he knew I'd removed it. I force it back in place and the impending fit of terror subsides. It seems the only panic attacks I've had are all Danny-induced, although he insists he does it for my own good. Maybe Axel was right all those months ago. Maybe I'm stronger than I think I am. The doubt floods in but I hold it back, because there's a sharp niggle in my mind that maybe Danny is wrong, and I can do this baby thing by myself after all...

I'd felt something shift in the shadows of my soul when I unleashed my rage on Axel. I felt my strength creep back in for the first time in months. But I never even argued with Danny. My stomach twists at the mere thought of confronting him and

I contemplate that while I make my plans.

* * *

The Broken Keg has a clarity about it tonight like nothing I've felt before. The voices of the patrons are sharper, as if the air isn't as thick.

I feel different, too. Last night I drew a line in the sand. I need help with the baby, but it's my child and I need to do what I think is best, not hand over our child's future to another person.

Flynn lands a warm smile on me and I veer off to see him. I didn't realise until now how long it's been since I spoke to him. His eyes have sunk into the shadows on his face, a hardness emanating from him that was never there before. With heart weighed down by guilt, I'm aware of how trapped in my own world I'd become. I should have seen his sadness long ago. With a forced blink he clears his head.

"How are you doing?" I ask gently.

He shakes off the shadows that flit over his expression, summoning back the smile he hides behind.

"Hey Will, I'm fine, but how's my favourite waitress? You look…different tonight."

His teeth shine white with honesty and I feel myself relax a little more.

"Hey, Flynn. I'm good…" I frown at him, suddenly aware that the persistent knot in my stomach is loosening just a little.

"What's wrong?" Flynn peers into my face with a light frown, his arms immediately uncrossed and his hands gripping my shoulders.

I respond with a glance that reflects my bewilderment, because I feel the warmth of his hands on me, his body so close to mine, and my pulse doesn't even stir.

"You're touching me." I breathe in wonder.

"Shit, Sorry, Will-" His hands disappear.

"No Flynn. It's okay. It really, truly is." I laugh, a light, incredulous sound that lifts Flynn's eyebrows.

Feeling spontaneously courageous, I slide my arms under his and lean against his chest in a quick hug.

Flynn gives me a quick squeeze, then peels me away.

"Care to enlighten me on what this is about?" He smiles gently.

"I don't know what it means, Flynn, but I can touch you, and I'm not even close to having a freak out! I have no idea what it means, but I don't feel sick at all. It's wonderful!"

I rest my hand on his arm and stare at it, feeling him shake beneath with amusement.

"You've reached out to me before, remember? A few times. Did you ever think that maybe it's not a "freak-out" but more of an intuitive response?"

Still gaping at my hand on his arm, I frown. "What do you mean?"

"Will, you don't know what we see in your drawings, do you? They're more than just pictures, they explain how you feel about someone. Just by looking at those images, I know that you trust Rain with everything you have and you view me as someone safe and wholesome."

I yank my hand away in surprise, but Flynn snatches my hand and rests it on his chest. The sturdy beat beneath my palm grounds me.

"No, hear me out. I haven't finished. Think about how sick you feel when you're in our company."

"I…I don't." I meet his deep blue eyes without a brush of fear.

"That's right, because everything inside you tells you we are safe. We're no threat to you, physically or emotionally. Our intuition finds possible threats even before the danger is obvious. I'm guessing what you believe are "freak-outs" are actually heightened, but perfectly, normal gut feelings."

Perfectly normal?

My skin chills at the thought. I flick my eyes with a measure of suspicion between my hand and Flynn's face while I struggle to process, then he shifts and drops my hand with a wink.

"Archer's opening up, Will. Everyone in their places; it's show time."

* * *

"What's up with you tonight, Willow?" Danny frowns, fingers dragging beads of humidity down his beer glass. The knot in my gut tightens and twists, and instead of pushing it down, I let myself feel it. It's been present for so long I can almost feel the frayed fibers straining.

"Nothing, Danny. I've just been thinking about...us, and I think we need to have a talk about what we really expect from this...relationship."

He scrunches the napkin.

"I see."

Those words should mean nothing, but the icy tone is laden with intent and my stomach churns.

I glance away, straight into the eyes of Flynn, his head cocked as he watches me.

I nod to him, hoping the simple gesture conveys my gratitude.

* * *

The last of the tables is wiped down, and I hum as I make my way to the bar.

Danny skipped dinner tonight, making excuses about an early meeting the following day, and the feeling of relief was instant.

"Another great night, Will. I'll be sharing out the tip jar in a minute; it's full again."

Archer splits the tips between the chef, Flynn and me, arguing he and Rain reap the lion's share with the nightly profits. He graces me with a rare smile.

"Whatever changed since last night, Will, I like it. You're more yourself than you've been in a long time. It's great to see that spark come back."

I thank him shyly, bursting inside with delight as I make for the door for my nightly dose of Mountain Plateau air. The sharp chill hits my face, my eyes flutter closed to focus on the invigorating sensation. My chest swells with the cleansing oxygen, and I lean my head against the cool brick wall. I feel like I've managed to crack open some huge cavity filled with strength and determination, and it tastes so sweet.

"You wanted to talk Willow? Start talking." My attention snaps on Danny's shape moving through the shadows, and the knot inside coils tight and crackles with ice.

"Danny? Oh, my god, you gave me a fright! I thought you'd left for the night." I stammer, the elation that soared through me moments before replaced by an oppressive foreboding.

He slithers beside me, expression so cold it freezes out the moon's reflection.

"So, start talking, sweetheart."

I fight to remain vigilant while my pulse quickens, avoiding his eyes while I struggle to recall what I wanted to tell him. Dread empties my thoughts, chips off my logic and breaks my reasoning, but I fight it. This time, I need to fight it.

"It's nothing, really, Danny. I j…just think I need to have more say in my baby's life. I mean, I'm grateful for your help, but I can't let you…" My voice dries up with my tongue.

His fingers brush a strand of hair from my face and I flinch.

"Look at you, Willow." He whispers with cold blooded calm. "That's not going to work. You need me to prevent the damage you'd do to the baby. If this child grows up thinking it's normal to jump at shadows and freak out at the slightest touch, their life will be no better than yours."

He's wrong, Willow. Fight for your baby!

It takes every ounce of effort to shake my head.

"N…no, Danny. I can do this. I will learn and I won't hurt my baby." I gasp, my breath labouring.

His curled finger forces my chin up.

"Now, Willow, don't think you know better than me. You imagine it will all be just peachy, but you can't see what I see. You're a mess, and your head is all over the place. Like us, for example. We're engaged, but you still refuse to allow me to touch you, then I see you throw yourself at Flynn. Now tell me how that shows me your gratitude for saving you?"

His eyes darken to black, the tone of his angry breaths deepening into a lustful timbre that steals whatever strength I have left.

He slams me hard against the wall, stars exploding in my head. My fingers claw, nails biting into flesh and digging.

He knocks my strikes aside, crushing my hands in his palm as his body jams against mine. He's too hot, too close, and panic makes my head spin.

"You're mine, Willow, and I've been patient with you, but I'm done waiting. I'm taking what you owe me."

His free hand yanks my skirt up, my thin choked wail too useless, my body weak with terror. My panties jerk down my thighs, and I feel the stinging pain as his fingers slam into my dry centre.

No no no!

I summon a scream but only manage a thick grunt. He withdraws his fingers and brings them to his nose, nostrils flaring as he draws it in. My tears pour free, blurring the sight of him sliding them into his mouth.

"So damned sweet, my Willow. No more holding back. Tonight I feast!"

Every memory roars to life with each painful thrust of Danny's fingers, so loud and clear that I do the only thing I know that can drown out the pain and the sound of my useless grunts for help. I retreat into the safety of my own head. It's all happening to someone else, the pain, the horror, the humiliation drifting into numb curiosity until I'm not a part of it at all. My last conscious thought registers my body going limp, and then I detach completely from Danny's brutal punishment and find a warm safe place far, far away from here.

I feel nothing.

CHAPTER 36

AXEL

*A*ngie crouches before me with her forehead creased.

"Are you sure you want to go home?" She asks for the fourth time.

I grab a handful of my hair.

"What else can I do? I told her I loved her, and she didn't believe me. She doesn't need me, Ange. She's chosen Dorian. She wears his ring. I have my answer."

"No, you're both right. She doesn't need you, and you don't need her. But you want each other! She still loves you, Axe, she already chose you. It was you who took that option from her. I can see it still burning inside her, but she's hurt and angry, and thrown off guard by you appearing out of nowhere and telling her the guy she's seeing is a bad man. What would you do in her position?"

"I loved you, once, and you would have known that if you'd read my letters."

She chose me. She came to me in fear, and gave her all to me, unfurling like a flower of prudence and finding a safe place in my arms. I earned her trust, her love, and then destroyed it as she stood before me, vulnerable and raw.

I growl. "I'd be sensible and listen to reason!"

"Like you were sensible and listened to reason when she told you she was pregnant? Bullshit! You reacted with as much pain and rage as Willow. We are not going home, you are going to go and talk to her. You're going to listen to her fury and she will listen to yours!"

For a tiny slip of a thing, Angie has some power behind her. She yanks me to my feet with determination thinning her mouth.

"And stop your damned sulking!" She snaps, shoving me hard into the passenger seat.

"She won't listen to me."

"Try." Angie snarls, peeling out onto the road.

"She's made up her mind."

"So change it!"

"It's no use."

The car stops so fast my head almost hits the windscreen, and dust overtakes the car as I stare at her in shock.

"Are you a man, Axe? I heard all these stories about how brave and fearless you are, but all I see now is a little boy who's ready to throw his happiness away because he's too cowardly to let the woman who owns his heart know it. Happily-ever-after's don't just happen, Axel, you fight for it!"

She spins the wheels, finds the bitumen again and we continue in silence.

The outside lights are out when we pull up out front of The Broken Keg, but Archer's car is still there so I walk straight in. Flynn finds me immediately, but I lift my hands in surrender. He eyes Angie with suspicion.

"What are you up to Axe? Willow was pretty messed up last night, thanks to you. I won't let you do any more damage to her."

He knows he'll lose to me, but I see it in his eyes. He's prepared to fight for her anyway. He knows her worth. I find myself warming to him all over again.

"I'm here to fight for her, Flynn. I love her."

It sounds foreign from my mouth, but it hangs in the air like a white flag between us, Flynn's eyebrows darting upward as his blue eyes land on Angie in confusion.

"Yeah, and I'm his work partner, Angie, since this big lug seems to have forgotten his manners."

Flynn's face softens as all the pieces fall into place, until eventually he smiles.

"Great to hear it, man. Uh, I haven't seen her around for a while. She must be outside getting her nightly dose of fresh air before we go." He frowns at his watch.

Fear collides with the tickle of anticipation. *Maybe if I can explain, maybe she'll forgive me.* My feet propel me to an unknown future.

The door slams open in my urgency and my blood turns to ice.

Dorian has her wedged against the wall, his hand under her skirt. Her body jerks with his movements, smearing a stain of blood behind her head. *Dorian's hurting her!*

But it's her expression that breaks me. Her face is lax and empty, her mouth parted so her pale lips can catch the tears that track steadily down. Her wide eyes are unblinking and vacant, so void of anything I wonder if she's even still in there.

"Willow!" My voice cracks in anguish.

Dorian rams his shoulder into her, snatching a blade from his unbuttoned pants.

"I had a fucking idea you'd show up again. You could have waited another five minutes." He growls, resting the blade between her breasts. He's crushing her hands in his grip so tight he's cutting her circulation, but she doesn't even try to fight him.

"Let her go! Your issue is with me, and I'm here, so let her go and I'm yours."

He snorts. "I'm not that much of a fucking idiot, Axel. You'd beat me in a second. You're stronger than me, faster too, thanks to the damned bullet in the foot you gave me, and luckier. This is the only way I'm better than you! I'm better with the girls. You can't satisfy them, so I'm here to do it for you."

"Don't do it, man. She's not like the others." My heart near liquefies when the blade tip draws a droplet of blood. She doesn't cry out, just continues that soft, keening whimper that tears at my heart.

"When you disappeared with Frostbite I was curious where the man who destroyed my career had got to. Apparently you managed to shatter just enough bones in my foot to dash any hopes I had of rising through the ranks, and I decided to find you to thank you personally. Imagine my surprise to find you perfectly happy with a great job and a stunning girl. You certainly wasted no time moving on instead of regretting what you did to me. That's when I decided I'd take it upon myself to teach you that no bad deed goes unpunished. I know she's not like the others, old friend. You love this one. That's why the reward is so much sweeter. She tastes so good."

My nostrils flair and retribution roars through me as he leans into her and licks his fingers. I lurch forward but he pushes the blade until the tip disappears and crimson wells beneath it. I scramble backwards. He knows my moves, and I know from experience he would follow through without remorse.

My lungs hiss in agonizing fear. I need her. I need her to come back and fight for herself. I need to give her the strength she needs to save herself.

Because I can't save her.

I answer Dorian but send my heart to Willow.

"You're right. I *do* love her. And I should never have let her go. Right from the beginning I knew she was something special. She invaded my head from the moment I laid eyes on her - from the moment she told me she spit in my breakfast. But I pushed it away, because I was too damned scared to love anyone after what happened with you and Janice. But the harder I tried to fight it, the more it enveloped me. Willow was in my thoughts with every low-life I put behind bars. Every time I wanted to buy the whole damned art supply shop for her but forced myself to bring her only a single notebook, so she wouldn't feel like she owed me anything."

My eyes are trained on Dorian, but the edge of my vision

is zeroed in on her face. Her lashes flutter and I feel the first stirrings of hope.

"I found myself seeking her out and hated myself for it. I was drawn inexplicably to her complexities; how she was so soft, but at the same time she was the strongest warrior I know. She has this…light about her that is so fascinating and addictive that every time I'm near her I'm in awe of it."

She blinks again, and my blood electrifies.

Come back to me, Willow. I know you can, baby.

"I don't give a shit, Axel. She's mine. We're engaged and pretty soon she'll forget all about you. Now, get the fuck away so I can take her home. You can see she's having a freak-out."

Dorian is so busy watching me he doesn't see her face begin to firm with awareness. He'll be concentrating on her sagging body and lack of resistance in her hands, but my girl is coming back, just not fast enough.

"No, Dorian. She's not having a freak out. She is having a normal reaction to bad people, and you've worn her down so thoroughly she's forgotten how to listen to what her body already knows. But she'll remember, because that's who she is. She's braver than either of us; stronger, too. You know, maybe she will forget about me, because Willow can do whatever she sets her mind to. But that's where she and I are different, because I will never forget her. I know it because I spent the last few months trying and failing. I know I don't deserve her, but I'm hoping she can find a place inside her that thinks I just might be enough for her."

She frowns, inches back to me with every breath that fights its way past her lips. But Dorian's done with my monologue.

"Shut up and leave, man. You had your chance, and it looks like you lose again." Dorian sneers as he presses up against her, eyes never leaving me.

"Get off her, Dorian!" I snarl, fists so tight my flesh threatens to split open.

Clarity strikes Willow's eyes as they seek mine, searching for something in me I hope with everything I am that she finds.

I show her everything, all the parts of me I was too scared to acknowledge. They're all hers now, no matter what happens next. I just need her to do something. Anything. If she fights him, he might turn his attention to her, leaving him open to an attack from me.

Help me to help you I silently implore her. Her eyes narrow to slits, whatever terror held her captive is chased away by her beautiful rage. Her breaths surge; furious breaths of justice.

Dorian smirks, then it evaporates suddenly when Willow's slack body jerks to life, the strength returning to her body in time to slam her knee into his groin so hard I feel it in my throat.

Dorian chokes on a scream, mouth opening uselessly for frozen vocal chords, eyes bursting with the agony inflicted.

Willow sinks to the ground bonelessly beside him.

The restraint I practised snaps the very second the knife drops from his startled fingers. White hot rage courses through my veins and I'm on him, my fists iron pistons of vengeance. I smell his blood. It fuels the adrenaline that charges my muscles and feeds my rasping fury as I rain blow after blow on the scum that dared lay a hand on my Willow.

"Axel?" The soft sound, tiny as a finch switches on in my brain and I leave the limp carcass and scramble to her on my knees, gathering her to me so tightly I can feel her racing pulse over mine.

"Will, baby, I've got you now. You're safe" I croon, my tears soaking her hair.

I feel her eyelashes stroke my neck as she blinks, and my exhale explodes in relief.

"I thought I'd lost you, baby. I was so scared you were gone and I'd never get to touch you again."

I barely register when Angie and Flynn burst through the door, the familiar conversation of Angie calling in for backup. As she barks orders down the line, Willow's head moves, and I loosen my grip enough for her to peer up at Angie.

"You're his partner?" She whispers as Angie ends the call.

"Yep," she grins, "Now, has he told you yet how much he loves you, or am I going to have to keep hearing about it every damned day?"

***

The ambulance arrives before Dorian regains consciousness. His silence is the only thing that keeps me from going back and finishing him off.

Archer hands them a copy of the security tapes to the police before they take him to the hospital.

Willow pushes me away long enough to drag his ring from her finger. I snatch it from her with a snarl, sending it deep into the night. Then I hold my girl.

"That was Dorian?" She asks, and I brush her hair from her face. The nurses patch her head. It's nothing more than a nasty gash that will heal as fast as it bled.

The bruising Dorian left on Willow's wrists will fade in a week, the damage he inflicted inside her was thankfully minimal, but only time will tell me if he's given her deeper, more permanent scars. I don't care. I'll take them, too, and dedicate every second to healing them.

"Yeah, but I had no idea it was him until I saw your drawing, and recognised him."

She looks lost and bewildered as the shock drains from her system and she begins processing. She wriggles in my arms and stares up at me with her huge, perfect eyes.

"You can let me go, Axe." She says, but I shake my head.

"I can't Willow. I let you go once, and I just can't do it again." My voice wavers, but she pushes on my arm and I open them, the warm hospital air feeling like ice where her warmth was.

She sits beside me, leaving air between us. It explains so much in the tiniest gesture, and my heart crashes.

"Will?" my whisper pleads.

She frowns at her feet and I feel space stretch.

"We need to talk, Axe. All the things we should have said, we need to say them now, because you need closure and I need to move on."

CHAPTER 37

WILLOW

I look at the desolation on Axel's face with an invisible fist crushing my heart, and know there are worse things in this world than dying.

He might think he loves me, but he doesn't know I'm carrying the baby he doesn't want. I couldn't keep breathing if I knew the man I loved with all my heart was with me out of duty.

"Please don't talk like you're saying goodbye, Will. Please don't do that." The pain in his strained whisper is so raw I have to look away.

"We need to talk about what went wrong. We need to talk about you running away and we need to talk about the baby."

Rip off all the bandaids and pull up all the scabs. Watch the blood spill. Because that's what we never did.

I watch his throat bob as he nods. He reaches out and drags my hand into his lap, running fingers over mine, focusing on our connection.

"You first." He invites, his deep voice tight and thin.

"I was so scared, Axel. I was too obsessed by you to think about the possible repercussions. I'll own that. I didn't think of protection, I didn't think about the possibility of us going so wrong. I wasn't able to think about anything outside of you. I was drowning in you and I just wanted to dive deeper. You can imagine what went through my head when I discovered I was pregnant. I'm broken. I'm damaged. I have no right being a mother, and I knew that if I tried I'd mess the baby up even more than I am. So I turned to the one person besides Rain that ever had my full trust, and you threw every single fear of mine in my face. I have never felt so utterly desecrated as that moment. And then you showed me how unworthy I was when you disappeared. I knew then that no matter how deeply I believed you could love me that I was wrong, and I started to mistrust my own instincts. It was easy then for Danny...Dorian to swoop in and eat away at my raw edges."

I fill my lungs with a shuddering inhale, and lift my eyes.

Axel's pewter eyes shimmer with unshed tears.

"I'm so, so sorry, Willow. You were right about me the whole way through. I was so scared to be in love that when I realised I was falling, I panicked. Deep down I knew you weren't the type to try and trap me, and it took such courage for you to tell me in the first place. Everything I did was a move in the opposite direction I needed to be in. But when you made up your mind on the spot to terminate the baby, I lost my head."

Anger heats my belly.

"I *hadn't* made up my mind, Axel! I was airing my fears to work out what I thought was best! I took my time, and made sure the decision I made was one I could live with, and the only person I had to discuss it with was Da...Dorian!"

Axel brings my hand to his lips, but I don't look. The drop of moisture detonates on my flesh and resonates through my heart.

"I know Will, and I'm so sorry. I guess I thought you'd talk about it with Rain-"

"Dorian convinced me not to tell anyone until I'd made my decision, or rather, until he'd convinced me to do what he wanted!"

Axel recoils, but I'm too bitter to care.

"I realise that, and I know you made the best decision you could at the time, and I'm just going to have to accept that."

The way he cringes makes my chest ache. This is nothing

compared to how he'll react when I tell him that I decided to keep it. He's going to hate me.

"What's with you and Dorian, anyway? I get that he hurt you by stealing Janice away, but it doesn't make sense. You told me that it broke your heart, but then you say you never loved her."

His hand squeezes mine, and his voice is so low I have to strain to hear him.

"I didn't love Janice. But I got her pregnant."

"Oh, Axel!" I gasp.

Silver eyes seal with a tirade of regret.

"I got her pregnant and was too young to know we could be apart and still co-parent, so we decided the only thing to do was to get married. Neither of us wanted that, but, well, we did what we thought we had to. The whole thing started getting her down, and that's when Dorian swooped in. He said all the right things and made all the right moves, and convinced Janice to leave me and be with him, so she left me."

Blood pounded in my brain, and the dots started connecting in my mind. The fractured conversations we'd had about it, the day I came home to find him weeping in my nest, and the 'solutions' Dorian had at the ready when he'd tried to steer my decision. Axel's tortured timbre brought the horrible truth into the light.

"I didn't know he had this loathing for me. I went with it, as long as Janice was happy. Then Dorian convinced her that they could only work as a family if she…"

"…terminated your baby." I finish. His lips tighten and his head dips.

The night I found him, tear-stained and raw in my nest, he murmured a name in the arms of sleep.

"Thomas?!" I gasp, eyes wide and woven with his.

"Thomas." He confirms grimly.

My head spins.

Dorian's reassurance springs to mind.

There's no hurry, Willow. I know a doctor who can terminate at twenty weeks.

Bile surges up, and I choke it down.

"He got her to terminate at twenty weeks! Oh, Jesus, Axe. You weren't angry at me because you thought I'd trapped you, you were crazy with grief that you thought I'd decided to terminate."

He digs his free palm into his eye.

"I'm so sorry I couldn't handle it. It's the only thing that kept me away, Will. I understand why you made that decision, and part of that's my fault, but I don't think that will ever stop stinging."

I bristle at that. He's too consumed by his own grief to think logically. Or he has already concluded that I'm the type of person who can reach my decision easily. Does he imagine I'd simply 'get over it' if I'd made that difficult decision? He notes the bitterness I radiate, his eyes widening as his timbre tightens.

"But it's okay, Will. I want to work past that. I want to be with you, and we can start over!"

"We can't just ignore it, Axe. It will eat at you until you won't be able to hide your feelings. I just can't watch you grow to resent me. I've had months to come to terms with my decision, but you need to go away and have a good think about what you want, too. You've spent so long fighting relationships that you've not had a chance to work out what you want with one.

"You see, I know what I want. When you're stuck in your own head there's not much else to do but work your way through the maze that brings you to the future you want. I want someone who I can rely on, someone to stand by me and hold my hand through the difficult decisions, and who will always be there when I need them."

He grips my hand so hard it almost hurts.

"I can do that Will. I promise!" His eyes dart between mine and I hold them, showing him my sadness and my hope.

"You need to hear me out, Axe. I have to make sure you understand. I want it all. I want marriage, I want kids, damn it, I finally decided that I deserve my happily ever after. And I need a partner, someone who will have my back. Someone who will be patient when my past gets too hard for me to face and sit with me through the darkness. I want honesty and understanding. Do you think you can commit to that? Can you tell me without a doubt you can be all of that for me?"

"Yes, Will. Yes. I can and I will!" His voice is rough with emotion.

"No, Axel. You can't. You need time to think about it, and then you need to come back and tell me what you need from me, if you decide you really want to."

My hand cuts him off when his mouth opens.

"The next thing is important, Axe. I want you to really consider who I am, and if you still decide I'm worth your time, you will have to ask the one question you never did."

There's a lump in my throat when I retrieve paper and pencil from my handbag and scribble some details down.

"Two weeks, Axe. Think about what I want, and what you want, and in two weeks, meet me here to talk. If you decide not to come, I'll understand."

He lets my hand fall from his when I stand, and I shiver the moment his warmth leaves me. Without his touch the grief slams into me, and I can no longer resist my need to reach for him. My hands slide over the stubble on his beautiful face, my thumbs exploring the heat of his lips. He moves quickly, lips finding mine with such hunger my head spins. I moan and open for him immediately, drowning in the feel of him, the smell of him, the taste I've craved for so long it aches. His arms crush me against him, but at that moment I feel my baby kick and I push Axel away.

He's not ready to meet you, yet, little gem.

I can't meet his eyes again, so I press the paper into his hand with tears in my eyes and leave the hospital room.

***

Harold Elwood is one of the best psychologists there is, Simone assures me.

"'Normal' is a term used to describe typical, or common behaviour. A desire to be 'normal' is simply another way of telling me you wish to conform. Is that what you really want? To cast aside your individuality and become a carbon copy of every other person in the world?"

I stare down at my hands clasped in my lap. Harold leans back in his chair, pressing his hands together, heavily peppered eyebrows shadowing his kind brown eyes.

"What components of yourself do you wish would conform with everyone else?" He invites.

"The way I freak out all the time." I murmur, my face heating.

"Oh, do you mean your heightened survival instincts? If you wish to control those responses, do as your friend Flynn suggested, and listen to your intuition. It will tell you when you're in danger. Believe it or not, Willow, but your reaction is pretty typical for a person who has experienced the kind of trauma you have. It's a learned response from a time it was necessary to protect you, and it served you well, numbing and cushioning your mind from what was happening to you. It's an incredible defence instinct, and one that allows a better response to healing. But if it's what you want, we can manage the thought processes of the eleven-year-old girl who found this way to cope, and your reactions will lose strength over time."

I make my way to the small cafe down from Harold's office and order an iced chocolate. And a cake, because my baby likes cake. My stomach swirls with a myriad of emotions. All I wanted was to be 'normal', but my life has been anything but typical. It's filled with pain and trials, strength and joy, love and despair, but I'm surrounded by good people who will help me through it. My hand rests on my stomach.

Two more months and I'll get to meet you, little gem.

I'm a little anxious about telling Rain about the baby, but no longer because I think she's going to be disappointed. She would have loved to have been with me the entire way through this, and she'll be hurt that I let her miss it.

A shiver runs through me as I seek the time again.

Axel has ten minutes to meet me here. I scan the cafe, but there's no sign of him. My cake suddenly tastes bland and I push the half-eaten slice aside. Maybe he's decided that he can't meet my terms. It was a lot to demand of a man who fears commitment.

Eight minutes.

Six.

Two.

As time slips away, the ache in my throat grows.

With thirty seconds to go, I force my limbs to lift my handbag from its resting place at my feet as my private heartache throbs.

Maybe it's a good thing I never told him I loved him.

CHAPTER 38

AXEL

*W*hy I had to wait for two weeks is beyond me. I don't care about her terms. I'll catch her a star if she asks.

Once I allowed myself to accept that I loved her, I charged ahead with everything I had to reach my goal. Well, not quite. In the back of my mind, that niggling itch that didn't sit right with me. Willow is courageous and resilient, and she can be damned stubborn at times. The way she was brave enough to keep facing me when she thought I couldn't stand to be around her, the way she fearlessly reprimanded me, and the way it would all melt away when she came to me with open arms; *that* is a woman who would fight for what she wanted. So why didn't she fight for our baby? Was it her lack of self-confidence that made her mind up, or was it me? Or had she made up her mind to keep it before Dorian sunk in his poisonous hooks?

I've walked into rooms filled with armed criminals. I've faced my own death more times than I can count. I've watched helplessly as my brothers in arms fell around me, the odds stacked against us, but I've never felt as terrified as I do in this moment.

Frozen to the concrete, I watch her make her way to the table in awe. Her movements are sturdy with that fire inside her I always knew was there. Now she wears it like a badge of honour, and it gives her an untouchable edge. She's never been so sure of herself, and that fills me with dread. Has she decided, now that she's stepped into herself, that I'm not enough for her? Male eyes all around drift to her, linger with hungry thoughts, and Willow is oblivious, but my fists curl.

My feet burn to take me to her, but I need another moment to soothe my frayed nerves. So much rides on this moment, and everything I've done before I managed to mess up. She's perfect, and any step I take towards her is another closer to failing again. I'm lost in the uncharted territory of my hopes and dreams, and all I can do is stretch out this moment, when I can still believe she could be mine.

She checks her watch and stands, her long hair arranged in that messy bun that sends me crazy, showing off the graceful lines of her neck. I watch her tuck her chair in, a habit from waitressing. Her head is high and proud as she walks away. She doesn't need me. I'll be broken and finished, but Willow will survive without me. She can survive anything.

Shit!

Then I'm running, the ache that will always be Willow spurring me on past the cafe.

I pull to a stop behind her, unsure what to do.

"Willow?" I manage.

Her back stiffens. Without turning, her sweet, strong voice carries.

"Axel?"

My heart catches in my throat, and she turns.

Wide oceans of blue land on me, wet tracks on her cheeks. It upset her to think I wouldn't meet her?

"I thought you weren't coming."

I'm so damned nervous all I can do is stare at her, reacquaint myself with the shape of her mouth, the soft angle of her chin. The gentle slope of her nose. Two weeks seems like years. Then she blinks and shakes her head.

"Come and sit, Axel. We need to talk."

It's the most frightening thing I've ever faced. It hurts to open up my own scars and lay them at her feet, but I give her everything. And she gives me hers. All the truths she faced in those foster homes, the ugly details of Kurt, and the others that followed. She lay all her damaged fragments at my feet, and I collected every last shard and tucked them all in my heart.

"What do you want from this, Axe? What do you need from me?" She asks gently as she puts her ghosts to rest for the moment.

"I just want you. I want it all with you. I want to marry you, and I want kids. I want to give you children more than anything." I breathe, swallowing the tears that threaten.

"And what happens if I'm pregnant, and we didn't plan on it?"

"Then it will be the greatest surprise ever, like it should have been the first time. I'm so sorry, Will."

She swallows hard and nods to herself, her mouth thinning.

"Is that all then?" She asks quietly.

"Yes. Wait. No. I don't want to make this any harder than it is, but there's one thing that I just have to know. Before…before Dorian stepped in. Our baby. What had you decided?"

She watched me, searching my face. Emotions crash so fast into one another in her eyes I can't decipher a single one. But I have to know, no matter how it hurts either of us.

"I decided to keep it."

My exhale explodes in relief, dimmed by sadness. She wanted our baby. If I hadn't run when I did, and Dorian hadn't injected his evil, my little son or daughter would be almost here. I swallow down my guilt, but Willow's moving. She lays a hand on my arm and its warmth sends those familiar tingles through my blood.

"Come on, Axel. I want to show you something, and we'll be late."

No matter what I ask, her mouth stays closed. She leads me by my hand into a building, dragging me into an elevator. A secret smile plays on her lips as she tugs me out.

The sign on the door reveals we're entering a doctor's suite.

"What is it Will? Are you sick?" I ask, but she puts a finger to her lip.

A doctor comes in, beaming at Willow.

"Good afternoon, Willow. You know the drill. I'll be back in a moment. What brings our medical miracle back again?"

Medical miracle?

"I brought someone who I thought should see this. Dr. Anna, this is Axel."

The doctor's eyes narrow on me, then widen. She scans me from head to toe until I squirm with discomfort. I frown, landing a puzzled look on Willow, but she releases my hand and lays back on the consulting table.

Dr Anna returns. I watch the small talk between the women, a comfortable conversation born of many visits.

What is so wrong that she had to come in so often? I can't stop the fist tightening around my lungs. *Do I finally have Willow in my grasp, only to lose her to whatever illness the doctor's treating?*

"Axel." Dr Anna's crisp tone demands my attention, and I give it all to her, desperate to discover why we're here.

"Have you ever heard of a cryptic pregnancy?"

I frown my impatience and she explains.

"It's a rare condition where a perfectly normal gestation occurs, but the baby sits just so that there is no outward evidence of the actual pregnancy."

"*Wha-*" My heart stops, and I cut to Willow and the wary smile that blooms there. Then the television screen lights up and my whole world implodes.

A grainy image in black and white fills the screen, a large head tucked down, perfect legs crossed, one tiny arm across the chest, the other lifted, tiny digits balled in a fist, a stray thumb jammed between tiny lips.

"Will?" I choke, reaching for the screen in disbelief.

Palm over the image, I stare down at her.

"Fuck, Will? Is this…?"

Tears of happiness stream from her face.

"Nothing on this earth could make me give up this precious gift from the man I love."

She grasps my free hand and presses it against her flat belly. Beneath it, her stomach shifts and rolls. The pressure beneath my touch intensifies.

The doctor's voice is soft with her smile; "Oh, look, Axel. That's your baby's hand. It wants to meet its Daddy."

Willow loves me, and she carries my baby. I'm the happiest man alive, and I fall to my knees, face pressed into the womb that carries my child, and sob with pure joy.

EPILOGUE

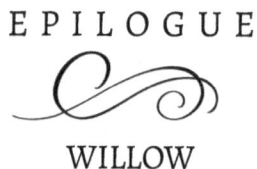

WILLOW

*O*ut in the garden, the warmth of the early afternoon sun holds Rain and me in thrall. There's nothing to be frightened of anymore, and with every day that passes I find myself that little braver, a little more...me. I smile, my arm reaching around Rain's waist, and like so many years ago, she rests her head against my shoulder.

"I'm sorry I didn't tell you I was pregnant. I wanted to, but I wasn't strong enough at the time to face your disappointment. When Da...Dorian suggested I keep it quiet, I just did what seemed easiest. The more time passed, the harder it got to tell you." I whisper my shame.

Her arm snakes around my waist in silent reassurance.

"Nothing you do could make me disappointed, Will. I've never been anything but proud of you. I understand, though. Dorian is a master manipulator. He feeds on his victim's doubts and controls them with it. From what Axel and Archer told of him, I'm not sure I would have picked up on it in your position, either. I want you to remember one thing, though, and that is no matter how scared you feel, or what doubt leaves you feeling uncertain, please, you can talk to me. Or any of us. We all love you. We all have your back. Can you promise me you'll never stop talking to me again?"

Her eyes are the softest brown. They are eyes that know every shadow and valley of my soul and never let me down.

"Before I promise you, there's one more confession I need to make. Axel and I are going to have a baby."

I laugh at the shock that she tries to hide, and she grins when she realises she's sprung.

"I'm sorry Will, but I wasn't judging. I was surprised that the two of you didn't waste any time. He's only been back a week. Isn't it too soon to tell?"

My grin widens, and Rain's eyes narrow suspiciously.

I take her hand and press it to my belly. Her gasp rips out when the baby kicks against the pressure, and her mouth gapes.

"No, Rain. I'm not pregnant *again.* I'm pregnant *still.* And from our calculations, you have less than two months to get used to it before I expect the godmother of this baby to be all-hands-on-deck."

The elated embrace that follows heals every moment of silence that fell between us in the months that passed, and knots together our future with the promises we make with our souls.

***

The fog of sleep lifts as I snuggle against his hard chest. The smell of raw pine and musk fills my lungs and makes me smile. I feel the gentle curl of his breath on my neck as he pulls me closer, his hand protectively over my stomach. The baby kicks, and Axel's hand zeroes in on the movement. I wriggle onto my back and take in the gorgeous man beside me. Everything about him is breathtaking. He's all muscle and power and pure masculinity. He's been adorable, obsessing over our little gem so much that even Flynn teases him about it. I stare at his lips, barely visible on the edge of dawn, remembering how they felt whenever they made up for lost time, which they did a lot of.

"If you don't stop staring, I'll take it as an invitation." Axel mumbles sleepily.

"Actually, I was just thinking that you're wearing me out. I think I need a holiday away from your demands." I smirk.

His eyes jump open and he moves so fast I squeal in surprise as he pins me beneath him.

He fills my vision with his broad shoulders, wide chest and my pulse races to attention.

"Is that so? Well, I warn you now that you'll miss me too much to stay away for long."

"Oh, you're so arrogant. And what is it I'll be pining for, Andre?"

He growls into my neck and I arch towards him, wrapping my legs around his waist.

"You'll miss my charm. That's a given." He nips my ear and my gasp makes him grin.

"And my muscles. You'll definitely miss my muscles."

I quiver as he lines himself up, my nails already impatient for his back.

"Oh, is that all?" I feign nonchalance, my breath rasping.

"Oh no…" His sexy voice rumbles "You'll miss *this* the most!"

And he fills me up, that stretching sting that connects us. He's hungry this morning, and he claims me hard. The pregnancy hormones have me wired, and he's taking me over the edge before he's barely started.

"Christ, Will, I love you so much." He growls as he plunges deep. The friction sends me wild.

"Oh, god, Axe, oh yes!" I buck and reach for him.

This time he comes with me, that sexy roar rattling his body with his release.

As our pulses slow, eyes locked on each other.

"I never thought I could be this happy, Axe. I couldn't imagine being capable of feeling this good. I love you so much.'

Axe blinks at me.

"You know, you nearly sent me mad, because I couldn't understand how the only person I wanted more than anything didn't seem to want anything from me. I don't think I'll ever get tired of hearing you say that."

I smirk.

"I hurt your ego pretty bad, huh?"

"You were scathing!" He winces, then so do I when he pulls out of me.

His hand spreads over my stomach for a while, then he plants a kiss there.

"Okay. Time to feed the munchkin."

***

"I *am* capable of making breakfast, Axe!" I roll my eyes to hide my amusement.

I curl my finger and he sheepishly hands over the bacon and eggs.

I've almost got it plated up when I see movement in my periphery, and my attention snaps outside. In the shadows, two figures stand facing each other, and even from here I can feel the tension radiating off one of them. In the half-light I recognise Flynn, spine fused as the stranger's mouth moves.

"Axe, what's Flynn doing meeting up with someone at this hour?"

Axel's head whips to the window, breakfast forgotten, bumping my side in his haste to see. His breath hisses out against my cheek.

"I know that uniform! But what the hell would a senior detective be wanting with Flynn? Simone's the one following up on his sister's case."

Outside, Flynn shakes his head at the detective, fists balled and taut, then the next moment his entire frame slumps in defeat. He nods, slowly. His face to the ground.

We both duck from view as the detective turns his back on Flynn, and strides to the car he parked out on the street.

I swallow nervously as I listen for the soft click of the front door as Flynn sneaks inside.

When he walks past the kitchen he sees our expressions, and his face drains of colour.

I watch it all, terror, futility, and finally resignation collide in the deep, turbulent sea of Flynn's eyes. Then it falls away, and all that remains is raw fear.

He attempts a smile and fails, frowning harder at the floor at our feet the longer the silence stretches.

"He's, uh, an old friend; just stopped in to chat." His mutter trips and falters.

"Flynn?" Axel's rumble startles him, and his glance is desperately heartbreaking.

"Please…just leave it alone?" He implores with a constricted whisper.

And Flynn slips away into the darkness of the hall.

Excerpt from RETICENCE

CHAPTER 1 - FLYNN

J'm Flynn; the nice guy. The unassuming friend, so easy to trust. The guy who'll be there for you with an empathetic ear and a shoulder when you need it, but nobody could guess that every element in my life is a tangled mess of deception and fear just waiting for the day it will be exposed.

Maybe I should have come clean when I first met Rain, but she had her own problems to deal with, and I was in desperate need of an ally, then before I knew it, the time for truth had passed.

But something's changed now. I feel it in the air; the icy chill that signifies the beginning of the end, and all I can do now is wait.

Shit floats, as Archer says, and he's right.

Because when you play the destructive game of reticence, nobody wins, and utter ruin is inevitable.

Also by Rowena Spark

STAND ALONE ROMANCE

HER WHOLE HEART

STEALING BRYNN

SCARS OF CREDENCE SERIES

CREDENCE (BOOK 1)

RETICENCE (BOOK 3 - COMING SOON)